37653005937399
Fletcher
FIC STEVENSON
Mrs. Tim gets a job.

**CENTRAL ARKANSAS
LIBRARY SYSTEM
JOHN GOULD FLETCHER
BRANCH LIBRARY
LITTLE ROCK, ARKANSAS**

DEMCO

Copyright, 1947, by D. E. Stevenson
Copyright © 1973 by Dorothy Emily Peploe
All rights reserved, including the right to reproduce
this book or portions thereof·in any form.

First published in 1947
New Edition 1974

Library of Congress Cataloging in Publication Data
Stevenson, Dorothy Emily, 1892–1973
Mrs. Tim gets a job.
I. Title.
PZ3.S8472Mp5 [PR6037.T458] 823'.9'12 73–12860
ISBN 0–03–012256–2

Printed in the United States of America

Mrs. Tim Gets a Job

by D. E. STEVENSON

HOLT, RINEHART AND WINSTON
New York   Chicago   San Francisco

Author's Foreword
to the Story of the Christie Family
by D. E. STEVENSON

The four books about Mrs. Tim and her family are being re-published during 1973 and early 1974, and the author has been asked to write a foreword.

The books consist of:
1. *Mrs. Tim Christie*
2. *Mrs. Tim Carries On*
3. *Mrs. Tim Gets a Job*
4. *Mrs. Tim Flies Home*

The first "Mrs. Tim" was written many years ago (in 1934). It was written at the request of the wife of a professor of English history in a well-known university who was a personal friend. Their daughter was engaged to be married to an officer in a Highland Regiment. Naturally enough they wanted to know what it would be like and what she would be expected to do.

There was nothing secret in my diary so I gave it to Mrs. Ford to read. When she handed it back, Mrs. Ford was smiling. She said, "I read it aloud to Rupert and we laughed till we cried. You could make this into a very amusing book and call it *Leaves from the Diary of an Officer's Wife*. It just needs to be expanded, and you could pep it up a little, couldn't you?"

At first I was doubtful (it was not my idea of a book), but she was so persuasive that I decided to have a try. The result was *Mrs. Tim of the Regiment* (recently reissued as *Mrs. Tim*

CENTRAL ARKANSAS LIBRARY SYSTEM
JOHN GOULD FLETCHER BRANCH
LITTLE ROCK. ARKANSAS

Christie). By this time I had got into the swing of the story and had become so interested in Hester that I gave her a holiday in the Scottish Highlands with her friend Mrs. London and called it *Golden Days*.

The two books were accepted by a publisher and published in an omnibus volume. It was surprisingly successful. It was well reviewed and the sales were eminently satisfactory; the fan-mail was astonishing. People wrote from near and far saying that Mrs. Tim was a real live person; they had enjoyed her adventures immensely—and they wanted more.

But it was not until the outbreak of the Second World War in 1939 that I felt the urge to write another book about Hester Christie.

Mrs. Tim Carries On was easily written, for it is just a day-to-day account of what happened and what we did—and said and felt. The book was a comfort to me in those dark days; it helped me to carry on, and a sort of pattern emerged from the chaos.

Like its predecessor, the book was written from my own personal diary but this time there was no need to expand the story nor to "pep it up" for there was enough pep already in my diary for half a dozen books.

It is all true. It is true that a German plane came down on the moor in the middle of a shooting party and the two airmen were captured. It is true that German planes came down to low level in Norfolk, and elsewhere, and used machine guns to kill pedestrians on the roads. Sometimes they circled over the harvest fields and killed a few farm labourers and horses. Why they did so is a mystery. There could not have been any military objective in these maneuvers. People soon got used to it and were not even seriously alarmed but just took cover in a convenient ditch like dear old Uncle Joe. Perhaps the German airmen did it for fun? Perhaps it amused them to see old gentlemen rolling into ditches?

PULASKI-PERRY REG. LIBRARY
LITTLE ROCK, ARKANSAS

An American friend wrote to me as follows: "Your Mrs. Tim has made us *think*. We have been trying to imagine what it would be like to have a man-eating tiger prowling around in *our* backyard."

She had hit the nail on the head for, alas, the strip of water which had kept Britain safe from her enemies for hundreds of years had become too narrow: The tiger was in our backyard.

To me this book brings back the past so vividly that even now —thirty years later—I cannot read it without laughter and tears. Laughter? Yes, for in spite of the sadness and badness of Total War, the miseries we suffered, and the awful anxieties we endured, cheerfulness broke through at unexpected moments— and we laughed.

When they were first published, these four books about Mrs. Tim were all very popular. Everybody loved Mrs. Tim (everybody except the good citizens of Westburgh who disliked her intensely). Everybody wanted to know more about her and her friends. But the books have been out of print and unobtainable for years. I was pleased to hear that they were to be republished and that they would all be available again. I was particularly glad because together they contain the whole history of the Christie family and its friends. Taken in their proper sequence, readers will be able to appreciate the gradual development of Hester's character and the more rapid development of Tim's. As the years pass by there is a difference in the children; Annie and Fred Bollings become more adult; Jack and Grace McDougall, having weathered serious trouble, settle down peacefully together. The Christies' friends are very varied but all are interesting and unusual. We are introduced to the dignified Mrs. London; we meet Pinkie, an attractive young lady whose secret trouble is that (although seventeen years old) she does not feel "properly grown up, inside." But, in spite of this, Pinkie makes friends wherever she goes. Her circle of friends includes all the young officers who are quartered at the depot and is enlarged by the arrival of Polish officers who have escaped from their war-shattered country and are billeted in Donford while they reorganise their forces and learn the language. There is a mysterious lady, swathed in Egyptian scarves, who is convinced that in a previous existence she helped to build the Great Pyramid. There is Erica Clutterbuck whose rude manners conceal a heart of gold, and two elegant American ladies who endeavour to persuade Mrs. Tim to go home with them to America so that they may exhibit her to their friends as "The Spirit of English Womanhood."

But the chief interest is to be found in the curious character of Tony Morley and his relationship with the Christie family. At first he seems to Tim and Hester a somewhat alarming personage. (To Tim, because he is a senior officer and fabulously wealthy: he drives a large and powerful car, owns a string of racehorses, and hunts several days a week. To Hester, because he talks irresponsibly and displays an impish sense of humour so that she never knows whether or not he means what he says.) Soon, however, they discover that beneath the surface he is a true friend and can be relied upon whenever the services of a friend are urgently needed. We find out how he uses his tact and diplomacy to smooth the feathers of a disgruntled cook and show her how to measure out the ingredients for a cake with insufficient weights. We learn how he helps Hester to save a naval officer from making a disastrous marriage and how he consoles and advises a young husband whose wife has deserted him. We are told of Colonel Morley's success with a battalion of raw recruits, how he wins their devotion, licks them into shape, and welds them into a satisfactory fighting machine by imbuing them with the necessary esprit de corps. We see him salute smartly and march off at the head of his battalion en route for the Middle East. Knowing his reputation for reckless courage,

Hester wonders sadly if she will ever see him again. But apparently Tony is indestructible. He has survived countless dangers and seems none the worse. He pops in, out of the blue, in Rome (where Hester, on her way home from Africa, is seriously embarrassed by her ignorance of the language). Tony Morley arrives in his usual sudden and unexpected manner. By this time he has become a full-blown general and, having learnt to speak Italian from an obliging enemy, is able to deal adequately with the situation. He also deals adequately with a little misunderstanding at the War Office where he sees a friend and pulls a string or two for Tim.

Meanwhile the Christie children, Bryan and Betty, are growing up rapidly. In fact they are "almost grown up," and, although they are still amusing and full of high spirits, it is obvious that they will soon become useful members of the post-war world.

We meet them at Old Quinings where their mother has managed to find a small house for the summer holidays. Here, also, we meet Annie and Fred Bollings, Grace McDougall and her boys, an old-fashioned squire with a pretty daughter, a schoolteacher whose unconventional views about free love are somewhat alarming, and a very good-looking young man who is studying medicine but is not too busy to open gates for a fair equestrienne. We meet the amiable Mrs. Daulkes and the far from amiable Miss Crease whose sharp eyes and caustic tongue cause a good deal of trouble to her neighbours. Another unpleasant visitor is Hester Christie's landlady, the wily Miss Stroude, who tries to bounce Hester and almost succeeds, but once again Tony comes to the rescue in the nick of time to defeat Miss Stroude and send her away "with her tail between her legs."

Betty says, joyfully, "This is the best holidays, ever" but Hester's pleasure is not complete until the arrival of Colonel Tim

Christie from Africa. Now, at last, she is happy with all her beloved family under one roof.

I cannot finish this foreword without voicing the grateful
thanks of Mrs. Tim to her many kind friends in America,
South Africa, Australia, and New Zealand who sent her parcels
to augment her war-rations. The parcels contained tins of fat,
packets of tea and sugar and dried fruit, bars of chocolate, and
boxes of candy for the children. These generous presents were
shared with friends and were worth their weight in gold.

Mrs. Tim Gets a Job

Monday, 4th February

This seems a curious day to start a diary. I ought to have started on the first of January, but felt too lazy and depressed. Today I have received a letter from Tim, who is at present in Egypt, saying he hopes I have started another diary, if not will I please begin at once. He is keeping one himself, and it will be fun to compare notes when he returns. "For instance," says Tim. "What were you doing on the 20th January at 1700 hours?"

After making a hasty calculation I discover that 1700 hours is five o'clock in the afternoon, so it is probable that I was drinking tea, either in my own house or somebody else's . . . but quite impossible to remember anything at all about it. Was that the day I went to tea with Grace Mac-Dougall and her twins behaved so badly, or was it the day Annie went out, and Betty and I had tea together in the kitchen and amused ourselves by telling fortunes with cards? (There is something rather alarming in the discovery that one's memory is so unreliable . . . the days slip by and are lost forever.)

Tim continues, "Now that you have finished counting on your fingers, and have discovered the time of day to which I refer, I hope you will be able to satisfy my curiosity. The fact is I had a very strange dream—having fallen asleep over a belated cup of tea—and I should like to know if it is founded upon fact."

Tim does not tell me his dream, which is most annoying of him. The remainder of his letter is full of a visit to the Sphinx and of enquiries as to the welfare of the children (how is Bryan getting on at Harton, and have I discovered a suitable boarding school for Betty to go to after Easter?) and I am so annoyed with Tim, and so full of burning curiosity about his dream that I decide to write at once and tell him that the Sphinx has nothing on him for tantalizing mystery.

At this moment the door flies open and Grace Mac-Dougall rushes in, full of excitement. "It's all right," she cries, waving a letter at me. "It's absolutely all right. Erica says yes."

Grace is frequently excited, for she is a young woman full of nervous energy, so her abrupt entry does not disturb me in the least. I point to a chair and ask her to be seated and congratulate her upon finding a nurse for the twins.

"A nurse!" exclaims Grace in amazement. "But I haven't! There aren't any. What on earth do you mean?"

" 'Erica says yes,' " I quote briefly.

"Erica!" exclaims Grace. "Oh, I see! Oh, of course I didn't tell you about it, did I? The fact is I didn't want you to be disappointed, and of course I didn't know what she'd say until I asked her, so I thought—"

"Who is Erica?" I enquire.

"Erica Clutterbuck, of course. I'm sure I must have mentioned her."

"I'm sure you haven't."

"Why?"

"Because it's a most extraordinary name."

Grace smiles. She has a very delightful smile which makes her look prettier than ever. "It's a good name," says

Grace. "The Clutterbucks are a very old Border family—that's why it was so sickening for poor Erica to be left so badly off when old Mr. Clutterbuck died. She had absolutely nothing except the house, and she didn't want to sell it, of course."

I nod gravely and assure Grace that I understand and sympathize with Miss Clutterbuck's predicament and add that I hope she will be able to manage the twins.

"Oh, goodness!" exclaims Grace impatiently. "I've told you already it has nothing to do with the twins, and anyhow I wouldn't have Erica as a nurse for the poor lambs if she were the only woman left alive. She'd probably knock their heads together in the first five minutes."

It is on the tip of my tongue to reply that quite a number of women might be tempted to commit this atrocity, but I manage to refrain.

"Well, anyhow," says Grace proudly, "the long and the short of it is I've found you a job."

"A job!"

"Yes, Hester, a job. You said you wanted a job, didn't you? And of course I understood *exactly* how you felt. I mean if it weren't for the twins, who take up all my time, and *more,* I should take a job myself. Now that Jack is away in Egypt life is simply *too* dreary—or would be, if it weren't for the twins. They keep me cheerful, of course. Hester, d'you know what Ian said this morning? It was *too* sweet . . ."

Grace chatters on, but I am much too preoccupied with my own thoughts to listen. Now that I think about it I have a faint recollection that in a depression of spirits following upon Tim's departure I *did* say I must get a job—

and probably meant it. Since then, however, I seem to have
recovered and the idea of a job is most unattractive.

"It's very unselfish of me," continues Grace. "You're
really my only friend—the only woman in the place with
a sense of humor—and I'm sure I don't know what on
earth I shall do without you to hold my hand when the
twins get colds or measles or tummy-aches. It will be just
too frightful," says Grace earnestly. "But I feel I'm doing
the Right Thing. You want a job, so I've found one for you
and you'll be much happier with lots to do; the time will
pass like lightning; and Erica seems only too pleased to
have you, so I've done two people a Good Turn," says Grace
with the air of a complacent Boy Scout.

Grace is so charmed with her project that I haven't
the moral courage to tell her I have changed my mind and
don't want a job, but only want to remain peacefully in
Donford until such time as Tim returns from Egypt. Instead I enquire faintly what sort of job is being offered me.

"A lovely job," declares Grace. "I'd take it myself
like a shot if it weren't for the twins. A terribly interesting
job. Erica has turned her house into a country hotel and
she wants you—"

"But I couldn't possibly!"

"Why?"

"Because I don't know anything about hotels."

"You'll soon learn . . ."

"I don't want to. . . . I couldn't!"

"Don't be silly," says Grace firmly. "It's just like house-
keeping on a larger scale—besides, Erica does everything.
Erica is tremendously capable."

"Then why does she want me?"

"To help her of course. She can't be in fifteen places at once."

"Grace—"

"No, listen," says Grace. "Just listen to me. What are you going to do with yourself when Betty goes to boarding school? You aren't going to stay on here at Donford with nothing to do except look after the house."

"There's quite a lot to do—"

"Nonsense," says Grace briskly. "Be sensible, Hester."

"—and the children will be here in the holidays."

"They'll be *there,*" says Grace. "I told Erica all about Bryan and Betty. She says they can go to Tocher House for the holidays."

"*What* is it called?" I enquire.

"Tocher House," says Grace. "It's very old indeed. It was built by a man called Sir Alexander Johnstone as a dowry for his daughter. She married a Clutterbuck, you see, and it's been in the Clutterbuck family ever since. Isn't it interesting?"

"Very interesting," I agree in tepid tones.

"You'll love it," declares Grace. "Bryan and Betty will have a lovely time there in the holidays. "They'll fish in the Rydd and climb the hills and—"

"They won't because I'm not going there."

"Hester, please listen—"

"I'm not going to Tocher House."

We argue heatedly. I learn that Miss Clutterbuck's mansion is about five miles from a small town called Ryddelton in the Scottish Borders. Grace stayed there several times when old Mr. Clutterbuck was alive and has exceedingly pleasant memories of its amenities and of its glorious situation amongst purple-heathered hills.

"Poor Erica!" says Grace with a sigh. "She's a funny old stick—must be fifty if she's a day—and very fat and ugly. Of course she hates everybody; that's natural, isn't it?"

"Natural to hate everybody!" I exclaim.

"The guests or clients or whatever you call them," says Grace impatiently. "It's only natural she should hate to see them throwing their weight about in *her house*. That's one of the reasons she wants you, of course. You'll be a sort of buffer between her and them."

The mere idea of being a buffer between Miss Clutterbuck and her guests is so alarming that I pull myself together and tell Grace firmly that nothing she can say or do will persuade me to take the job.

Grace leaves immediately saying she does not understand me at all.

Wednesday, 13th February

Betty and I have breakfast together as usual and—as usual—Betty is full of high spirits. As I look at her, eating her porridge, I begin to realize how much I shall miss her "bright morning face" when she goes to boarding school. She announces with relish that this is the thirteenth. What do I think will happen? Reply that I am not affected by that particular superstition. Betty says Annie once lost her brooch on the thirteenth. It was a lovely brooch, given her by Bollings before they were married, so it was frightfully unlucky, but that was a Friday, which is worse. Fortunately she does not wait for my reaction but goes on to remark in her haphazard way that she's sick of school and Miss Clarke is an awful ass.

Feel that this is the wrong attitude for a child of twelve and endeavor to rectify it.

Betty says with brutal candor, "She's getting old, of course."

This seems the right moment to mention boarding school, so I take a long breath and mention it.

Betty considers the matter. "I wouldn't mind," she declares. "It might be rather fun. I suppose I couldn't *possibly* go to Dinwell Hall? Jane Carter has gone there and she likes it awfully. It's near Edinburgh, you know."

"I don't see why you shouldn't."

"But what about you?" says Betty, looking at me doubt-

9

fully. "It would be frightfully dull for you without me, wouldn't it?"

"Frightfully dull," I agreed. "But that can't be helped. I shall see you in the holidays."

We discuss the matter thoroughly—in fact we discuss it so thoroughly that Betty is late in starting for school.

When she has gone I ring up Mamie Carter (the mother of Betty's friend) and make searching enquiries about Dinwell Hall. Mamie says it is *ideal* and urges me to send Betty there; she gives me the name of the headmistress and tells me to write at once. Feel that things are moving much too fast and go upstairs, in a dejected mood, to make the beds.

Am still in the throes of bed making when Annie brings up the letters.

"None from the Colonel, today," says Annie in commiserating tones. "But there's no need to worry. I got one from Bill and he says the Colonel's in fine form. Bill says they went and saw the spinks; it's a sort of War Memorial."

Bill Bolling is Annie's husband and also Tim's batman. They have both been with us for many years and are definitely part of the family. I am, therefore, much more interested in Annie's letter than in my own two letters which Annie has placed upon the dressing table.

We discuss the various items of news contained in Annie's letter and the possibility of wives being permitted to join their husbands in Egypt . . . which leads in turn to the problem of Betty's future. Annie seems resigned to the idea of boarding school which surprises me a good deal.

"She'd like it," Annie says. "That Miss Clarke was all very well when she was little. Betty's getting too old for Miss Clarke, that's what's the matter. . . ."

It is all quite true, of course.

My letters are both addressed in unknown handwriting and, looking at them, I wonder idly why two complete strangers have found it necessary to write to me on the same day. Annie is interested too. She points out that one of them bears a London postmark and advises me to open it first.

I open it and am immediately plunged in gloom. The letter is from my landlord and announces that owing to a change of plan he is obliged to ask us to vacate Winfield by the end of March.

"It's the thirteenth," says Annie. "I felt in my bones there'd be something bad happen today. I was almost afraid to open Bill's letter—but this is it."

"This is it," I echo in despair.

"What about the Colonel's uncle?" suggests Annie. "The one who lives at Cobstead. It wouldn't be bad at Cobstead now the war's over and no bombing. Or perhaps Mrs. Loudon would have us at Avielochan for the summer."

These are possibilities of course, but I hate the thought of dumping myself upon relations or friends for indefinite periods. It seems odd that half an hour ago I was quite happy and settled, and now I am a homeless wanderer upon the face of the earth.

"We've been here so long," says Annie thoughtfully. "I'd begun to think Winfield belonged to us . . . I'd got used to it, if you know what I mean."

I know what she means only too well.

Annie sighs and takes up her duster. "Don't you worry," she says comfortingly. "Something'll turn up—it always does. I remember what a fix I was in when Mother died—and then I got your letter saying come on Friday."

"That wasn't yesterday," I tell her, trying to smile.

It is some time before I recover sufficiently to open my other letter. The writing is large and determined but exceedingly difficult to read and the signature beats me entirely until a sudden brilliant inspiration suggests it may be Erica Clutterbuck, all run together into one word. Having decided that it can't be anything else I turn back to the first page and set to work, and after some struggles I discover that Miss Clutterbuck is exceedingly glad to hear from Grace that I am coming to help her with her hotel. She is willing to engage me immediately—the sooner the better—and she will take the children in the holidays and "give them the run of their teeth." She mentions the salary she is prepared to offer, and hopes it will be acceptable, but, as this part of the letter is quite illegible, I cannot tell whether it is acceptable or not. Grace has told her I have no experience, but Miss Clutterbuck does not mind as long as I have my head screwed on the right way. Miss Clutterbuck has had to sack her former assistant because she was a fool—no head at all and apt to take the huff when her shortcomings were mentioned. Miss Clutterbuck would like me to run the bar—no, it can't be that—run the *car,* which has seen its best days but is still useful for shopping. The linen will be in my charge. Grace has told her I am patient and tactful, so (as she herself is neither the one nor the other) she thinks I am the right person to look after the social side.

Am so impressed with the coincidence of the two letters that I despatch a wire saying yes, and have no sooner done so than I am filled with apprehension and dismay.

Thursday, 14th February

Spend a sleepless night worrying about my future plans. How could I have been so mad as to accept Miss Clutterbuck's offer? What am I to do with Annie? Where is Betty to go for the remainder of the term? At six o'clock I decide I cannot lie in bed a moment longer, so I rise and dress and go down to the dining room and start a letter cancelling the whole thing.

Dear Miss Clutterbuck,
    On second thoughts I feel I am not at all the sort of person you require to help you . . .

No, that sounds humble. There is no need to be humble about it.

Dear Miss Clutterbuck,
    You will have received a telegram from me, accepting the post of receptionist in your hotel but on second thoughts I have come to the conclusion . . .

No, that won't do either—much too clumsy.

Dear Miss Clutterbuck,
    Since wiring to you I have changed my mind . . .

No, I don't like that either. Of course I have changed

my mind but why proclaim myself a weathercock to Miss Clutterbuck?

Dear Miss Clutterbuck,
    It was most kind of you to offer . . .

No, it wasn't the least kind of her. She is obviously desperate for an assistant and would take anyone short of a murderess. I seize another sheet of notepaper and begin again.

   Dear Miss Clutterbuck . . .

At this moment Annie comes in to lay ·the breakfast. She, also, has lain awake all night but her night thoughts have been more fruitful than mine and she is full of plans.

   "It's wonderful how things work out," says Annie cheerfully. "I thought at first ·it was all too difficult, but—"

   "It *is* too difficult, Annie."

   "Nothing's too difficult if you give your mind to it. Besides it looks to me as if it was Meant . . . you getting those two letters on the same day and Betty leaving Miss Clarke's. I was thinking we could find a school for Betty near the hotel so we could see her weekends or whatever's allowed."

   "*We* could see her!" I exclaim.

   "Of course I'm coming too," explains Annie, in a matter-of-fact tone. "You couldn't get on without *me,* and I daresay that Miss Chatterback will find a job for me, so you won't have to pay my wages. The Colonel said—"

   "Annie! I'm just writing to say I can't come."

   "Yes, that's what I thought," says Annie, with a glance

at the wastepaper basket. "But it seems a pity. It does, really. There isn't much for you to do in Donford—to take your mind off—and there'll be less when Betty goes away—and where will we stay when we're turned out of Winfield? It *does* look as if it was Meant."

I remain dumb.

"Lots of ladies do things like that nowadays," continues Annie persuasively. "Nobody thinks the worse of them for it—"

"It isn't that, at all," I assure her hastily. "I don't mind a bit what I do."

"What is it, then?"

"I'm afraid I'm not capable of tackling the job, and—"

Annie smiles. "Oh," says Annie. "You're quite capable when you set your mind to it. Look at the way you ran the Welfare! And I'll be there to see you don't get put upon," adds Annie firmly.

Spend the day swithering between hopeful confidence and blank despair. After tea Grace arrives in a contrite mood and says she is very sorry she was such a beast about the Erica Clutterbuck affair. She has been thinking it over seriously and talking to Mamie Carter and of course the job is quite unsuitable. I couldn't do it.

This annoys me—quite unreasonably, of course—and I reply that I think I could do it without much difficulty.

Grace says no. She and Mamie discussed it thoroughly and both of them are of the opinion that I couldn't do it. I'm not the right type. The sort of person Erica needs is a person with plenty of drive, a person full of initiative and resource—

Break into Grace's description of the ideal hotel assistant to point out that I have succeeded in running my household through six years of total war.

Grace says she knows, but this is different. She and Mamie have decided, definitely, that I mustn't go to Erica. Fortunately, says Grace, fortunately when she was looking at the *Times* this morning she happened to notice an advertisement for a dentist's receptionist. That would be the ideal job for me.

Reply that it is sweet of her to bother but I have decided to take the Clutterbuck job and have sent a wire to that effect.

Grace is horrified. She says I must be mad; I have no experience of running a hotel and have no idea what I am letting myself in for.

Reply that Miss Clutterbuck knows I haven't had any experience.

Grace says it would be too arduous. I should be worked to death . . . a dentist's receptionist would be far easier and I could live in London, think of that! She knows exactly what a dentist's receptionist has to do because her dentist has one—a delightful girl, of very good family, but unfortunately with a pronounced squint. All you do is to make appointments for people and hold the bowl for them to spit into after an extraction.

Say feebly, I would rather not.

"But, Hester," says Grace impatiently. "It wouldn't be every day—and as a matter of fact you would probably have far worse things to do if you went to Tocher House."

"Nothing could be worse," I murmur.

"You don't know Erica," retorts Grace. "Erica has a farouche manner—positively terrifying."

This certainly ought to put me off, for I dread people

with terrifying manners, but for some unknown reason it has the reverse effect. I am now confirmed and strengthened in my intention to proceed to Tocher with all speed. I point out to Grace that on Monday she was insistent that I should take this post.

Grace does not blink an eyelid. "Yes," she agrees. "Yes I know, but I've thought it over carefully. I've thought over all you said on Monday and I realize you were right. I mean I see your point, Hester."

"I've thought it over carefully and I see yours."

"It would be far too strenuous for you."

"But Grace, you said I should be much happier if I had lots to do."

"You said you had no experience of running a hotel—and you have none," Grace reminds me.

"And then you said Miss Clutterbuck would manage everything."

"I *know*," says Grace impatiently. "But then you said why did she need an assistant—and of course the answer is *to stooge for her.*"

"Then I shall stooge for her, Grace."

Grace glares at me so fiercely that I begin to laugh, and the next moment we are both laughing helplessly.

"Oh well," says Grace, blowing her nose. "We seem to have convinced each other pretty thoroughly. I still think a dentist's receptionist would be—"

"No, Grace."

"Oh well, if you've made up your mind there's no more to be said about it," says Grace. She hesitates and then enquires, "What will you do with Annie?"

Of course I know quite well what this question implies. Grace would like Annie for the twins, but I also know that this would never work because Grace is not Annie's sort of person. Annie is one of the family and, as such, she is given and takes liberties which Grace wouldn't tolerate. She was never a well-trained maid, and never will be, but she is a true friend which is a good deal better in my opinion. In the last few years, when maids were unobtainable, Annie and I have worked together and have got to know one another and to appreciate one another as we never should have done in ordinary circumstances. I look back at the raw, rather self-assertive girl who came to me as housemaid when we were at Biddington and realize how much Annie has changed. She has changed not only in appearance and in speech but in a more fundamental way as well. . . . No, Annie could never go to anyone else as maid or nurse, she would be miserable; but fortunately she will not have to. It is all decided that when Tim is free and we go to Cobstead to settle down there—and never move again—Annie and Bollings will be with us and will settle down, too.

All this passes through my mind in a flash and I explain to Grace that Annie and I are sticking together, and if Miss Clutterbuck wants me she will have to take Annie as well.

Grace sighs and says she might have known and of course Erica will have Annie like a shot, she'd be a fool not to.

Monday, 18th February

Although I have practically decided to send Betty to Dinwell Hall it is unthinkable to do so without seeing the place and interviewing the headmistress, so having made the necessary arrangements I start off from Donford at crack of dawn—this being the only manner in which I can accomplish my mission in one day. The first sight of Dinwell Hall impresses me favorably; it is a large square house situated in a pleasant park and it looks comfortable and peaceful. An elderly female opens the door, and on hearing my name says Miss Humble is expecting me. Conducting me to a room at the back of the house, she pokes up the fire and goes away. The room is full of contradictions—or so it seems to me—some of the furniture is old-fashioned, some of it strictly utilitarian and up-to-date. For a moment or two this puzzles me, and then I remember there are two Miss Humbles—co-partners in the school—and I decide that one of the ladies must be matter-of-fact and the other sentimental. The rolltop desk, the chair made of steel tubes and leather and the oak bookcase (unvarnished and perfectly plain) all belong to the matter-of-fact Miss Humble. The Victorian armchair, the occasional table, and the cabinet full of Dresden china belong to her sister, of course . . . also, of course, the Sheraton console table bearing a large dish of wax fruit, the mere sight of which makes my mouth water. The pictures display the same duality of taste, for it is obvious to the meanest intelligence that a woman who admired the brightly colored clear-cut cubist painting which hangs over the desk would never have chosen to suspend "The Huguenot Lovers" over the mantelpiece. All this is easy, it would have been child's play to Sherlock Holmes—even Watson might have guessed it—but which of the ladies chose the text, that large, illuminated text which hangs in the place of honor facing the window and enquires in red and blue and green lettering with gilt edges:

WHO HATH BELIEVED OUR REPORT?

Riven from its context and plastered upon the wall of a schoolmistresses' sanctum, its significance is somewhat startling. One wonders what significance it bears in the minds of the Misses Humble. Are they aware that parents are an incredulous set of people? Have they taken this unusual means of keeping the fact ever before their eyes? I examine my own reaction to reports which I have received from scholastic establishments (reports upon the attainments and behavior of my offspring) and am bound to admit that I have usually received them with a grain of salt. If the report is favorable one has an uncomfortable feeling that it is insincere, if tepid one springs to the conclusion that one's child is misunderstood.

I am indulging in these interesting reflections when I am surprised by the incidence of the Misses Humble. They welcome me with cordial dignity and introduce themselves. The large fat one (in the well-fitting coat and skirt) with close-cropped grey hair and flashing spectacles with tortoiseshell rims is Miss Humble, herself; the small thin one (in a green linen overall) with shaggy brown hair and bright brown eyes is Miss Lena Humble. Miss Humble looks after the scholastic side and cares for the children's minds; Miss Lena is the domestic one and cares for their bodies. All this and more is explained to me by Miss Humble, clearly and rapidly in a few well-chosen words; it is obvious that every prospective parent is treated to the same little speech of explanation.

I listen and nod and examine the ladies with interest. Although they are quite unlike one another in build, feature and personality, the fact—most curiously—remains that anyone would know they were sisters. I was right about them, of course. Miss Humble is the owner of the desk, the steel-tube chair, the bookcase and the cubist picture; Miss Lena is the owner of "The Huguenot Lovers," the occasional table, the china cabinet and the wax fruit. As for the text I am not so sure . . . perhaps Miss Humble chose the text and Miss Lena painted it, or perhaps it was painted by a pupil with an eye for color and a particularly neat hand.

We chat in a friendly manner. As is natural, they want to know all about Betty and my only difficulty is not to tell them too much. I endeavor to assume a "sensible" attitude, to convince the Misses Humble that I consider Betty an ordinary child, neither particularly charming nor outstandingly bright, but the Misses Humble are old hands at the game and I feel sure they see through me like a pane of glass. Just another foolish mother, they are saying to themselves as they nod and smile and egg me on to further foolishness, just another fond mama who thinks her duckling a swan.

"And when would you like her to come—if you decide to let us have her?" enquires Miss Lena Humble with interest.

I reply by telling them my predicament and explain that I intend to leave Betty at Donford; she can board with Miss Clarke until the end of the term.

The ladies look at each other. "Yes," says Miss Lena, nodding.

"Yes," says Miss Humble. "We can take Betty at once if that would suit you. The fact is we have a vacancy. One of our pupils left unexpectedly because her parents went south and wanted to take her with them. I thought it unwise, but—"

"It was very unwise," declares Miss Lena.

They shake their heads over the unwisdom of parents.

"We don't usually take children in the middle of a term," continues Miss Humble. "But in view of the special circumstances we would be willing to relax our rules."

"For Betty," adds Miss Lena, smiling kindly.

This would suit me admirably, of course, but I feel unreasonably downcast. I feel as if the trap were closing upon my child; I have almost lost her already. Is it possible that in my heart of hearts I hoped that Dinwell Hall would be unsuitable?

"The children are very happy here," declares Miss Lena. "We feed them well—as well as we possibly can. We have a Home Farm, you know, and that helps a lot."

"You would like to see the classrooms," suggests Miss Humble.

"And the dormitories, of course," adds Miss Lena.

We make a tour of the school and no fault can be found with the arrangements. The children, hard at work in sunny classrooms, look cheerful and well fed. In spite of this—or perhaps because of it—my spirits sink lower at every step and when I take leave of the Misses Humble at the front door I am almost speechless with misery.

"Then we shall expect Betty next week," says Miss Humble cheerfully. "I feel sure she will go straight into Form Four. Miss Wentworth is *most* competent."

"I shall meet Betty at the station," says Miss Lena in friendly tones.

"Clothes . . ." I murmur, clutching at a straw. "I don't see how—"

"Do what you can about clothes," says Miss Lena. "We have some secondhand garments—perfectly good, of course —so we shall be able to help in that way, but it would be nice if you could spare enough coupons for a reasonably complete outfit—nice for Betty, I mean."

"Don't worry too much about clothes," says Miss Humble firmly.

Betty's fate is sealed.

Larder completely empty this morning (except for a very small bone which Annie says she will boil for soup). This necessitates an expedition to the shops so I leave Annie to turn out the drawing room—a task in which I had intended to take part—and sally forth to see what I can find. My expedition is satisfactory, by present-day standards, and I return triumphantly with a loaf, a pound of sausages, three oranges and two very small haddocks. Grace is waiting for me and has brought me three eggs, so we are now stocked for a prolonged siege and can get on comfortably with the cleaning.

I feel a little dubious about accepting the eggs from Grace, the gift being so munificent, but Grace says, "Take them and be thankful, but don't ask where I got them, that's all."

Reply that I should not dream of making such an unnecessary enquiry.

This being settled Grace sits down on the arm of the sofa and says she intended to come and see me yesterday afternoon but she had to take the twins to the dentist for their biannual inspection. She wanted to ask me if I listened to the talk on Sunday night. "You should have listened," says Grace. "It was most interesting—all about how kind and brotherly the Russians are."

"Are they?" I enquire.

Grace says she was surprised, too. She has never been to Russia, nor does she know any Russians, so the only way she can judge them is by their actions.

"Quite a good way!" I suggest.

Grace says it's rather puzzling. The speaker has just returned from Russia and he says they are a most delightful people, they spend their time singing and dancing, they drink vodka and eat smoked salmon and exude brotherly love at every pore. It sounded lovely, says Grace, and of course he must know, but she finds it a little difficult to reconcile this account of them with their actions. She pauses for breath and then continues, "I mean if you went round Donford accusing me of being a mischief-maker, trying to put people against me, I shouldn't put down your activities to sisterly affection. In fact I should be inclined to think it a little unfriendly."

"Unreasonable of you, Grace."

"I think it's all rather frightening," declares Grace, looking at me with large serious eyes. "Yes, *frightening* . . . and if there ever should be another war I should like someone to kill me before it starts and bury me very, very deeply in the ground, because—to tell you the truth—I just . . . simply . . . couldn't . . . bear it."

We are silent for a few moments.

"However," says Grace, pulling herself together with a visible effort. "However I didn't come here to cry 'Bogey, bogey!' I came to ask you about your visit to Dothegirls Hall."

"It's perfect," I reply in tepid accents.

"They do the girls well?"

"Yes, the food is good and the education leaves nothing to be desired."

"The girls are well fed and well dinned."

"Really, Grace—"

"I know," says Grace repentantly. "I'm a bit upset, that's what's the matter. Tell me all about it, Hester."

I tell her all about Dinwell Hall, and all about the Misses Humble, and all about the interesting psychological data revealed by their private sitting room. Grace listens and nods—she is particularly struck with the text and murmurs with a thoughtful air that it is a new one on her.

" 'Who hath believed our report,' " says Grace. "Poor old things! What a life! It's pathetic, isn't it?"

The Misses Humble did not strike me as pathetic—not in the least—and I assure Grace that she need waste no sympathy upon them. They are neither poor nor old, but well-off and only middle-aged, and to all appearances perfectly happy; and as a matter of fact (I assure Grace) I have never seen two pegs in more comfortably fitting holes.

"Holes!" exclaims Grace. "That reminds me. I knew there was something I wanted to tell you. It was yesterday when I was taking the boys to the dentist. Ian was dancing along, full of the joy of life, but Alec seemed terribly depressed and listless. I was rather surprised because they're usually in the same sort of mood; I mean they're usually both cheerful or both broody. Then Ian said, 'I don't mind going to the dentist. I haven't got any holes in *my* teeth. Alec's got a hole. It hurts when he eats sweets. You've got a hole, Alec.' 'I think so,' said Alec in a sad voice. Then his face brightened and he added, 'But perhaps Mr. Barnes won't find it.' "

Grace's stories about her twins are often rather silly, but I like this one.

Wednesday, 27th February

After nearly ten days of complete chaos, order has emerged; everything is settled and I am leaving Winfield tomorrow, spending the night in Edinburgh and taking up my appointment on Friday. It is true that Winfield is ours until the end of March but the Fates have conspired to hasten our departure. Miss Clutterbuck wants me immediately and has agreed to take Annie as second housemaid and pay her a good wage, so Annie has gone to her sister for a holiday and will come to Tocher House later. Betty has gone to Dinwell Hall, taking with her a trunkful of garments for which Annie and I have surrendered every coupon we possessed. In addition to all these arrangements and activities I have had to cope with a shower of cables from Tim, urging me to look before I leap and beseeching me to go to Cobstead or to Mrs. Loudon or to take rooms in Donford; and I have been obliged to reply at length explaining my actions. I have interviewed the house agent and the painter; I have toiled through the inventory of Winfield and endeavored to replace broken or missing china and worn out pots and pans; Annie and I together have cleaned and washed and polished, turned out cupboards, packed boxes and tied up large bundles for the Jumble Sale. Our labors were complicated and interrupted by visits from various friends in Donford who made a habit of dropping in at the most inconvenient moments to say good-bye. One good thing about all this hurry and confusion is that I have had little time to think, for now that the time has come to leave Donford I find I have become very fond of it. We have been here all through the war, we have shared in Donford's wartime activities, shared in its anxieties, in its privations and its victory celebrations. Better to leave quickly rather than brood over our departure for another month.

Today I am alone in the house. I wander about like a lost spirit—for there is nothing left to do. I wander amongst corded boxes and packing cases and although I am extremely weary it is impossible to rest.

At lunchtime Grace comes in, accompanied by the twins, and discovers me eating bread and cheese in the kitchen.

"Hester!" exclaims Grace in horrified tones. "Why didn't you come to lunch with me?"

"Too tired," I murmur. "Too fed-up. Besides bread and cheese and coffee is a perfectly good meal."

"It's letting down the flag," says Grace reproachfully. "It's backsliding—that's what it is. I wouldn't have thought it of you, Hester. Think of the men who change for dinner every night on desert islands!"

"I've never really believed in them," I reply, helping myself to another wedge of cheese. "And anyhow, I've slid. I'm a displaced person."

"Displaced person!" cries Grace. "What nonsense, Hester! You've got a job. If you don't like it you can come and stay with me—or go to Cobstead. Displaced person my foot!"

Grace is doing me good as she always does. Sometimes she annoys me considerably but that does me good, too. It is not the least of my regrets in leaving Donford to be leaving Grace.

"Are you going straight to Tocher House tomorrow?" enquires Grace.

Reply that I am going to Edinburgh tomorrow to stay the night with Pinkie Loudon and do some necessary shopping before taking up my appointment on Friday.

Grace says, "Pinkie!" in scornful tones . . . for, most regrettably, Grace does not like Pinkie and never has. It always seems odd when two people, whom one likes enormously, show marked antipathy to one another, and the case of Grace and Pinkie is a case in point. Pinkie is a dear, completely natural and unspoilt. When she stayed with us for nearly two years, she was a delightful addition to the family, helping me in all sorts of ways and keeping me cheerful company while Tim was in France. And we were happy when she met Guthrie Loudon (the son of our old friend Mrs. Loudon of Avielochan) and became engaged to him.

"I suppose she's married, now," says Grace after a short pause.

"Yes, they're married now. Guthrie's ship is at Rosyth so they've taken a little flat in Edinburgh. It will be fun to see Pinkie again."

"I don't know how you can be bothered with the child," says Grace impatiently.

"I don't know why you dislike her," I retort.

"She's such a little wretch. She led you a fine life when she was staying with you . . . first she had all the subalterns dancing attendance on her, and then she carried on with those Polish officers."

"It was all quite innocent, Grace. As a matter of fact Pinkie can't help it; she's perfectly lovely to look at and men just—"

"I don't admire her at all," snaps Grace. "I can't stand that big, bouncing, blonde type of girl."

"A little unfair," I murmur with a smile. "Just a little unworthy of you, Grace."

But Grace is not listening. She glances at her own reflection in the kitchen mirror and obviously admires what she sees. (Her own mat complexion and dark curls and the slim elegance of her own figure are more to her taste than Pinkie's pink and gold charms.)

"Oh yes, you're beautiful, too," I tell her, trying to look as solemn as an owl.

During the foregoing conversation the two little boys have been wandering round the kitchen poking their noses into everything like a couple of strange dogs, but now they have finished exploring and are ready to talk.

"Aunt Hester's like Old Mother Hubbard," says Ian, the elder, in conversational tones.

"That's rude, Ian," admonished Grace.

" 'Tisn't rude, it's true," declares Alec. "The cupboard was bare and so the poor dog got none."

"Aunt Hester is going away," explains Grace. "She took everything out of the cupboard and packed it. Besides, she hasn't got a dog. You know that, don't you."

"What about the mice?" enquires Ian. "What will the mice do?"

"The poor little mice!" cries Alec in pathetic accents. "No cheese, no nothing for the poor little darling mice!"

Grace murmurs, "So tenderhearted," and looks at her offspring with an adoring smile which annoys me excessively.

"The poor little darling mice will starve to death," I remark in a brutal manner.

"Oh *no!*" cries Grace. "Aunt Hester is only joking. The dear little mice will go next door for their dinners."

"I know what to do," says Alec brightly. "If Aunt Hester leaves a teeny piece of cheese we could put it in the cupboard for the mice to eat."

"We could poison it," cries Ian excitedly. "Alec, we could poison it."

"Oh yes!" cries Alec, hopping about with glee. "Do let's poison it. Then Ian and me could come in on our way home from school—"

"And *sweep* them up," cries Ian, making sweeping gestures. "We could *sweep* up dozens and dozens of dead mice all over the floor . . . and bury them."

"So tenderhearted!" I murmur.

"But, darlings," says Grace earnestly. "Listen to Mummy a minute. You wouldn't like to see the poor little mice, all dead."

"I wouldn't mind," declares Alec. "I saw a dead cat, yesterday."

"You didn't," says Ian indignantly. "I saw it first and it was only a kitten."

"It was *nearly* a cat," objects Alec. "I believe it would have been a cat if it had lived a week longer."

"Poor little thing," says Grace. "I expect you were sorry about it, weren't you?"

"Not awfully," says Alec truthfully.

"We didn't know it, you see," explains Ian. "It might have been a *horrid* kitten for all we knew."

"It *was* a horrid kitten," says Alec in reminiscent tones. "It had been dead for a long time. It was all covered with—"

"Alec!" says Grace firmly. "Alec, I want you to say a poem to Aunt Hester—the one you learnt at school. Aunt

Hester is going away tomorrow and you won't see her again for a long time. You know that sweet little poem about the children playing in the garden. You'll do it to please Mummy, won't you?"

Alec says he won't, and I don't blame him.

"But I will," says Ian with a seraphic smile. "I'll say a sweet little poem for Aunt Hester. It's about some children playing near a stream."

"The one Uncle Tubby taught us," says Alec, giggling. "Oh yes, Ian. I'll say it too."

"I'll say it myself—"

"No, together. Please, Ian."

"Say it together, darlings," says Grace fondly.

They stand up together, hand in hand—two lovely little boys with dark hair, blue eyes, and pink and white complexions, two lovely little boys, so alike that one can hardly tell them apart except that Alec, the younger, is slightly taller and sturdier than his brother. Grace beams on them, of course, and in all fairness I must admit she has reason to be proud of their appearance.

"Go on, darlings," says Grace. "Aunt Hester and Mummy are listening."

Thus adjured the twins open their dear little mouths and say the poem in unison—the sweet little poem that Uncle Tubby taught them:

"Three little children were playing near a stream,
    Mummy heard them shouting, Mummy heard them scream;
    Mummy picked them up and threw them in the water
    (First her little sons and then her only daughter),
    Murmuring so sweetly as she drowned the third,
    'Mummy's little darlings should be seen, not heard.'"

Thursday, 28th February

When I find myself actually in the train on the way to Edinburgh, with all my luggage complete, I am not only surprised but slightly smug at my cleverness. I pull up the window, sit back in my seat and review the situation. Here am I suspended between two worlds, the known world of Donford and the unknown world of Tocher House. It is slightly alarming, of course, for I have never before done anything like this on my own responsibility, but there is a curious elation in my bosom; I feel brave and capable and optimistic. I feel free. For the moment I have no responsibilities—not one. I have sloughed them as a snake its skin; husband, house and children—not to speak of the various committees and social duties connected with the regiment—are all shed and for today at least I am my own woman. Today I am myself, Hester Christie, and the freedom of the world is mine. I am aware, of course, that this sense of freedom may turn into forlorn despondency, homesickness may set in and make me yearn for my chains, but just for the moment all is well and the sun is shining.

Pinkie meets me at the station. I have not set eyes on her for months, but I am delighted to see she is exactly the same Pinkie, as large and beautiful as ever. She falls upon me with cries of joy and nearly squeezes me to death in the exuberance of her welcome. In fact she is so excited that I am quite alarmed, for I am aware that inordinate excitement in Pinkie prompts her to perform Catherine Wheels and these would be slightly out of place on the platform of the Waverly Station.

"Darling!" cries Pinkie. "Darling Hester . . . but I'm terribly angry with you. Where's your suitcase? Give it to me. I'll take that, too—and that." She seizes two suitcases, a holdall, a large basket of provisions and a brown-paper parcel and marches off with them.

"Stop! Let me carry something!" I cry, galloping after her.

"It's nothing," says Pinkie. "I'm as strong as a lion— and we'd better hurry because I've got a taxi waiting, unless of course he's deserted us and gone off with somebody else. He isn't there! Hester, isn't that sickening! Oh no, *there* he is, waiting quite patiently, poor soul. I know him by his funny little moustache—rather like Hitler, don't you think? Perhaps he *is* Hitler—or are you one of the people who think Hitler is really dead? Guthrie is sure he isn't. Guthrie thinks Hitler went off to Ireland and left one of his doubles to die with Eva Braun. . . . *There* you are!" exclaims Pinkie rapturously to the taxi driver. "I thought you'd gone when you weren't there."

"We're not allowed to wait over there, miss," explains the man.

"Well, I didn't know, you see," says Pinkie. "But anyhow here you are. It was awfully nice of you to wait and not go off with an American Officer who would have given you a pound and not asked for change."

The man smiles and says there are not as many of those about as you'd think from reading the papers and anyway he said he'd wait.

"I can see you're a man of your word," says Pinkie, handing me in.

We crawl up the slope from the station and buzz along Princess Street at a terrific pace.

"And now, Hester," says Pinkie, looking at me with her large blue eyes. "Now perhaps you will explain what you mean by this. I'm terribly angry with you—and so is Guthrie. We're both absolutely furious. . . ."

At this moment the taxi swerves violently and Pinkie clutches my arm. "Oh Heavens!" she cries. "Look at that child! I thought we were over it! People ought to take more care of their children and teach them not to cross the road without looking. Guthrie says people here are terribly careless compared with other countries. I know you always used to tell Betty to look both ways . . . how is Betty? And Bryan—how's dear Bryan? I simply love Bryan, he's the most adorable creature. . . . No, it's here on the left!" cries Pinkie, leaning forward and knocking on the window. "Yes, that's right . . . no, no, on the *left!*"

The taxi zigzags across the street from left to right and back again and finally stops with a jerk opposite Pinkie's door.

"Sorry, miss," says the man. "I thought you said left, and then I thought you said right."

"It was my fault entirely," declares Pinkie, beaming at him. "I said left, which it *was,* and then I said that's right. You see?"

The man says, "Oh, that was the way of it!" and pockets his money with a satisfied air.

Pinkie's flat is at the top of the house, so we climb three flights of stairs and arrive in a breathless condition. It is a small flat but very comfortably furnished and it has a gorgeous view over the Forth to the Fife hills.

"There," says Pinkie proudly. "Isn't it divine? Isn't it the darlingest little flat you ever saw? I simply adore it—and so does Guthrie. This is your room, Hester—rather small, I'm afraid, but—"

"Lovely!" I declare. "Terribly nice, couldn't be nicer. I shall sleep like a top in this comfy bed."

Pinkie bustles round while I am taking off my things and in a few minutes we are sitting cosily by the fire, having tea.

"Why are you annoyed with me?" I enquire, as I munch my scone.

"Not just *annoyed,*" says Pinkie earnestly. "Guthrie and I are both in the most frightful rage, Hester. You knew quite well you could come here and stay as long as you liked. You knew we'd love to have you."

"But Pinkie—"

"I stayed with you for years," continues Pinkie. "I had the most heavenly time, one way and another, and of course I met Guthrie. If it hadn't been for you I should never have met Guthrie at all. Everything nice that I've got is because of you—*everything*. And now," says Pinkie, reproachfully, "now you've gone and fixed yourself up with a horrible job . . . Well, of *course* I'm angry."

"Pinkie, you see—"

"I can't *imagine* you doing a job, Hester. Honestly, I can't. What sort of things will you have to do?"

"I shall just do what I'm told."

"It sounds frightful," says Pinkie.

I explain the circumstances to Pinkie at great length and show how one thing led to another and all things put together practically forced me into accepting the post. I explain my feelings too: Tim is in Egypt and the children both at school and unless I have some definite work to keep me occupied I shall become dull and mouldy. My eloquence is such that I manage to convince Pinkie and her anger is somewhat appeased.

"I wouldn't mind quite so much if the woman wasn't a friend of Mrs. MacDougall. Somehow or other I don't *like* Mrs. MacDougall," says Pinkie with a surprised sort of air. "I know you like her, Hester, so of course she must be nice, but . . ." she shakes her head sadly and leaves it at that.

"Do you think she's pretty?" I enquire with interest.

"Very," replies Pinkie without hesitation. "She's more than pretty—in fact she's just the type of person I admire, pale and dark and slender," says Pinkie with a sigh. "Quite lovely, really. But all the same I don't like her. It's funny, isn't it? Guthrie thinks—"

"Pinkie, I do *not* want to hear what Guthrie thinks."

"Why?" enquires Pinkie in amazement.

"How would you like it if I were to keep on telling you what Tim thinks about every single subject we discuss?"

"Oh . . ." says Pinkie, doubtfully. "Yes, I suppose it would be rather boring."

"I'm very fond of Guthrie, but I don't want to hear his opinions secondhand."

"No, of course not," agrees Pinkie. "I'll have to watch that. It might become a habit."

"It might," I reply. "And women who get into the habit of reporting their husbands' opinions are almost as bad as the ones who talk about their children—but not quite."

"Tell me about your children, darling," says Pinkie, drawing her chair nearer the fire.

A large railway station is always an interesting study for a woman who is interested in her fellow creatures. People rush about madly, clutching baskets and suitcases. Their faces are drawn with anxiety, their eyes are wild. Small children buttoned into coats, too tight for them, are pulled hither and thither by one hand and endure these discomforts and humiliations with resigned expressions. Occasionally they burst into loud roars of grief or pain, but these occasions are the exception, not the rule.

Pinkie accompanies me to the station. She finds a corner seat for me (we are very early) and piles my luggage in the rack.

"There," says Pinkie. "Now you'll be all right, won't you? The man says the train stops at Ryddelton so you won't have to change . . . and don't forget if you can't stick it you must come straight back to me."

"Don't wait, Pinkie."

"No, I won't," says Pinkie. She takes leave of me affectionately and away she goes, striding down the platform with the air of a young goddess.

How sensible of Pinkie not to wait! Valedictory conversations are so trying and so fruitless, and the more one likes one's "see-er-off", the more agonizing they are. One comes to the end of everything one has to say, and still there are five minutes left . . . one searches feverishly for something and nothing can be found.

But this disability is not universal. Some travelers think it their due to be seen off by their friends, and would feel insulted and neglected if the said friends did not remain by their sides until the train actually started upon its way. There is, for instance, a tall woman in a bright green hat who stakes out a claim at the other end of the compartment and having done so leans out of the window and discourses with two girls who have come to see her off, and it is obvious she is enjoying her role of departing traveler and glorying in her importance. A nice-looking woman, she is, clad in tweeds, and her hair beneath the brim of the green hat is well-waved and soignée. Unfortunately her voice is less pleasant than her appearance—it has a monotonous twang. This woman is a past master in the art of valedictory conversation, she chats brightly and keeps up such a constant flow that, malgré moi, I cannot but admire her. She sends long messages to Uncle Bob and Sylvia; she asserts that she has enjoyed her visit to Edinburgh immensely—especially the Zoo. She wishes there were a Zoo at Carlisle. Will it be dark when she reaches Carlisle, she wonders. She points out a very ordinary-looking woman leading a fox terrier up the platform and exclaims in amazement at the sight. There was a pug in the carriage with her, traveling in the same compartment as herself when she came to Edinburgh, and she embarks upon a long story about it, but breaks off at the sight of two sailors carrying kit bags and says they are too sweet. The girls do not help her much. They murmur yes and no. They glance at their watches surreptitiously; they fiddle with their handbags; they stand first on one leg and then on the other . . . but, these signs of strain have no effect upon Green Hat. She prattles on.

This exhibition of social competence is so enthralling

that I scarcely notice a tall man in a khaki overcoat who comes into the compartment from the corridor and takes the seat opposite me. Indeed it is not until the train begins to move and Green Hat, having waved enthusiastically, settles down into her corner with a satisfied smile, that I can take my eyes off her and give some attention to my other companion. He has now removed his overcoat and stowed it in the rack, and his crowns proclaim him a major, his buttons an artilleryman. His medal-ribbons show he has seen service in France and North Africa—quite an interesting little dossier in fact. For the rest he has a thin brown face with rather a high forehead, well-marked eyebrows and intelligent grey eyes.

The train gathers speed. The suburbs of Edinburgh flash past and soon we are amongst green fields dotted with browsing cattle; there are bare brown trees, skeleton hedges and an occasional half-frozen pond. The tops of the distant hills are covered with snow and the sky is very blue. It is curious to think that, at this very moment while I am sitting with frozen toes and numb fingers, Tim is probably finding it too warm . . . not really hot, of course, for Egypt is a pleasant place in March.

I glance at the major again, and discover to my embarrassment that he is staring at me. Our glances meet . . . whereupon he leans forward and asks in a very deep voice if I would like him to close the window. This is an unoriginal gambit, but it does well enough and we continue to chat about the weather and the countryside. Green Hat is interested in our conversation and doubtless would like to take part, but the major gives her no opportunity to do so. Perhaps he heard her chatting to her friends and is aware that if once she starts there will be no stopping her.

After a few minutes the major leans forward and says, "Do you know Tim Christie?"

"Tim!" I exclaim, idiotically. "Of course I know Tim!"

"Then you *are* Mrs. Tim! I was sure of it!" declares the major.

At this I am even more surprised and demand how he can possibly have discovered my identity as I make a point of having no large labels attached to myself or my luggage.

He replies in some confusion that he has seen my photograph.

"My photograph!"

"Yes. As a matter of fact I met Tim in France at the very beginning of the war; we were billeted in the same town. It was like this," he says confidentially. "Oh, by the way my name is Roger Elden. I don't suppose you've heard Tim mention my name because I didn't know him well. . . . Tim managed to get hold of a case of whisky by some unlawful means, and, being hospitably inclined, he was always asking us round to his quarters. He had your photograph hanging on the wall and one day I asked him who it was."

"So he told you."

"Not exactly," says Major Elden smiling. "He said it was his pin-up girl, but I heard all about you from one of the other fellows in the regiment."

Being only human I long to know who it was and what he said about me, but of course I can't enquire . . . being only human I am pleased and flattered to hear that Major Elden has remembered me all these years and recognized me from my photograph . . . being fairly sensible I am somewhat astonished at the feat.

"He got away all right," says Major Elden after a short pause.

I reply that he managed to get away after adventures that would put a shilling shocker to shame, and add that, since then, he has been all through the European Campaign and is now in Egypt.

"We travel around, don't we?" says Major Elden with a smile. "I suppose you'll be going to Egypt one of these days, when things settle down a bit."

"Well, of course I should like to," I reply. "But Tim seems to think it will be some time before wives are allowed. We shall have to wait and see."

He asks me about the children, and as he seems interested I tell him about them, but I refrain from telling him about my arrangement with Miss Clutterbuck as I have a feeling he is an old-fashioned type of man and would not approve.

Green Hat, who has been listening with all her ears, breaks in to ask if the train stops at Carlisle, and as I am aware that Green Hat knows full well the train stops at Carlisle I feel slightly annoyed with her.

Major Elden says, "I beg your pardon," and, on Green Hat's repetition of the idiotic question, replies, "Yes, all trains stop at Carlisle."

"I wondered if I would have to change at Carstairs," says Green Hat plaintively.

"No," says Major Elden.

"Sometimes you do," asserts Green Hat. "I knew a lady who was going to Carlisle and found herself in Glasgow."

"This train goes through to London, stopping at Carlisle on the way," says Major Elden firmly. He then turns his shoulder to Green Hat and we resume our conversation.

It is now his turn to be informative. He tells me he is a lawyer in private life and is about to be demobilized. ("I am taking felt next week," says Major Elden with a smile.) During the war his business has wilted away but this does not seem to worry him unduly. "It will be nice to be a free man," says Major Elden. "Of course I shall want a job later, but not just at once. I have a little daughter; she's at school of course, but we're going to have a good time together in the holidays. Sheila is all I've got, you see. My wife died soon after she was born."

Green Hat has been very quiet for the last ten minutes and I now observe she has gone to sleep. She is less attractive in this condition, her hat has slipped to one side and her jaw has dropped. Major Elden says it isn't often you see women asleep in trains. Men frequently seize the opportunity for forty winks, but not women. He has thought about this phenomenon a good deal and has come to the conclusion that vanity keeps them awake, what do I think about it. I have given the subject no consideration but feel inclined to disagree with him (in spite of Green Hat's unlovely pose which is certainly an argument in favour of his theory) so I reply with suitable gravity that a woman's subconscious mind forbids her to sleep unguarded; it is a primitive instinct, persisting from the Stone Age. Major Elden glances at Green Hat and says he sees what I mean, but he still thinks it is vanity—and nothing more.

It is much easier to talk now that Green Hat is asleep and Major Elden becomes more confidential. He tells me about Sheila and about her school and about his difficulties in buying clothes for her and making arrangements for her holidays.

"Haven't you anyone to help you?" I enquire. "Haven't you a sister or—"

"Nobody," replies Major Elden. He hesitates for a moment and then adds, "There's a possibility I might marry again . . . if the lady will have me."

"She'd be silly not to!" I exclaim, and this is true, for Major Elden is the sort of man who would make an excellent husband.

He laughs and replies, "You had to say that, of course!"

There is a short silence. We both look out of the window. Then he leans forward and says, "I wonder if—I mean would it bore you frightfully if I told you about it and asked your advice? It sounds mad to talk like this to someone you've never seen before—"

"Sometimes it's easier to talk to a stranger."

"I think it would be easy."

"Go on," I tell him encouragingly. "You've never seen me before and you'll never see me again, so—"

"Oh, I wouldn't go as far as that! Why shouldn't we meet again, someday?"

This question requires no answer, nor does he seem to expect one. He frowns for a few moments, marshaling his thoughts and then continues, "You mustn't think it's just because of Sheila I want to marry again. It would be nice for Sheila, of course, but . . . no, I must start at the beginning. You see when my wife died I thought I should never want to marry again. We had been blissfully happy. Eva was the most marvelous person. It could never be quite the same. Nobody could ever take Eva's place—if you know what I mean—but I'm very fond of Margaret and I feel sure we could make a good thing of life together. We enjoy the same things, we understand each other . . . at least I thought we did." He pauses and sighs.

"Something has gone wrong," I suggest.

"Yes," he says. "Yes, I'm afraid so, but I must tell you more about her. I met her about four years ago when I was billeted near Chichester. She was a companion to an old lady, a disagreeable old dame who worked her like a slave. I used to drop in and chat to the old lady and then drag Margaret out for a walk. She likes walking and so do I; we had some good times, one way and another, and we—well, we came to an understanding. We couldn't be openly engaged because the old lady would have been furious, she was that sort of person. Then I was bundled away to North Africa. We played about there for a bit and eventually took ship for Italy where we had more fun and games. . . . I got home about a month ago. The old lady is dead now, so I thought it would be plain sailing, but Margaret seems to have changed her mind. I can't understand it, really, because we wrote to each other constantly; everything seemed all right until I got home. Now everything is all wrong. Of course if she really has changed her mind that's that—I can take it—but somehow I'm not sure. What should I do?" enquires Major Elden, looking at me earnestly.

"How can I tell you!" I exclaim. "If I knew your Margaret—but I don't know anything about her. I don't know what she's like."

"I thought you might advise me whether to wait a bit and then try again," explains Major Elden. "You see I know very little about women, that's the trouble. People say that women often say no when they mean yes."

"People say a good many silly things!"

"Then it isn't true?" he enquires.

"It depends on the person. Is Margaret like that?"

"No, she isn't. She's a pretty definite sort of person."

"Well, then . . ."

"But she's had a rotten time lately and she says she wants to be free. I wondered if she would go on wanting to be free—or is it a passing phase?"

"Has she any money? Enough to live on, I mean."

"Oh yes," he replies. "The old lady was comfortably off. She left everything to Margaret. Money doesn't enter into it, one way or the other."

"I should wait for a little and give her another chance."

He smiles at me. "You really think so? I hate the idea of badgering her but I do feel we could be happy. I know she felt the same until just lately."

"Perhaps she thought you were taking it all too much for granted."

"I wonder—" he says, thoughtfully. "No, I don't believe it's that, somehow."

"You must give her another chance."

"You're an advocate for marriage?"

"Yes, definitely. A woman once said to me it was better to be unhappily married than not to be married at all. I wouldn't go as far as that, but—"

"I wouldn't, either," declares Major Elden, laughing.

By this time we have left Carstairs behind and are in the midst of rounded hills, covered with yellowish green grass and brown heather. The train is laboring up a gradient; the engine is puffing and panting with the strain. We talk about other gradients in various parts of the world, in the Himalayas and in Italy; now we have reached the summit and are flying down the other side and we rock to and fro gathering speed in a most alarming manner. Major Elden seems unalarmed, he cleans the window, which has become a little steamy, and says that's a most attractive-looking burn. He would like to have a day's fishing amongst these hills; perhaps he will before he's much older.

Miss Clutterbuck meets me at Ryddelton Station. It is quite a small station and there are not more than a dozen people on the platform, most of them railway officials, so there is no doubt at all as to the identity of my employer. She stands near the bookstall, a solid figure in a Lovat tweed coat which is somewhat shabby but very well cut. She stands with her feet well apart and her hands in her coat pockets, a cigarette in a cherry-wood cigarette holder is stuck in the corner of her mouth. She is short-necked; she is hatless, her grey wavy hair is slightly tousled with the evening breeze. For some strange reason Miss Clutterbuck reminds me of Mr. Churchill, Mr. Churchill in one of his belligerent moods.

Miss Clutterbuck's eyes fall upon me as I alight from the train, fall upon me and move on without interest (it is as if she said, No, that is not my new assistant) and this denial of me is so alarming that in a moment of panic I turn to climb back into the train . . . but the train only halts here for a few moments and already Major Elden is handing out my luggage to the porter so it is too late to change my mind. The whistle blows, the train moves off and I am marooned upon the platform.

Miss Clutterbuck, having glanced at the other passengers who have alighted from the train, and having decided that the young woman with the two small children is not her new assistant (nor the man with the fishing basket on his back . . . nor the aged female in the long black coat . . . nor the platinum blonde with the plucked eyebrows who has attached herself firmly to a member of the Air Force) advances upon me with a firm step. "You are Mrs. Christie," she says.

I agree that I am no other.

"I thought you would be—different," says Miss Clutterbuck.

As I know this already there is nothing to be said— nothing to be done, either. It is with difficulty I refrain from apologizing for being as I am; but I manage to refrain and follow her to the waiting car without further speech. Did she think I would be older—or younger? Did she expect her new assistant to be better-looking, or worse? Perhaps she hoped for a woman with a commanding presence to overawe recalcitrant guests.

"This is the car," says Miss Clutterbuck. "It's old, but it still goes. You can drive."

"Yes. . . . Oh yes, I can drive."

Fortunately she does not expect me to drive tonight. She cranks the car in a competent manner and off we go.

Grace said Miss Clutterbuck was alarming—and so she is. She alarms me so much that I am speechless and as Miss Clutterbuck's attention is taken up with driving the ancient and somewhat temperamental car we accomplish the five mile drive in almost complete silence. In any other circumstances I should enjoy the drive for the country is lovely. The light is fading and the sky is pale, but there is a glow in the west which clothes the high, rounded hills with radiance. All along the valley there are little farms surrounded with fields . . . a man is ploughing a steep piece of ground with two horses . . . there are woods here and there, woods of closely growing conifers, and a narrow river winds along by the side of the road. Miss Clutterbuck, in a rare burst of loquacity, waves towards it with one hand and says "The Rydd," and I now remember that Grace spoke of the Rydd and told me that it flowed through the town of Ryddelton.

Presently we mount a steep hill, turn in at a stone gateway and roar up a drive through a park dotted with beech trees. This is Tocher, I presume, and I look about me with interest. The first thing that strikes me is that the place is exceedingly well kept, which is rather unusual in this period of postwar dilapidation. The drive itself has been re-metaled, the railings are in good order and painted dark green. Tocher House stands upon a slight eminence; it is a large rambling building which obviously has been added to at various times. I have a swift vision of windows flashing brightly in the evening sun, and the next moment we pull up with a jerk before the pillared doorway with its short flight of stone steps.

Miss Clutterbuck says, "Todd will see to the luggage," and leads the way into her house with a firm step. The hall is large and airy, the lounge leads out of it to the right. I catch a glimpse of people sitting there, of a man reading a paper, and a woman knitting a scarlet jumper, as I follow Miss Clutterbuck's broad square back across the hall. There are two women lingering here, and these show signs of a desire to converse with their hostess, but she ignores them completely and stumps up the stairs. We mount three flights in silence; we stride along a winding passage, mount three more steps to a small landing with several doors, Miss Clutterbuck opens a door marked 45 and shows me in.

"This is your room," says Miss Clutterbuck. "It's an

74 08870
PULASKI-PERRY REG. LIBRARY
LITTLE ROCK. ARKANSAS

odd shape because it's in the tower. This is the oldest part of the house. I'd have given you a better room but the place is full of people. I've had to move up to this landing myself."

I assure her that I am charmed with the room, and this is true, for it is extremely pleasant and comfortably furnished. Red rep curtains hang across the window, there is a red eiderdown on the bed and a large armchair stands near the dressing table . . . my eye falls upon an electric radiator and a small bookcase, containing books.

"It's not bad," agrees Miss Clutterbuck looking round. "You can sit here and read if you want to. The bathroom's next door and there are two small rooms which will do for your children. I'm at the other end of the passage if you want anything."

I express my gratitude for these arrangements in suitable terms.

Miss Clutterbuck takes no notice of my gratitude. It seems to bore her. She says dinner is at seven-thirty and goes away.

My luggage is brought up by a short stocky man with red hair—presumably Todd; he arranges it for me, says it's a nice evening and goes away.

I sit down on the armchair and deliberate. I can't stay here, that's obvious. Miss Clutterbuck dislikes me and I am so frightened of her that I cannot open my mouth. Why on earth did I come? What malign spirit influenced me? But there is no time to brood over my predicament. I must unpack and change; the navy blue woollen frock will do.

The door opens suddenly and a tall gaunt woman appears. She is clad in black, with a white apron, and wears a starched cap perched at a rakish angle upon her somewhat scanty hair. She is so extremely proper that I feel conscious of being insufficiently clad, though as this is my own room and I am changing for dinner my embarrassment seems unreasonable.

"You'll be Mrs. Christie," says the woman dourly.

"Yes," I reply, seizing my frock and diving into it.

"I'm Hope," says the woman.

Hope seems a misnomer for my visitor, she looks more like Retribution, but as it is important to make a good impression upon the staff I endeavor to chat with her in a friendly manner and remark (as I brush my hair) that Miss Clutterbuck met me at the station, that the country is very pretty and that I am delighted with my room. Hope answers in monosyllables or not at all so we do not get much further. She has brought two towels with her (as an excuse for her visit which I am certain is prompted by curiosity and nothing more) and these she arranges upon the towel horse.

"You'd best not be late," she warns me as she goes away. "Miss Clutterbuck likes folk to be there when the gong sounds."

Thus adjured I hasten my preparations and run downstairs and, the gong sounding as I reach the hall, I march straight into the dining room and am conducted to a small table in the corner near a large bay window where Miss Clutterbuck is already seated.

The dining room is filling rapidly, every table seems occupied. I comment upon this circumstance to my companion who replies gloomily that it's impossible to keep them away. She'd hoped the place would be emptier in the winter but it's always full and she's deived with letters arriving by every post, asking for rooms. She's put up her prices twice but nobody seems to mind. . . . "You'll have to deal with them," she adds.

This seems a good opportunity to tell her that I have decided not to stay at Tocher House but I am too cowardly to take it.

"The trouble I have with them!" continues Miss Clutterbuck savagely. "They have no sense—that's what irritates me. People come here for a week or ten days and then they find they can't get rooms elsewhere, so they expect me to keep them on. You wouldn't turn us out into the street, would you, Miss Clutterbuck? they moan. It's beyond all bearing. Where do you stay when you go to London?"

The question takes me by surprise when my mouth is full of macaroni. I swallow it hastily and reply that we belong to a private club, called the Forty Club, and can usually manage to get a room there.

"Why forty?" she enquires.

"It was started by forty people, I think."

Miss Clutterbuck eats her macaroni in silence for a few minutes and then continues her previous train of thought. "You can take over the social side," she says. "You can talk to them. I can't talk to them. It dries me up when I think of them paying for their food."

"Why shouldn't they pay for their food, Miss Clutterbuck?"

"It's my house," she replies shortly.

I reflect upon this (it is easy to reflect because Miss Clutterbuck obviously sees no necessity to make conversation with her assistant) and come to the conclusion that she feels she is outraging the laws of hospitality by filling her ancestral home with paying guests. This is the only explanation I can find, but it does not altogether satisfy me for it means that Miss Clutterbuck has more sensibility and less horse sense than I have given her credit for.

"You can talk to them," she says again after a long silence.

"Will they want me to?" I enquire.

Miss Clutterbuck does not reply. She has a habit of ignoring questions she does not want to hear . . . or perhaps she is slightly deaf, that might account for it.

"Bridge," says Miss Clutterbuck suddenly. "You play, I suppose?"

I reply firmly that I don't, and am about to add that if she would like to find somebody able and willing to make up a four when required I can easily leave tomorrow, but before I have time to formulate these sentiments Miss Clutterbuck continues.

"That's a mercy," she says firmly. "Miss Andover was forever playing bridge when she could have been better employed counting the linen."

"But didn't you tell her—"

"She was needed to make up a table. What could I do? Bridge seems a most extraordinary game," says Miss Clutterbuck. "It brings out the worst in human nature. Mr. Whitesmith, for instance—" and Miss Clutterbuck indicates a man with very black shiny hair sitting by himself—"Mr. Whitesmith in his normal senses is quite an agreeable person, but sit him down at a small square table with three of his fellow creatures and two packs of cards and he becomes insane."

I look round the room and wonder which of the diners are Mr. Whitesmith's partners. There is a big-boned rangy-looking woman with lank hair—does she play bridge? There is a party of three at a round table, obviously mother, father and newly demobilized son; there is a large pale-faced woman, who has beside her dog of mixed ancestry—a dog which requires more exercise and fewer tidbits, to judge from its bulging sides—and then there are the Americans, of course. Do they play bridge?

Miss Clutterbuck notices my wandering gaze and says in a hoarse whisper, "Americans . . . traveling together . . . from Connect-i-cut."

"Nice-looking," I murmur, "and refreshingly well-dressed."

"No clothes coupons in America," says Miss Clutterbuck.

We have an excellent dinner (to tell truth I have not felt so comfortably full of food for years) and immediately we have finished Miss Clutterbuck gets up and goes, leaving me sitting at the table alone. As she has given me no instructions I may consider myself free to do as I please so I retire to my room and write up the events of the day in my diary. Decide quite definitely that I will tackle Miss Clutterbuck tomorrow morning and ask her to find somebody else . . . her manners are outrageous.

Saturday, 2nd March

Wake early and watch the grey light of dawn seeping into my room through the open window. In spite of my worries I have slept well and feel rested and refreshed. Last night I decided definitely to leave Tocher House as soon as possible, to beard Miss Clutterbuck in her office and tell her she must find somebody else, but this morning things look a shade less black. Perhaps it is because I feel more able to cope with them. Miss Clutterbuck is the snag, of course (in other respects Tocher seems quite bearable) but wouldn't it be cowardly to run away from Miss Clutterbuck? Wouldn't it be ignominious to run away with my tail between my legs and confess myself beaten? And what about Annie? Annie is coming here to be with me, am I to desert her?

Sir Walter Scott in his diary gives a description of his own feelings in times of stress. He says, "Nature has given me a kind of buoyancy . . . that mingles even with my deepest afflictions and most gloomy hours. I have a secret pride . . . which impels me to mix with my distresses strange fragments of mirth . . ." His afflictions were a thousand times worse than mine, which are merely temporary, yet through them all his spirit was unbroken. What a fine man he was! As I think of him I feel a buoyancy rising in me; I, too, have a secret pride which I must draw upon to see me through. Having thus decided I rise and look out of the window and I find myself looking out over bare treetops towards high but softly rounded hills, clear cut against the brightness of the eastern sky . . . and, even as I watch, the light brightens and glows and the sun peeps over the hilltop and floods the scene with gold. Before, the land was painted in acid colors, but now a sudden transformation has taken place and the golden flood of sunshine runs down the side of the hill, gilding the walls and trees and strengthening their shadows upon the ground.

Thanks to Sir Walter and the morning sun I have started the day in buoyant mood, and this buoyancy carries me down to breakfast and enables me to smile quite cheerfully at Miss Clutterbuck as I take my seat opposite her at the little table. There are screens round our table this morning, whether to hide us from the guests or the guests from us it is impossible to say, but the result is rather pleasant, giving an atmosphere of privacy, and as our table is in the south window we have a gorgeous view upon which to feast our eyes. The trees have been cut to give a vista of the valley and of the windings of the Rydd as it meanders down towards the sea. There is no sea in sight—the distances are shrouded in delicate veils of mist—but somehow or other one has a definite feeling that the sea is there.

". . . and of course you can write to them," says Miss Clutterbuck.

I come to myself with a jerk (a spoonful of porridge halfway to my mouth) and gaze at my employer in alarm. Has she been enumerating my duties? Have I been daydreaming and failed to register a word?

"Write to them!" I echo feebly.

"Answer letters," she explains, handing me a sheaf

which have just arrived. "People don't seem to be able to read my writing for some reason."

"It *is* a little difficult," I murmur with a sudden recollection of my own struggles to elucidate Miss Clutterbuck's hand.

"Why?" she enquires bluntly. "It's large enough in all conscience."

As I feel unable to discuss the matter I change the subject hastily and enquire whether Lady Foreland can be given the accommodation she requires.

"No, she can't," says Miss Clutterbuck firmly. "She wants a large suite overlooking the garden, doesn't she? Tell her she can have a double room facing east but her maid will have to sleep upstairs."

"She wants a sitting room," I murmur.

"Nonsense. I can't turn the house upside down for her. You had better take the letters up to the office and answer them there."

"How?" I enquire, looking at Miss Clutterbuck boldly. "I mean how can I possibly answer them until I know what rooms are likely to be vacant?"

"You can't," agrees Miss Clutterbuck. "I'll help you of course. We'd better make out a plan of the rooms; it's getting too complicated for me to keep the whole thing in my head. We'll do it after lunch."

The morning passes in a whirl of activity. I follow Miss Clutterbuck round the house; I am sent hither and thither with messages; I am discovered by Miss Clutterbuck in the act of hanging clean curtains in a bedroom which is being prepared for a new arrival and requested to desist.

"That's Hope's job," says Miss Clutterbuck. "If I'd

wanted another housemaid I would have got a woman from the Labour Bureau."

"But I don't know what my job *is*," I cry in despair.

"You'll soon find out, Mrs. Christie. It's not hanging curtains, anyway," says my employer in trenchant tones.

We tackle the letters after lunch. Miss Clutterbuck opens them and reads them out, interpolating instructions and remarks; while I, seated at the table pen in hand, endeavor to keep pace with her.

" 'Dear Madam,' " says Miss Clutterbuck. " 'I shall be much obliged if you will reserve three single rooms adjoining for the first half of May, for myself, my husband and my daughter who has just been demobilized' . . . she can have number ten, it's double, but the girl will need to go upstairs and they must leave on the twelfth because Mrs. Fairway is coming—tell them that. Oh, there's a dog! Tell them there are two dogs already so unless they can keep it under control they had better not bring it. Here's another. 'My wife is very delicate but I have been told your hotel is comfortable. Have you box-spring mattresses and comfortable chairs? My wife must have milk puddings, she cannot eat anything fried or made up' . . . Faddy!" says Miss Clutterbuck, tossing the letter onto the table. "Tell the man we're full. Here's a Miss Glass; she says, 'My brother and I are going for a walking tour and a friend told us to be sure to stay at Tocher House. Can you reserve two rooms for us on the sixth of April for three nights?' Let me think! Yes, the Americans are leaving on the fifth—say yes."

"Miss Clutterbuck!" I exclaim, throwing down my pen in despair. "I can't do shorthand. I never said I could. It's hopeless!"

"Hopeless!"

"I'm sorry but you'll have to go over them again, slowly."

"Mark the letters yes or no as I give them to you, then you can write them later."

"But what am I to say? Supposing I say something that puts them off?"

"You won't," replies Miss Clutterbuck. "The only way to put them off is to say the place is full and even then they keep on writing. Here's a man, for instance . . . I didn't like his letter so I said we were full up till October and now he writes to ask if I couldn't put up a camp bed for him somewhere. I don't want hordes of people," explains Miss Clutterbuck, stabbing out the butt of her cigarette and fitting another into her holder. "I'm running the place as a hotel because I've got to do it, but I'm not going to pack the place like a sardine tin—and I may as well have decent people while I'm about it, people that will take what they're given in the way of food, people who know how to behave themselves."

"That's only sensible."

She raises her eyes and glowers at me. "Yes, I'm sensible," she declares. "If you see anything in this house that you don't think sensible, you can tell me about it."

This remark is rhetorical, of course. Miss Clutterbuck rises as she speaks and obviously expects no reply, but somehow or other I am not quite so frightened of her now, and a demon of mischief lurking deep within me prompts me to take her at her word.

"There's just one thing, so far," I tell her. "Quite a small thing, of course. I wondered why you had put those notices in all the bedrooms asking guests to bring their own towels."

"Because I want them to bring their own towels, of course!" exclaims Miss Clutterbuck in wrathful amazement. "I can provide enough towels for residents, but not for people who only come for a couple of nights. I had those notices printed and hung in all the bedrooms—"

"Yes, I realized that—but you see, Miss Clutterbuck, by the time you arrive in your bedroom it's too late."

"Too late!"

"Much too late. You've either brought your towel with you—or not. And, if you haven't had the foresight to bring it with you, no notice in large clear type hung upon the wall of your bedroom will alter the fact."

"Hrrmph!" exclaims Miss Clutterbuck. (She does not really say "Hrrmph," of course. The ejaculation is made by Miss Clutterbuck clenching her teeth and emitting a short deep grunt; if she happens to be smoking at the time—and rarely is she not—smoke issues from her nostrils in two clouds which adds to the horrific effect.)

"May I suggest—" I continue, sweetly—"may I suggest that we have small slips of paper printed so that these could be enclosed when I write to people and offer them rooms?"

"May I suggest that your meekness is deceptive?" retorts Miss Clutterbuck fiercely, but there is a latent twinkle in her eye. Is it possible that Miss Clutterbuck's ferocity is deceptive, or perhaps only skin-deep?

Monday, 4th March

Decide that today I must really get down to things and evolve some sort of routine instead of pottering round and accomplishing nothing. This laudable intention is frustrated by Miss Clutterbuck who says will I please take the car and do the shopping in Ryddelton. The Grants are arriving this morning (Miss Clutterbuck says) and she had better be here to see them and show them their rooms and deal with any complaints as to aspect or unsuitability. Here's a list of the shops—she has accounts with most of them—and here's a list of shopping and two pounds for extras.

I take both lists and the two pound notes and endeavor to look businesslike and intelligent.

Miss Clutterbuck adds that the battery has run down so she's told Todd to start the car and I can park it on a hill when I get to the town to avoid cranking. . . . Oh, and I had better get a large notebook for the linen cupboard, and some ink so that I can make a list of the linen . . . adds that she forgot to write down soap powder, she doubts if I'll get it but no harm to ask . . . adds *that* reminds her Cook needs curry powder and Hope wants powder for the baths, and I had better get oil for the sewing machine while I'm about it.

At this point Cook rushes in and says has Mrs. Christie gone, because she wants a scraper, not a door scraper but a thing for scraping carrots, and Todd wants half a pound of carpet tacks, and has Miss Clutterbuck remembered the knife? Miss Clutterbuck strikes herself on the forehead and says she knew there was something—a sharp knife for skinning rabbits.

Cook says she hopes Mrs. Christie is going soon or they won't keep the fish.

Miss Clutterbuck asks if I think I'll manage.

Reply with confidence (which I am far from feeling), "Of course I'll manage!" Throw on hat and coat, seize two baskets and rush out to the garage where I find the car has been started by Todd; the engine is puffing and panting and clouds of blue smoke are issuing from the exhaust.

There is a youngish man in the garage. He is attired in overalls and is tinkering with a bright blue sports car. He looks up as I approach and says have I seen Todd, because he's got a leak in his carburetor and Todd will know what to do. Reply that I have not seen Todd.

The youngish man looks at me and says, "Oh, you're the new dogsbody, of course. My name's Wick if that's any interest to you."

Decide that I do not like Mr. Wick and that his name is of no interest to me whatsoever, but manage to refrain from saying so. As I climb into the driving seat Mr. Wick leaves his car and comes over, spanner in hand, and asks incredulously if I intend to take that thing out on the road. It ought to be in a museum, Mr. Wick thinks, or at Darlington Station alongside Puffing Billy. Reply that the car is the property of Miss Clutterbuck so these suggestions should be made to her.

"Not likely!" exclaims Mr. Wick turning away.

Drive slowly down the avenue, trying various gears and discover they are not only extremely difficult to engage but,

when engaged, behave in an incalculable manner; also discover that it is impossible to get into top unless the car
is practically stationary which seems an inconvenient arrangement. Decide that Miss Clutterbuck had every excuse
for her taciturnity on the night of my arrival as the car
takes the whole of one's attention . . . discover at the gate,
where I endeavor to slow down, that the foot brake is not
working, but fortunately the hand brake *is,* otherwise it
would have been difficult to carry out my instructions to
park on a hill.

The town of Ryddelton is bright and spacious, or at
least that is the impression it produces upon me. It consists
of one very wide street and several very narrow ones; the
wide street is divided by trees planted up the middle and
by a war memorial surrounded by green painted seats. Some
of the buildings look old and are slightly crooked, while
others are solid sensible Victorian structures of dressed grey
stone. There are three large churches, which seems an ample
provision for a smallish town, and a municipal hall with a
clock in the tower. It is some little time before I discover
a parking place; there are plenty of hills but most of them
are too steep or too narrow and are therefore unsuitable for
the purpose, but eventually I discover the ideal spot and
blocking the wheels with stones I take the baskets and begin
my shopping. There are no queues here, except at the fish
shop (how different from Donford where nearly every
catering establishment had its queue) and before I have
stood very long in the fish queue I discover it is quite a
social occasion. It is in the fish queue that the worthy people
of Ryddelton meet their friends, enquire after wee Jeanie's
tonsils and Andrew's rheumatics; it is here they discuss the
news of the day or arrange to go to the pictures. Two

tweed-clad women in front of me carry on a conversation more germane to the matter in hand. Lovat Tweed is older than Grey Tweed but seems a tyro at the game.

"What funny looking fish!" she remarks. "The ones with the red spots on their backs."

"Plaice," replies Grey Tweed succinctly.

"What does one *do* with them, Jean?"

"One fries them if one has enough fat."

"And if one hasn't?"

"I suppose one could grill them," says Grey Tweed doubtfully.

Lovat Tweed sighs and says she wonders if it's worth waiting, it looks as if there wouldn't be anything left except the spotty fish and she doesn't fancy them, somehow.

"They're quite nice," declares Grey Tweed earnestly. "I shall wait; my butcher has nothing."

"Not even sausages?"

"Nothing. Jean, do you ever get a kidney?"

"Sometimes, if I plead with him, but I'd rather use my persuasive powers to get a bit of liver, it goes further."

"My dear!" cries Grey Tweed in amazement. "My butcher has no liver—ever—and no heart."

The woman behind me is less patient in adversity than her fellows. She heaves several deep sighs and says to her friend she wonders if there'll be enough to go round. "We were in Edinburgh on Saturday," she says in complaining tones. "We were at the Zoo and the keeper was *throwing fish to the sea lions*—believe it or not."

"It's an idea," declares her friend. "But I doubt if we'd be as good as the sea lions at catching them." She says this with a completely serious expression, but I (who am not of Scottish extraction) cannot emulate her gravity.

"Thamas said—" declares the first woman—"Thamas said it was an awfu' waste of good food."

"You should have sent Thamas in among them," replies the second. "The keeper would never have noticed . . ."

Thus whiling away the time in pleasant manner the fish queue moves slowly forward to its goal, is fed with parcels of fish and dispersed to the four winds. Soon it is my turn and I enquire for Miss Clutterbuck's usual order.

"The Tocher fish!" exclaims the girl as she glances at me with interest. "It's ready. Where did I put it? Clem, where did I put the Tocher fish?"

Clem produces an enormous flabby parcel and hands it over, gazing at me the while. "You're new here?" she enquires. "It used to be a fat wee woman with scrunty hair."

This description of my predecessor interests me quite a lot but I have no time to linger, so I agree pleasantly that I am new, stow the parcel into one of my baskets and hurry away . . . and now I am too busy to observe my fellow shoppers, for I have to find the shops, buy what I can and mark off my purchases on the list; but my fellow shoppers are not so engrossed that they cannot take note of me and presently I begin to have a vague feeling that everyone in the town is interested in me and my doings. These people are too polite to stare at me openly, but their eyes follow me and bore into my back.

Wherever I go I meet the same people—the people who stood beside me in the fish queue. At the baker's, for instance, I hear the tag end of the story about the sea lions, and I bump into Grey Tweed coming out of the grocer's. I discover the ironmonger's shop in a back street, and endeavor to buy a scraper for Cook, and while I am doing so Grey Tweed appears and asks for screws. By this time she and I seem old friends; Grey Tweed says it is a lovely day and I agree enthusiastically.

"You're new here, aren't you?" says Grey Tweed. "I heard you say Tocher House—are you helping Erica Clutterbuck?"

"Yes, I'm the new dogsbody," I reply smiling.

"I don't envy you," returns Grey Tweed. "It must be a frightful job . . . no, I'm afraid those screws won't do. I want them with round heads."

Both my baskets are now full to bulging point and extremely heavy so I stagger back to the car, fairly well satisfied with my morning's work. I have managed to obtain nearly everything I was told to get—I have even managed to obtain the elusive soap powder—and the car consenting to start up quite agreeably on the hill, I drive back to Tocher House without further adventure.

Todd is waiting for me at the gate and seems surprisingly pleased to see me. He explains that I've been on his mind the whole morning; he had intended to be there when I started to warn me about one or two things, but he was called away to attend to the refrigerator and I had gone when he got back. "You'd find the gears a wee bit different," says Todd looking at me anxiously.

"Quite different," I reply.

"And the brake," adds Todd. "It's not the newest kind of brake, Mrs. Christie. I've done my best with it, but it's just not very reliable."

"Not very," I agree.

"But you managed fine," says Todd, looking at me questioningly.

I assure Todd that no lives have been lost and rush off to find my employer and make a report of my mission.

Thursday, 7th March

A hotel such as this is a study in psychology and it is interesting to observe the different proportions of tiger and ape and ass in one's fellow creatures. Many of the people are shadowy; they are average people and there is nothing outstanding about them; they are neither good-looking nor ugly; they have no peculiarities to awaken and hold one's interest. To me these people are like a flock of sheep, yet to their families and their friends they must be individuals. Other people one notices at once and has no difficulty in remembering their faces and their names. There is Miss McQueen, for instance. She is by herself and obviously prefers to be, for she speaks to nobody and brings a book to every meal. Miss McQueen is about thirty-five and is tall with golden-red hair and a pale complexion, her thin face has a curiously tragic expression and I decide she is suffering from unrequited love. Mr. Wick also is alone, though by no means lonely for he speaks to everyone and his roving eye is always on the alert to sum up new arrivals, especially if there happens to be a good-looking young woman amongst the party. I have met Mr. Wick, of course, so we know each other now, or at least are acquainted sufficiently to wish one another good morning if we meet on the stairs. Mrs. Maloney is fat, with a fat white dog which she feeds at meals in a surreptitious manner. Mrs. Ovens is young and good-looking in a fluffy way. Her husband is in Germany. To be frank, I should not have noticed Mrs. Ovens particularly if it were not for her complaints about towels; she is constantly pursuing me and asking me to change the towels in her bedroom. Then there are the American ladies, of course. They are both "Mrs. Potting" which is a little puzzling until one discovers that they have married two brothers. Mrs. Wilbur Potting is tall and dark, Mrs. Dene Potting is tall and fair, they are the greatest friends and are pretty and lively and vitally interested in their fellow creatures. There is Mr. Whitesmith, who is mad on bridge and is forever trying to induce three of his fellow creatures to join him in a rubber. Mr. Whitesmith consults the barometer every morning and looks cheerful when it falls. There are the Stannards, mother, father and son, who fish industriously but so far have caught nothing. They have impressed themselves upon my notice because they are often late for dinner, and because Miss Clutterbuck dislikes them even more intensely than her other guests. There is a bald, middle-aged man who seems to do nothing from morning to night except read the *Daily Telegraph*. It is impossible that he should be reading it all the time, of course (for any literate person could read every word of our shadowy wartime newspapers in a couple of hours), but the fact remains that whenever my eyes fall upon this particular individual he is reading the *Daily Telegraph*. His wife is small and thin, she knits incessantly. There is the tall big-boned woman who resembles a horse —her name is Dove which is so unsuitable that I can remember it easily; she has lank brown hair, too long to be tidy, too short to be gathered into a bun. Miss Dove writes letters far into the night, a most inconvenient habit. The lights in the lounge must remain burning till Miss

Dove has licked the last stamp. . . . Miss Clutterbuck has no patience with this lady's peculiarities. There are two young women, they are nurses and have come to Tocher House for ten days' holiday, so one would imagine that they would welcome the chance to get right away from all thought of the ills which beset the human frame, but not so. I sit near them in the lounge, having my tea, and listen to their conversation, not because I want to listen to it, but because I cannot help hearing it unless I leave my tea and go away.

"It was awful," declares the pretty one with the curly hair. "I couldn't remember the difference between the two comas. I was just going to shoot a hundred grammes of glucose into the woman and then suddenly I wasn't sure—"

"It's easily done," declares her friend. "I remember the first time I saw an insulin coma—diabetés mellitus it was. Sister called me to see it because she knew I'd be interested . . ."

There is something very sad about this—or so I feel; I would rather hear these two nice-looking young women discussing their love affairs.

So far I have made no effort to talk to any of Miss Clutterbuck's guests, for one thing I have been too busy and for another too shy. Some of them have spoken to me in the way of business, Mr. Wick at the garage and Mrs. Ovens on the subject of towels, but there has been no social chat, and social chat is a part of my duties so I decide to tackle it bravely. There are not many people in the lounge after tea and Mrs. Maloney looks approachable; I approach somewhat diffidently and the lady smiles and suggests it is a nice day. I agree rapturously, and the ice is broken. We talk about Mrs. Maloney's dog, a devoted animal with (according to its mistress) a really beautiful nature, but as I have seen it snap at some of the other guests I am inclined to doubt her word and refrain from blandishments.

"You're helping Miss Clutterbuck, of course," says Mrs. Maloney. "Such a capable woman, isn't she? But of course she can't do everything, and I'm sure you must be a great help to her. How delightful for her to have you—but not quite so delightful for *you.*"

"Oh yes," I declare. "I mean it is very nice for me— very nice indeed . . ."

"You are brave," says Mrs. Maloney. "Ah yes, believe me I can see how courageous you are—always so cheerful and bright. It's so sad for you to be parted from your husband," adds Mrs. Maloney, looking at me with large moist brown eyes—like a cow.

This remark surprises and annoys me (but surprise at the circumstances that Mrs. Maloney knows so much about my private affairs is almost completely swamped by annoyance)—how dare the woman tamper with my feelings! I am so annoyed that it is difficult to resist the temptation to shock her, to tell her that there is nothing I like better than to be severed from Tim, and that Tim is thoroughly enjoying his delightful holiday in Egypt.

"So dreadfully sad for you both," continues Mrs. Maloney; she continues to probe, and to invite my confidence by telling me of other unhappy wives parted from their nearest and dearest, who have poured out their troubles to her. The fact is Mrs. Maloney is a professional sympathiser, her bosom is damp with tears . . . or so she would have me believe.

Already I am regretting my impulse to speak to the woman, but there seems little hope of escape. My unwillingness to confide in her is too obvious to be overlooked —even by Mrs. Maloney—but she has other means of approach.

"I am so glad you spoke to me," she declares. "I'm sure we shall have lots of nice little chats and get to know each other better. We have much in common—I felt it the moment I saw you. Miss Clutterbuck is *so* different. Very capable indeed and quite a lady but rather unsympathetic —just a teeny weeny bit hard. Some people might not notice it, but I notice anything like that at once. I'm terribly sensitive—the least sign of hardness *withers* me."

I commiserate suitably with Mrs. Maloney.

"Yes, that's what I'm like," she says sadly. "It's a great handicap in life to be so sensitive, especially for anyone absolutely alone in the world, but there are compensations, of course. I mean if I happen to meet a kindred spirit I can recognize them at once, something goes out from me— a flow of sympathy." She pauses for a moment but I can find nothing to say so she sighs heavily and continues, "Poor Miss Clutterbuck! One ought to be sorry for her, of course. It isn't her fault at all. I often think spinsters get like that—just a teeny weeny bit hard—I expect you've noticed it."

"No, I don't think so, Mrs. Maloney."

"You mean you haven't noticed?"

"I mean I don't agree."

"They're different," says Mrs. Maloney smiling gently. "There's something in marriage . . . it has such a softening effect."

On the brain, perhaps, I think to myself.

She waits for my comment in vain and then, leaning

forward, she places her hand on my knee. "Ah, you and I *know,* Mrs. Christie," she says confidentially.

The hand is soft and fat and the fingers are heavily bedecked with rings—I can hardly bear it lying upon my knee, in fact I can't bear it. I rise saying I must go and I go with all speed.

This attempt to get in touch with Miss Clutterbuck's guests has not been a success—or perhaps it has been too successful. I decide to be more careful in future, to be less friendly and more dignified; in other words to keep myself to myself. But this intention is frustrated by my employer who announces at dinner that the American ladies have invited us to take coffee with them in the lounge. She adds that she, herself, prefers to have her coffee comfortably in her room, but I had better drink mine in their company. I suggest it is really Miss Clutterbuck they want, not her assistant, but Miss Clutterbuck pretends not to hear.

"I think you should come," I tell her firmly, raising my voice a trifle.

"All right," says Miss Clutterbuck. "I'll come. I'll pass a few remarks with them, but I'll take my coffee upstairs as usual."

The American ladies welcome us to their table with gracious smiles, and the elder, a really beautiful creature with fair wavy hair, makes the introductions, exhibiting a social aplomb which I admire but could never hope to emulate. She is Mrs. Dene Potting and her companion is Mrs. Wilbur Potting. They assure Miss Clutterbuck that they are enjoying their stay at her guesthouse and ask her to tell them the correct way to pronounce its name.

"Tocher," says Miss Clutterbuck laconically.

Mrs. Wilbur smiles and says Scotch names are difficult.

"You could call it Dot," suggests Miss Clutterbuck and with that she goes away.

The two ladies are somewhat surprised at her unceremonious departure and I find myself explaining that she has important business to transact, but my explanations are not very convincing because even important business could hardly excuse such peculiar behavior. Mrs. Potting says she has very natural manners and Mrs. Wilbur adds she is a busy woman of course, but it is obvious they are not deceived.

The coffee comes and we talk about this and that. Mrs. Wilbur returns to the subject of Tocher and says she did not understand what Miss Clutterbuck meant. I explain that the house was built by one Sir Alexander Johnstone for his daughter and given to her as her marriage portion, or tocher.

"You hear that, Marley!" exclaims Mrs. Wilbur. "It was her dot."

Mrs. Potting nods and says it's very interesting indeed.

They are anxious to know further details of Tocher's history, what year it was built and when the additions were made and whether it has always remained in the same family. In fact they are so eager for information and so surprised when I am unable to satisfy their thirst that I feel very much ashamed of myself and decide to ask Miss Clutterbuck all about it.

Soon after this Curry comes over to the table to collect the coffee cups and I remind her not to charge Mrs. Potting for my share.

Mrs. Potting says nonsense, she invited me to have

coffee and wishes to pay for it. She never heard of a guest paying for her own entertainment—never in all her life.

There is something in this, of course, but I explain that as I get my food free—as part of my salary—there would be no sense in Mrs. Potting paying for it.

The two ladies consider the matter carefully (while Curry waits for the verdict). Finally Mrs. Wilbur laughs and says it's very amusing, isn't it Darthy. If they want to entertain Mrs. Christie they will have to take her to Edinburgh for the day, and Mrs. Potting says she never would have thought of it, and she must remember to tell Dene.

Curry goes away.

Feel that perhaps I have been a little ungracious, so begin to explain matters all over again, then suddenly have a feeling I am explaining too much and stop abruptly.

Mrs. Potting smiles at her sister-in-law and says she gets a kick out of the way I talk. Mrs. Wilbur agrees rapturously. This has the unfortunate effect of rendering me speechless—or nearly so—and, making my apologies with some difficulty, I escape upstairs to deal with the correspondence which I left unfinished this afternoon.

The office is quiet and pleasantly warm. I read the letters carefully, consult the plan of rooms, and indite tactful replies. Miss Clutterbuck has consented to have slips of paper printed urging her prospective guests to bring their own towels but until the slips are ready I am incorporating the request in my letters . . . "P.S. Please bring your own towel," I write and smile to myself as I write it.

Miss Clutterbuck comes in and asks what I am doing. This is not the time for writing letters, and if I can't get them done in the afternoon I can leave them till the next day. I had better go and talk to somebody, Miss Clutterbuck says.

Reply that I have talked enough for one day.

Miss Clutterbuck says she saw me talking to Mrs. Maloney, what a woman!; and the Americans are not much better.

Reply that the Americans are very much better, and add boldly that I think Miss Clutterbuck was somewhat rude.

"I know," she replies. "I told you—I can't talk to people who are living in my house and paying me for their food. That's why you're here, Mrs. Christie."

"Surely there's no need to be rude to them!" I exclaim.

"Hrrmph!" says Miss Clutterbuck, with the usual clouds of smoke. "Well if you don't want to talk take a book and read it. There are books in your room—"

"Yes, I'm reading *Emma*—for about the fifth time."

"You are?" enquires Miss Clutterbuck with interest. "I've read it oftener than that. There's nobody like Jane Austen to my way of thinking. I like the saltiness, the restrained satire. When I'm more than usually irritated and deived with the guests I get out *Northanger Abbey* or *Persuasion* or one of the others and have a good read. I find them soothing. Jane Austen had as little patience as I have with the vagaries of her kind."

This is the longest speech I have heard from Miss Clutterbuck and easily the most interesting. I am anxious to hear more and suggest in a tentative manner that Miss Austen might have found the denizens of Tocher House an interesting study.

Miss Clutterbuck says she doubts it.

Friday, 8th March

Today I receive a letter from Tony Morley. To think Tim's and my very great friend is now a Brigadier, and as such, a Very Important Person. It is six years since I saw Tony, but we correspond occasionally and his letters are so vivid and so much a part of himself that he remains very clear in my thoughts and today as I hold his letter in my hand I can see Tony quite distinctly, "Tall and fair and devil-may-care" as the old song has it. Tony's Brigade is in Bombay at the moment, or at least it was in Bombay when he wrote to me last, but this letter is headed "A camp in the hills" and runs as follows:

"You will be surprised, my dear Hester, to see the address from which I am writing, and may even think it slightly vague. This vagueness is not due to military necessity (we need no longer shroud our movements from Hitler's or from Hirohito's all-seeing eyes) nor is it due to a desire upon my part to tantalize you by keeping you in the dark as to my whereabouts. The fact is I, myself, am slightly vague as to my whereabouts. The Powers That Be, always so considerate and thoughtful of those who have served them faithfully and well, decided that it was time this particular servant had a spot of leave, so this particular servant decided to betake himself to the hills, being somewhat weary of the sight of his fellow creatures and particularly of his Brigade Major, a most worthy and estimable person but addicted to a squeaking pipe. India has its compensations and amongst these the excellence of one's retainers ranks high. I expressed a wish for solitude and peace to Dost Mohammed and left the troublesome details in his most capable hands. Bearers, mules, tents and provisions, even the itinerary of our journey were left to him, and here we are encamped somewhere in the hills, encompassed with solitude and peace. Hester, I wish you could be here—and Tim, too, of course (for you would not be completely happy without Tim and complete happiness is essential to the enjoyment of this carefree existence). Yes, I would willingly share the mountains with you and Tim. Let me tell you a little about our journey. There was one day when we camped on a hillside overlooking the plains, and there was a sea of mist over the plains but through the mist I could see the silver ribbon of the Ganges winding its way along. To the west rose the hills, grey and green, changing to purple and blue in the distance . . . but we did not linger there. We struck camp and climbed on. There were goats feeding in the little valleys. We met a goatherd, or perhaps it was Pan, himself. He had a reed pipe and he consented to play upon it for me—it was such a sad little wandering air. We passed scattered villages and terraced fields which were irrigated by runnels of spring water. Then we came to woods of Himalayan oak, stony ridges and enormous boulders—the Himalayas do everything on a giant scale, even their boulders. It was cold here, of course, but the sun was warm and in sheltered hollows I found gentians and milkwort and a red flower which Dost Mohammed says is the flower of Nepal. There were pine trees and cedars, and a tree which reminded me of our English holly, but with a leathery sort of leaf. These lower hills—though steep enough by any ordinary standards—stretch out towards the plains in long ridges with valleys in between them. Beyond these lower hills tower the mountains covered with snow and extraordinarily bright in the fierce bright sunshine. I must tell you about the hunting, though as a matter of fact I was not out for killing but only hunted for the pot. We saw bear and some pheasants which reminded me of home and of those terrific shoots we had at Charters Towers before the war. Somehow I don't feel I shall want to do that again, even if it is going to be possible (which I doubt). Perhaps I have done enough killing to last me a lifetime, could that be the reason? Dost Mohammed was slightly annoyed with me when I refused to shoot more game than we could eat. Such weakness is beyond his understanding. I saw a panther, and would have shot it without compunction but unfortunately I hadn't my rifle with me at the time. It was a beautiful creature, sleek and glossy and sinuous as a film star—it had that well-groomed look! We climbed higher still, through thick forests which smelt of damp rotting wood, and wound our way up by the side of mountain torrents and at last we reached a plateau of grass and rocks and boulders. That's where I am now, Hester, so now you know! As far as I can make out we must be about ten thousand feet up, it's magnificent. The wind blows all the time. The sun is hot and the nights are cold. The air! O Hester, the clear crystal air! After the hot dusty used-up stuff that we have to breathe in the plains this air is something to write home about . . . so I'm writing home about it!

Yours ever,

Tony"

For some reason Tony's letter depresses me. It is a grand letter, of course, and a very cheerful letter and I ought to feel pleased that he is having such a good time, but instead of that I feel depressed. It is a grand letter—but what a lonely way of spending his hard-earned leave! Tony ought to be married, he ought to have a wife and children, he ought not to wander off into the Himalayas alone. The fact that he seems to be enjoying himself does not make it much better in my opinion. Long ago I tried to find a wife for Tony but my efforts were unavailing and I was told to mind my own business in no uncertain terms; since then I have minded my own business carefully!

But in addition to my depression on Tony's account I am depressed myself—a black cloud has descended upon my spirits. His letter, by reminding me so vividly of him, has reminded me of the old happy life which now seems far away. I have been here for a week and although I am settling down and finding my way about I still feel terribly alone—I am homesick, I suppose. Before, when Tim was away, I had the children to care for, I had a definite home. Now I have nothing and nobody, I have never been so absolutely alone in all my life. As there is half an hour before dinner I am at liberty to indulge in an orgy of self-pity, and this I proceed to do. I miss Tim so badly; I miss Betty and Bryan; I miss Grace—I even miss her spoilt little boys. If only there were somebody, somebody from the old life, to whom I could talk, if Tony were here, or Pinkie could be torn away from her adoring husband to keep me company!

I am still very busy pitying myself when the door opens and Hope stalks in.

"Oh!" says Hope. "I'm sorry I'm sure. I didn't think you'd be here."

There seems no answer to this remark, so I say nothing.

Hope lingers. "Could I have the key of the linen closet," she enquires.

Hitherto I have always complied with this request, but

I have decided to comply no longer, for the linen is my responsibility and when Hope is let loose amongst the linen she rearranges it so that I can find nothing. Such is the havoc she wreaks that I am beginning to suspect she does it on purpose to bewilder me and make my task more difficult.

"The key of the linen closet," repeats Hope, holding out her hand.

"What do you want it for, Hope?"

"Mrs. Ovens wants a towel," declares Hope triumphantly.

"She must ask me—or Miss Clutterbuck. Mrs. Ovens has had three clean towels this week."

Hope's eyebrows are dark and thick, they meet across the bridge of her thin bony nose. Beneath them her eyes are almost black, black and shiny like boot buttons. "Are you staying here, Mrs. Christie?" she enquires.

"Staying in my room?"

"Staying at Tocher."

There is a moment's silence.

"We did all right before you came," continues Hope, in a mumbling tone. "Miss Clutterbuck and me can run the place ourselves."

"Miss Clutterbuck doesn't seem to think so."

"We managed fine," declares Hope.

It is not surprising to find that Hope dislikes me. She resents my presence and shows it in all her actions. The cup of tea which she brings me in the early morning is set down upon my bedside table with an ungracious clatter; my curtains are pulled roughly and crookedly across my windows, my hot-water bottle is always lukewarm. These may seem small details and unworthy of notice, but no

servant has ever treated me like this before and the treat-
ment hurts me and makes me unhappy. Isn't there any
way of getting at Hope, of finding out why she dislikes
me, and putting things right?

"Hope," I say, trying to speak in a friendly manner,
"just listen to me a moment. You and I are both working
for Miss Clutterbuck, there's no difference between us except that we do different sort of work. Why can't we pull
together?"

"There's no need for you here, Mrs. Christie."

"If Miss Clutterbuck wants me I shall stay."

"She doesn't," says Hope in a low trembling voice. "I
can do it all . . . I'm not afraid of work . . . I can do the
linen and everything . . . she doesn't need you."

"In that case I feel sure Miss Clutterbuck will tell me
so, herself," I reply with a calmness which I am far from
feeling.

Mrs. Wilbur Potting and I have a heart-to-heart talk. It is in the lounge, after tea. I am sitting there in a corner by myself and am run to earth by my American acquaintance. She asks if she may sit down beside me and on receiving permission sits down and lights a cigarette. Mrs. Wilbur says she is trying to understand the Spirit of English Womanhood as she is going to lecture upon that subject when she returns to the States, but so far the essence of the matter has eluded her. She has made copious notes, of course, but they cancel each other out in the most puzzling way and she feels she must be starting from the wrong end. She gazes at me as she speaks and her gaze is so intense that I am assailed by the uncomfortable sensation that Mrs. Wilbur looks upon me as the embodiment of her theme . . . I murmur that it is always difficult to generalize about people. You can't put them all into one box and label it neatly. Mrs. Wilbur agrees but says there *is* something, she hasn't got it yet, that's the trouble.

After a short silence Mrs. Wilbur says may she ask me a *very* personal question and, on being assured I have no objection, she enquires what emoluments I am receiving for my services. I tell her I am receiving three pounds ten a week and my keep. There is another short silence and I can see that Mrs. Wilbur is translating my salary into dollars and is somewhat surprised at the answer. She hesitates for a moment and then asks a trifle diffidently if I am doing the work for fun.

Hastily review my day and decide fun is the wrong word.

Mrs. Wilbur says she can't understand my standpoint on the subject of money. For instance I was careful to save Marley the expense of my coffee but I am working like a slave for inadequate pay. These two facts are incompatible in the same person. I consider this carefully and reply that although money does not mean a great deal to me I don't like to see it wasted. Mrs. Wilbur points out that it is better to earn enough to make small economies look silly. I see her point of course but am not quite sure that I agree. Are economies ever silly? Mrs. Wilbur says yes if they are unnecessary, because they take time and trouble. The right thing is to see that you are paid what you are worth and circulate the money freely: that is good citizenship. She quotes Kant to uphold her contention. "Act so that every action is worthy of being made into a universal law, worthy of and suitable for adoption by all," says Mrs. Wilbur earnestly.

She is quite right, of course, and I am convinced that my behavior is antisocial.

Mrs. Wilbur then leans forward confidentially and asks if I will come back to the States with her.

I gaze at her in dumb amazement.

"Why not, Mrs. Christie?" says Mrs. Wilbur in persuasive tones. She then proceeds to explain that she is offering me the post of housekeeper in her American mansion. I should have very much less work, plenty of parties and three times my present pay. I would run the house for her, which would leave her free for her committee work, and I would help to entertain her guests. They would be tickled to death, says Mrs. Wilbur, looking at me with a serious air.

Needless to say I am flattered by this proposal. In fact, to borrow Mrs. Wilbur's phrase, I am tickled to death. I can't accept it, of course, because Tim would have a fit if he heard I was racing off to America without him—and there are the children's holidays to be considered—but it is exceedingly pleasant to be asked. Why have I been asked, I wonder. Is it on account of my capabilities as a house-keeper, or because Mrs. Wilbur has taken a fancy to the shape of my nose? I have a feeling that it is neither; that, in fact, Mrs. Wilbur is making the offer in the same spirit as she would make an offer for an objet d'art. She wants to exhibit me to her friends (she might even exhibit me on the platform when she gives her lecture on The Spirit of English Womanhood). Mrs. Wilbur's friends would come and listen to me talking and would murmur as they went away, "Isn't she cute? I wonder where Darthy found her."

All this rushes through my mind in a moment and makes me smile. "Why do you want me—honestly?" I enquire.

Mrs. Wilbur says that's very difficult. There are at least a dozen perfectly good reasons why she wants me. Perhaps the chief reason is that I always seem happy and it would be pleasant to have me in her home.

This surprises me vastly and I tell her so.

She asks if I am really happy, and if so, why.

Feel quite unable to answer these questions offhand.

Mrs. Wilbur says thoughtfully that she has come to the conclusion English women are happier than their American sisters and she can't think why, because it seems to her they have a pretty poor time of it. Is it their natures? Is it something in the air? Do I think she should take that as her jumping-off point when she gives her lecture upon The Spirit of English Womanhood?

I enquire why Mrs. Wilbur thinks happiness is so important.

She looks at me in amazement and says the pursuit of happiness is one of the chief aims set forth in the Declaration of Independence.

This silences me completely, but Mrs. Wilbur insists that I must explain my views on the subject. She presses me so hard that at last I am forced to admit that I think the pursuit of happiness an ignoble aim and a selfish aim and, as selfish people are never happy, a foolish aim.

Mrs. Wilbur exclaims, "Happiness foolish? Not to this chicken!" and looks so shattered that I feel I may have hurt her. However she soon recovers and to my surprise comes back for more, assuring me that she can take it.

I continue by saying that in my humble opinion happiness is a privilege, not a right. It comes, not to those who pursue it for themselves, but to those who try to give it to others. The more you pursue happiness the more it eludes you—*vide* Maeterlinck's *Blue Bird*—and those who grasp at happiness attain despair.

Having got completely carried away by my own eloquence my courage suddenly deserts me and I come down to earth with a bump. Dumbness descends upon me and I wish the parquet floor of the lounge would open and swallow me up. Mrs. Wilbur is also afflicted with dumbness —and no wonder!

After a few very uncomfortable moments I manage to pull myself together sufficiently to rise and make my apologies and stagger away.

Thursday, 14th March

Miss Clutterbuck remarks suddenly at lunch that it's a fine afternoon and if I like walking I could do worse than take a dander up the hill. This, obviously, is her gracious way of offering me the afternoon off and I accept with gratitude. As I sally forth, stick in hand, Todd sees me and runs after me. Todd and I are now on the best of terms, he is not only willing and eager to help in any way he can but is also most capable. He can deal with any household emergency, a torn flex or the castor of a chair or a window cord are child's play to Todd; he prefers something really difficult. His hobby is carrier pigeons and he has converted the loft over the stables into suitable quarters for them. Tim and I have always been interested in carrier pigeons (once we are settled at Cobstead we intend to breed them ourselves) so Todd and I have had some earnest discussions upon the subject. There is no time for a long discussion today, but there is time for a few minutes chat. I learn that Max—the best and most beautiful of all Todd's pigeons— has been entered for a race next week. He will be sent away in a basket and will fly home ... Todd is certain that Max will win a prize.

"Are you going on the hill?" enquires Todd, when we have finished discussing the pigeons. "It's a nice walk on a breezy afternoon. You can take the path through the wood and you'll find a gate leading onto the moor. Puss-hill, it's called," he adds nodding.

"Cats?" I ask, looking up at the sloping contours crowned with rocks. "Wildcats, I suppose—or does it mean something quite different?"

"It means hares," replies Todd. "That's what it means, Mrs. Christie—and if you're lucky you may see some fun."

This prophecy puzzles me somewhat, for although I have seen quite a few hares in my time, I have never got much fun out of them. I have seen them loping about in turnip fields or streaking across moors with kangaroolike bounds, I have even operated upon them, spread out upon the kitchen table—but that wasn't fun, either. I explain all this to Todd but he refuses to elaborate his prophecy.

"If you're lucky you may see some fun," repeats Todd smiling mysteriously.

"Can I go anywhere I like?" I enquire.

"Anywhere," says Todd, giving me the freedom of the hills with a large gesture. "Shut the gates after you, that's all."

As I walk off Todd shouts out an injunction to refrain from knocking down the walls, an injunction which seems unnecessary on the face of it. (Later I discover that it is not as crazy as it sounds, for the fields which stretch up the side of the hill are all enclosed by dry stone dykes which are difficult to climb without dislodging loose stones.)

The day is fine. There is a cool breeze and a warm sun. My spirits rise as I leave the shelter of the wood and set my foot to the brae. Great white clouds sail majestically across the blue sky and trail their shadows after them across the bare hills. A lark starts from a clump of grass and soars upward singing. There are sheep in these fields, ewes which will soon be lambing, and I see an occasional hare loping its way along. The path stops suddenly at a little spring which is a drinking place for the hill's inhabitants, as is shown by the tracks of hooves and paws in the surrounding mud. Here come the heavy ewes, here come cattle, and here is the unmistakable print of a fox's pad. There is no real path leading upward from the spring so I continue across the grass, marking how coarse and yellow it is and how poor and stony is the hill pasture. Presently I arrive at a wall which is shoulder high but offers excellent foothold for a bold climber and I scramble over taking care not to disturb the precariously balanced stones; and now I have left the enclosed fields behind and I am on the open hill. For a few moments I stand still with my back to the wall and savor the freedom; there is not another human being in sight, and the hill is mine for the taking . . . but no, the hill has already been claimed, this is Pusshill and here are its owners.

There are at least six full-grown hares in sight, big brown creatures with long silky ears . . . perhaps there are more than six, I can't be certain of the number because of their strange antics. This is March, of course, the month when Hank goes mad, and there seems to be a good deal of truth in the old saying. A hare starts up, almost at my my feet, and alarms me quite as much as I have alarmed him; he gives a great leap straight up in the air and rushes away with kangaroolike bounds. Then suddenly he stops and whizzes round and crouches on the grass. A second hare appears from behind a rock and careers across the hill pursued by a third hare . . . suddenly he stops, and turns and crouches. Number three, instead of continuing the pursuit stops dead and crouches too. Number one now springs up and dashes off and, as he goes, two other hares appear as if they had materialized from the bare hillside and follow him. They run round in a wide circle, sometimes stopping and crouching, sometimes leaping straight up in the air, sometimes jinking in a zigzag manner from tuft to tuft. This game of follow-my-leader is curious enough, and I watch it entranced.

Suddenly two very large hares dash out from the shelter of the wall and, having leapt and capered and whizzed round several times in a thoroughly crazy manner, they run straight at one another and begin an absurd sort of boxing match, rotating on their hind legs and hitting one another with their front paws. I rub my eyes (for it is almost incredible) and look at them again . . . yes, there they are, two large brown hares with long silky ears boxing each other, hitting each other on the body or the head, dodging and capering and leaping in the air and then going for each other again. The oddest thing about it is the silence —no sound comes from the combatants—and the combat is in no way a ferocious affair. In fact it is not a fight at all but a friendly sparring match . . . these creatures are full of high spirits, mad with the joy of Spring. They feel the stir of the rising sap and they caper and crouch and bound across the moor.

Suddenly they have vanished. Where have they gone? To my inexperienced eye there seems to be no cover at all upon the bare hillside. There are a few biggish stones and tufts of rushes, there is grass and withered brown heather . . . and that is all.

The play is over, and now I begin to wonder if it really happened or whether I imagined the whole thing . . . but somehow my heart feels gay and my step is lighter as I take my way up the hill.

It is a good pull up to the top and the wind is strong

and gusty, it whistles through the stones of the little cairn and flattens my skirt against my legs. The view is lovely, I can see far down the valley of the Rydd. Far below lies Tocher House with its parks and trees and its square walled-garden laid out in neat rows . . . but the wind is too strong and cold to be pleasant, I must find a sheltered place to sit.

On the lee side of the hill there is a great outcrop of rock and seeking shelter there I stumble upon Miss Mc-Queen—stumble upon her quite literally, for I almost fall over her outstretched feet as I turn the corner.

"How did you know I was here!" exclaims Miss Mc-Queen fiercely. She is annoyed at my sudden appearance, of course, and one cannot blame her, for the place is so high and solitary that here, at least, one would expect to be free from interruption.

"I didn't!" I stammer, surprised into foolish babbling. "I mean I didn't know you were here; how could I? If I had known you were here I wouldn't have come! Todd said I could go anywhere—"

She laughs, somewhat mirthlessly, and apologizes. "You gave me a fright," she declares. "I was thinking about something—that's all."

I turn to go without more ado, for there is plenty of room upon the hill for two women to think their thoughts in peace, but Miss McQueen calls me back and says a trifle shyly that it's sheltered here.

"There are other sheltered spots," I reply, hesitating.

"Nòt many," she says. "I come here every day so I know it pretty well. Sit down, won't you?"

She makes room for me to sit on her mackintosh. I sit down and clasp my knees and we look at the view in silence. From this point there is nothing to see but hills, yellow and green and brown, with an occasional clump of wind-blown firs to relieve the monotony; hills and hills and hills . . . a hundred hills huddling one behind the other into the misty distance. There is one small farm which lies in the valley below—how lonely and deserted it looks— but apart from that there is no sign at all of human beings or human occupation.

The song of Tennyson's shepherd boy comes into my head:

"Come down, O maid, from yonder mountain height:
 What pleasure lives in height (the shepherd sang),
 In height and cold, the splendour of the hills?"

But there *is* a pleasure that lives in height, and a strange peace. Here, where one is high above the little world of men, one can get one's values right. Paltry troubles look paltry beside the grandeur of God's hills . . . how could I have allowed Hope and the linen to disturb my equilibrium!

"What a fool I am!" I exclaim suddenly.

"It affects you like that, does it?" enquires my companion.

"Silly little worries look silly," I explain.

She is silent for a few moments and then says she heard me talking to the American woman in the lounge— she couldn't help overhearing bits of our conversation— and she wonders if I really believe happiness comes from self abnegation. If so she ought to be blissfully happy, says Miss McQueen bitterly.

I feel rather out of my depth here, for obviously Miss

McQueen is far from happy, and I wish, not for the first time, that I had not allowed my tongue to run away with me.

"You said happiness was a privilege," declares Miss McQueen. "But surely one has a right to a little happiness —or at least a right as a human being to be less than outrageously miserable all one's life."

"I said it was no use to pursue happiness."

"I never pursued happiness, but I've attained despair all right," says Miss McQueen grimly. She shuts her lips in a firm line after this, as if to make sure of saying no more, but there comes a time when the proudest and most self-contained can be silent no longer and I have a feeling that Miss McQueen has reached bursting point.

"Why?" says Miss McQueen after a few moments' silence. "Why is one person happy and another miserable? Is it fair? If you do what you think is the right thing . . . there ought to be some . . . not reward exactly, but some sort of—of compensation. If you knew beforehand . . . but even then . . . what can you do when everything seems fated? You have no choice, really . . . no choice at all, so it can't be your fault when things go wrong. Can it?"

As I can find no answers to these incoherent questions, I shake my head sadly and say it is all very difficult. Fortunately Miss McQueen takes this as an expression of sympathy—which it is—and settles down to tell me about it more calmly. She has spent the last six years looking after an aunt who was very delicate and required a great deal of care and attention. Now the aunt is dead and Miss McQueen is alone in the world, absolutely untrained and practically penniless. The old lady had always told Miss McQueen that she would leave her everything and left a will to that effect, but as all her capital had been invested in an annuity there was nothing to leave except a few pounds in the bank, her clothes and a little jewelry. "I don't blame her, really," says Miss McQueen. "I mean she had every right to do what she liked with her own money, and of course she ensured herself a much better income, and was more comfortable . . . I doubt if she really understood that when she died there would be nothing left for me. She was very vague about money matters . . . but if I had known I might have managed to train myself for something, at any rate I would have been prepared for this. It has been a shock. I'm tired, too," she continued with a sigh. "Dreadfully tired. She was ill for weeks, you see, and I couldn't get anyone at all to help me. I didn't feel it so much at the time—just went on from day to day managing as best I could—but now I feel absolutely done."

"Haven't you anyone belonging to you, any friends?"

"I have—one friend," she replies in a low voice. "That's another—problem. He wants to marry me, you see. I don't know why on earth I'm telling you."

Half an hour ago I should have been surprised to hear this piece of news, but my feelings have changed and I realize that there is something very attractive about Miss McQueen—perhaps it is her voice, which is low and melodious, or perhaps it is because I am looking at her with new eyes. She is like a wood nymph, with her red-gold hair and pale skin, there is an ethereal quality about her. "The Lass with the Delicate Air," describes her admirably.

"Well?" she enquires, smiling at me a little.

I realise that I have been staring and daydreaming, which is a bad habit of mine.

"You're surprised," she continues. "It *is* surprising that any man should want to marry me."

I assure her that my thoughts were far otherwise.

"It surprises me," she says.

"Don't you—like him?" I ask her doubtfully, for it seems to me marriage would be the ideal solution of her problems.

She does not answer at once. She is busy poking a hole in the ground with her stick. "Oh yes," she says at last. "Yes, I like him. Nobody could help liking him; he's a splendid person, but—but I don't really want to marry him nor anyone. I want to be left in peace."

"You need a rest."

"Yes, but I can't rest . . . and there's the question of money. I ought to be looking about for a job. I should never have come here, of course, but I had to go somewhere —and now I'm too tired to move on. Tired," says Miss McQueen in a flat voice. "Not physically tired—I can walk miles."

"Nervously tired."

"The elastic has gone out of me. The spring has run down or something. Did you see the hares?"

"Yes, they were full of life, weren't they?"

"Full of life," says Miss McQueen wearily. "It made me tired to look at them—and of course it should have had the reverse effect. . . . I'm all wrong, you see. I'm all tangled up and I can't get straightened out . . . if I could sleep it might help. It's silly not to be able to sleep, because there's no need to *worry*—there's no *sense* in worrying, it only makes things worse—and I shan't starve. I'll get some sort of job—something—but I don't *want* a job. I'm used up, you see. There's nothing left, no goodness left in me, no warmth or life . . . that's why it wouldn't be fair to *him*. Oh, what a fool I was!" says Miss McQueen, beating her hand gently on the turf. "Oh, what a fool! I was caught, you see. I went at the very beginning of the war to stay with her for a fortnight and she got a bad chill so I stayed on and looked after her—and then the maid was called up —and I stayed on. How could I walk out and leave her? How could I? She couldn't possibly do everything herself. I might have nursed soldiers—I had been all through my V.A.D. training—I might have gone abroad and nursed soldiers and done some good in the war; but I was caught. They exempted me of course—well, of course they had to— I was caught." She is silent for a few moments and then adds, "I wish I knew what to do."

"Give yourself time," I tell her.

"I can't," she declares. "I can't just leave everything and rest because I can't rest until it's settled—besides it isn't fair to *him*. I must decide now—and I have decided, really, but he keeps on writing."

"Were you engaged?"

"Yes," says Miss McQueen. "Yes, but now—oh, how can I explain! If I married him *now* it would be because I don't want to work, and he's too good for that."

"If you had been independent—" I begin, because it seems to me that this is the whole trouble.

She catches me up at once. "Oh yes," she says. "If I had been independent I could have married him without feeling that I was marrying him for a home, for safety, for security. It would have been quite different, then." She hesitates and then continues in a lower tone, "Besides how do I know that he will want to marry a penniless woman?"

"You should explain—"

"No," she says. "No, I couldn't. He would marry me of course—he would be *more* determined to marry me, not less, if he knew my present circumstances—but I don't want him to marry me because he is sorry for me. It would be unbearable."

"I don't think you're being fair to him," I tell her.

"It wouldn't be fair to saddle him with a useless wife." She lies back against the rock. "It goes round and round," she says in an exhausted voice. "I get no further—and I can't sleep. I keep on telling myself there's no need to worry. I could serve in a shop, couldn't I?"

"Why a shop?"

"Why not? It would be mechanical sort of work and that's the only sort of work I could bear. I couldn't look after anybody—all that part of me is used up, the part of me that fills hot-water bottles and shakes up pillows and measures out medicine."

"Couldn't you look after a child?"

She shakes her head.

"You don't like children?"

"I do like them," she replies. "They interest me tremendously, but it wouldn't be fair to the child. Children need an interesting person, and I'm not interesting any more. I'm not . . . anything."

"It will come back when you've rested," I tell her.

She sits up suddenly, pulling herself together. "Heaven knows why I'm boring you like this!" she exclaims.

"You aren't boring me."

"Nonsense. You must be bored stiff. If a strange woman started to tell me the history of her life I should scream—and go on screaming." She rises and dusts her skirt. "Don't talk about it," she adds.

"Of course not—unless you want to . . ."

"I shan't want to—ever," says Miss McQueen firmly.

I watch her go down the steep slope and turn the corner of the hill.

Saturday, 16th March

Am very busy writing letters in the office when there is a knock on the door and Mrs. Wilbur Potting comes in. Since our talk I have avoided Mrs. Wilbur, partly because I am ashamed of having let myself go and partly because I was not sure of Mrs. Wilbur's feelings on the subject. Mrs. Wilbur asks if I am too busy to talk to her and without waiting for a reply she sits down in Miss Cutterbuck's chair and crosses her long silken legs. Have I thought over her suggestion that I should come back to the States with her, she enquires.

I reply that I thought she might have changed her mind.

Mrs. Wilbur says on the contrary she wants me more than ever, she likes people with definite ideas and admires people who express their ideas in forceful language. As to my ideas, says Mrs. Wilbur, she has been thinking over what I said and it's all very very interesting. She doesn't see how she could use it in her lecture upon The Spirit of English Womanhood, as it is too iconoclastic, but Marley thinks I might give a few lectures myself.

I assure her that I am incapable of lecturing.

Just drawing-room lectures, says Mrs. Wilbur. She seems quite certain that I could accomplish the feat without difficulty and I must admit that after the exhibition in the lounge she has some justification for her belief.

"No—honestly I couldn't. It's impossible!" I cry.

Mrs. Wilbur smiles and beseeches me not to get up in the air. I shall do exactly as I like about that. She is so charming and so pretty, and I am so glad she is not annoyed with me that I feel tempted to accept her offer straight off and go to America with her, but of course I know that this is just my "headlong impulsiveness" which Tim so often deplores, and that if I don't pull myself together and behave like a sensible woman I shall regret it. So I pull myself together and explain that I can't go to America, much as I should like to do so.

Mrs. Wilbur says Miss Clutterbuck can be compensated for the loss of my services, she herself will talk to Miss Clutterbuck and she guarantees to make her see sense.

Explain that it isn't so much Miss Clutterbuck as my family. The children are coming here for their holidays, so—

Mrs. Wilbur claps her hands and declares that she just loves children and of course they must come too—all of them. Wilbur will arrange passages on the boat, he's good at that sort of thing.

This manifestation of American hospitality almost takes my breath away, for it is obvious that Mrs. Wilbur is perfectly serious, and is willing, nay eager, to welcome a comparatively strange Englishwoman and an indefinite number of completely unknown children to her home. While I am still speechless for lack of breath Mrs. Wilbur is sitting bolt upright, and with shining eyes is enumerating the delights in store for her guests, delights unobtainable in a land ravaged by total war. Their meals will consist of fried chicken and ice cream and they will eat candy all day long. . . .

She is so kind that it is difficult to refuse without seeming ungracious, but I do my best, and being sensible as well as kind she realizes quite soon that I mean what I say and accepts the inevitable. Before she goes she gives me her card and says that if I change my mind about it I am to write straight off and let her know and Wilbur will arrange everything.

Mrs. Wilbur has no sooner gone than Miss Clutterbuck comes in and says what did that Mrs. Potting want? If she wants to stay on longer she can't because the rooms are let from the sixth of April.

"She wanted me," I reply in casual tones.

"She wanted you!"

"To go to America with her."

"I suppose she offered you three times the salary!" says Miss Clutterbuck in disgust.

This surprises me, and I ask quite innocently how Miss Clutterbuck knew.

"Three times!" exclaims Miss Clutterbuck, looking at me in such evident amazement that I realize she did not know, but was only speaking in a metaphorical way.

"Well—yes," I reply. "But of course it's different in America—and I can't go, anyhow, so what does it matter!"

"She thinks you're underpaid, and so you are," replies Miss Clutterbuck. "You won't believe this, of course, but I had made up my mind to give you more."

"I didn't mean to—"

"I know that. It's not difficult to see through you," says Miss Clutterbuck grimly. "I've told you already that I had made up my mind to pay you a decent salary before I heard a word about that American business."

"You're giving me enough, really. I mean—"

"Don't be a fool. You're a great deal more capable

than you look," says the amazing woman. She goes away after that and leaves me pondering over her words and wondering what exactly she meant by this backhanded compliment.

Sunday, 17th March

There is snow, today. Not very much, of course, but enough to make the little world of Tocher a fairyland. The lawns sparkle in the sunshine, every branch of every tree is outlined in white. Mrs. Everard's children have run out into the garden and are snowballing each other, shouting with glee . . . the scene resembles an old-fashioned Christmas card.

Miss Clutterbuck offers me the morning off and says I can take the car and go to church at Ryddelton if I want to. I decide to accept the offer and, dressed in my best clothes, sally forth to the garage. The car looks at me in a malevolent fashion as I go in (perhaps this is my fancy, or perhaps it is the effect of the crooked head lamps which gives it the appearance of possessing such a disagreeable squint). Summoning up my courage I take my seat and press the self-starter—nothing happens. I try the starting handle without result.

Todd now appears and says she ought to start quite easily because the battery has been pepped up and he cleaned the plugs yesterday. He'll have a go at her.

He has at least a dozen goes at her but she does not respond.

"I doubt it'll be the mag. again," says Todd frowning. "It'll take the best part of an hour to sort her . . ."

"Don't bother," I tell him quickly, for Todd (like myself) is attired in Sunday garments and obviously means to attend Divine Worship at the Tocher village church.

"Well . . ." says Todd, weighing the matter carefully. "Maybe I'd best leave it till the afternoon. You'll not get to church, anyway, for it wouldn't be done in time and I'd like fine to be at the kirk this morning. It's my second cousin's brother-in-law that's preaching."

"Then of course you must go!" I exclaim.

"M'ph'm," says Todd. "It's a pity, but it can't be helped." He hesitates and then adds, "I'll need to be here this afternoon, anyway. Maybe Miss Clutterbuck will have told you the Countess of Ayr is coming."

"To Tocher!" I exclaim.

"It's about the turn into the main road," says Todd, and with these cryptic words he wheels out his motor-bike and vanishes down the drive.

I hurry back to the house. It seems odd that Miss Clutterbuck has not warned me of the Countess's visit. Will she be here for tea, I wonder—surely I would have been told if she intended to stay the night!

Miss Clutterbuck is in the hall when I return. I explain about the car and add that it is just as well I have not gone to Ryddelton as I had better see cook about special cakes for tea.

"What's up?" enquires Miss Clutterbuck.

"Todd said the Countess of Ayr is coming, so—"

"Special cakes for the Countess of Ayr!" exclaims Miss Clutterbuck in obvious amazement.

It is obvious I have made a faux pas. I murmur something feeble and run upstairs to change.

By the afternoon the remains of the snow has vanished

and the sun is quite warm. I seat myself near the window in the lounge, from whence I hope to have a good view of our distinguished visitor's arrival; but—alas for my plans—I have no sooner taken up my position than Curry comes in and says Miss Clutterbuck wants me in the office. I glance down the drive again, but no car is in sight, so I am forced to relinquish my post and obey my employer's summons.

Miss Clutterbuck is in conclave with a burly gentleman in tweeds who rises politely as I enter and is introduced as Mr. Denham.

"Mr. Denham is a very busy man," explains Miss Clutterbuck.

"No busier than yourself, I'm sure," replies Mr. Denham gallantly. "And never too busy to come over to Tocher House—if I may say so."

This sort of talk gets nowhere with Miss Clutterbuck. "Well, that's all, isn't it?" she says, gathering a sheaf of papers together and stuffing them into a drawer.

Mr. Denham takes the hint. "That's all," he agrees. "I'll see what can be done about the corner. It ought to be better marked, anyway."

"Mrs. Christie will give you some tea," says Miss Clutterbuck in final tones.

I realize at once that this is the reason I have been sent for and remove Mr. Denham forthwith. We descend to the lounge and order tea—fortunately I am able to procure the table near the window. Mr. Denham is slightly heavy on hand and conversation is difficult . . . I remark that we are expecting the Countess of Ayr to arrive this afternoon.

"That's me," says Mr. Denham, helping himself to a bun.

"That's you!" I exclaim in amazement.

Mr. Denham nods. "Yes, I'm the County Surveyor, Mrs. Christie. Of course you wouldn't know—Miss Clutterbuck didn't mention it, did she? You may think it a bit queer that I should come over on a Sunday to see that corner she's complaining about—I can see you're a bit surprised."

"Just a little," I murmur.

"I'm a busy man," he explains. "Miss Clutterbuck said I was busy and she was right. The fact is I happened to be in this part of the County so I fitted it in. You see how it was?"

"Yes, of course," I reply in feeble accents. "Yes, of course—why not? I might have known—"

"You couldn't know," he declares. "You're new here, aren't you?"

"Quite new," I agree fervently.

Mr. Denham smiles at me. "Well, anyway, there's no harm done, Mrs. Christie."

"No harm done," I agree, more fervently than before . . . and I heave a sigh of profound relief as I realize that nobody—except myself—knows what an idiot I have been.

Wednesday, 20th March

The days pass very quickly at Tocher House. I have found my proper place in the ménage and have settled into it comfortably. Hope is still extremely difficult, but she is now the only pea in my mattress for my ideas about my employer have suffered a sea change. I like her now; in fact I like her quite a lot. She even looks different to my eyes, which seems odd when I have time to consider the matter. Obviously Miss Clutterbuck can't have altered "all that much" in the short time I have been at Tocher. She can't have altered at all! Nearly fifty years have passed over her head and for twenty of them she must have looked much the same as she does now. Let me try to describe her: tall, strongly built with square shoulders and a short thick neck, sturdy legs, but nice feet; square face, somewhat weather-beaten, grey eyes and short hair; large mouth, firm chin and excellent teeth—rather a deep voice. The woman has a curious flavor, all her own. She has rigid ideas and lays down the law with authority, but I have found she has a soft core beneath the hard, rough shell. One of her rigid ideas is upon the subject of sweated labor, and nobody in her house is allowed to work more than seven hours a day. It is amusing to hear Miss Clutterbuck "telling off" Todd for working after hours. She rates at him ferociously for this egregious fault while he stands before her, slightly sheepish but obviously enjoying the joke. I, also, have been in trouble for this offense and have decided I must not be found out committing it again.

It is difficult for me, of course, for my work is not a set routine. Some days are busier than others and there are certain jobs which must be done after hours. There is the linen room for instance. I have now banished Hope from the linen room but the muddle has never been straightened out and I realize that the only way to straighten it is to take everything off the shelves and make a list. This is a gargantuan task and it has been on my mind for days—I quail when I think of it. The linen room is a small square room with a skylight window; there are shelves and cupboards all round from floor to ceiling; two large wooden boxes full of extra blankets stand in the middle of the floor. It will be impossible to take out all the linen and sort it into piles unless I can use the landing, and I cannot use the landing during the day. I must do it at night, that's all. I must wait until everybody —including Miss Dove—has gone to bed and quiet has descended upon Tocher House.

The plan is brilliant, only marred by the unfortunate fact that when I go to bed I am tired; however that can't be helped and by dint of reading a detective story and pinching myself at intervals I manage to stay awake. At half-past one I issue from my chamber attired in the navy blue siren suit —a faithful copy of Mr. Churchill's—which I wore at Donford for A.R.P.; I creep downstairs to the next floor and set about my task.

It is quite as difficult as I feared and even more strenuous for the piles of linen are unexpectedly heavy and there is more of it than I expected. Sheets hemstitched, sheets plain, pillow slips of different patterns and sizes and textures, dozens of bath towels and hand towels, table linen of

all kinds, extra pillows, bolsters and eiderdowns. I take them
out of the cupboards and down from the shelves and lay
them in neat piles all over the landing.

I am in the middle of the job, the landing is piled with
linen and I am wading about in the midst of it, notebook
in hand, when I hear a slight sound and looking up behold
Miss Clutterbuck descending the stair from her bedroom.
She is wearing a pink flannel nightdress with a frill round
the neck and a royal-blue dressing gown of ample proportions. Her hair is standing on end and her eyes are wide and
half-dazed with sleep.

"What the hell?" exclaims Miss Clutterbuck in muted
accents—muted so as not to disturb her sleeping guests.

"It's all right," I assure her. "There wasn't time to do
it during the day."

"You're daft," says Miss Clutterbuck firmly.

"It won't take long."

"Clean daft. Do you think I want you on my hands with
a nervous breakdown?"

"I'm very strong."

"If I'd wanted you to work twenty-four hours a day I'd
have said so at the start."

"I need the landing," I explain, waving my hand at the
piles of linen.

"It's a straitjacket you need."

"Honestly, Miss Clutterbuck—"

"Mrs. Christie, you know my views . . ."

This conversation takes place in whispers of course, and
in whispers we continue to argue, quite fruitlessly, until at
last I ask Miss Clutterbuck what she wants me to do as it is
impossible to leave the landing strewn with linen.

"Have a little sense," says Miss Clutterbuck. "Leave it

and go back to your bed. Hope will help you in the morning."

"Thank you," I reply, infuriated. "I'll either do this myself, now, or I'll leave this house tomorrow."

Miss Clutterbuck is defeated but she goes down fighting. She says she'll save her breath to cool her porridge. She ties the cord of her dressing gown tightly round her waist, wades into the linen and begins sorting out pillow slips.

"Miss Clutterbuck!" I say in firm accents, which lose a little of their potency from the necessity to speak in whispers. "Miss Clutterbuck, the linen is my job. Please go back to bed and leave me to do it in my own way."

"Mrs. Christie," says Miss Clutterbuck. "I have no intention of going back to bed until the job is done."

We glare at each other.

"Please, Miss Clutterbuck, go back to bed."

"I will not," declares Miss Clutterbuck. "You're a stubborn woman—but so am I. There's precious little to choose between us." She pauses for a moment with an embroidered pillow slip in her hands, "And what's more," she says fiercely, "what's more I'll not work with any woman in the small hours and continue to address her by her surname. The thing is utterly ridiculous."

She looks so fierce—and so funny—standing there in her night attire with the absurd pink frill round her neck that I am taken with sudden and uncontrollable laughter and am forced to bury my head in a feather bolster which happens to be conveniently near. When I have overcome my weakness I raise my head and behold Miss Clutterbuck with her face buried in an eiderdown quilt; her whole body heaving and quivering with the violence of her emotion.

It is some minutes before we are able to resume work

. . . it is nearly an hour before we have finished. The linen is now back upon the shelves, laid out in neat piles and duly listed. The task has been arduous but well worthwhile and I survey the result of our labors with a satisfied air.

"Well, I hope you're pleased," says Miss Clutterbuck— or Erica, as I must try to call her (to be frank I find it extremely difficult to summon up the necessary cheek).

"I'm delighted," I reply. "It's simply splendid. I can't thank you enough for helping me."

"Hrrmph!" says Erica disgustedly. She hates being thanked.

Having completed our task and locked the door of the linen room we descend to the kitchen premises in search of food. Erica says she is ravenous, hard work always affects her like this which is the reason she can't get down her weight.

"I've lost my beauty sleep, and this extra meal will put me up half a pound," declares Erica in grumbling tones as she raids the larder for cold meat and the remains of a syrup tart . . . and now Erica shows another human weakness, a weakness which surprises me in a woman of her determination and strength of character. Erica is frightened of mice.

Friday, 22nd March

Today I receive two letters, one from Bryan and the other from Tim. As Bryan's is the shorter I read it first.

"Dear Mum,
Edgeburton has asked me to go with him to stay with his grandfather for the first fortnight of the holidays. Would this be all right? I could come on to Tocher House for the second fortnight. I daresay you remember me telling you about old Hedgehog's grandfather, he is Sir Percy Edgeburton and lives at Langmer's End. Hedgehog is terrified of him and says it will be awful if he has to go alone, that's why he wants me. Langmer's End is a big place and there are horses for us to ride so it ought to be quite good fun, especially as Hedgehog says his grandfather will not bother about us and we can do as we like as long as we are in time for meals. I think I should go, don't you? It would be a new experience for me. Let me know soon so that we can write and tell Sir Percy.
                    Lots of love from
                                        Bryan
P.S. E's G. asked him to bring a friend so it will be all right."

This letter amuses me a good deal for Edgeburton is an old friend of Bryan's; they were at prep school together and went on together to Harton, and although they sometimes fall out they have stuck together consistently through thick and thin. Edgeburton's grandfather is well-known to me by repute; he writes long letters to his grandson which Bryan says are "full of long words" and which necessitate the use of a dictionary. Bryan, who has a ready pen, usually helps to compose a suitable answer. As regards the visit, Bryan must certainly go; as he says himself it will be a new experience for him and a fortnight at Tocher will probably be quite enough.

I lay aside Bryan's letter to answer and take up Tim's.

". . . Don't stay a moment longer in that dreadful hotel," writes Tim firmly. "I can't bear to think of you slaving for that extraordinary woman. Chuck it, for goodness sake, and go and stay with Aunt Posy at Cobstead. I thought it sounded most unsuitable when you first told me about it (you're awfully apt to dash into things, you know) and I am all the more worried because I am so far away and don't know what is happening. However there is no harm done. You must give the woman a week's wages, or whatever the arrangement is, and leave at once."

Of course this letter is in answer to the letter I wrote Tim on my arrival at Tocher House when I felt anything but cheerful. I had no intention of worrying Tim, and purposely refrained from disclosing the full story of Miss Clutterbuck's peculiar behavior, but Tim must have read between the lines and despite my care in its composition my letter must have had a plaintive tone. By this time Tim will have received another letter—a cheerful one—so I can only hope he has stopped worrying and is quite happy about me.

Looking at myself in the mirror I am suddenly assailed by a queer sensation . . . am I really myself? Am I really Tim's wife and Betty's mother or somebody else—Miss Clutterbuck's assistant? *This* me, the Hester of Tocher House, is quite different from the Donford Hester, she has quite different thoughts and a different attitude of mind. Instead of being completely occupied with the full-time job of wife and mother she is completely occupied with the job of running a hotel. *This* Hester is so busy, so caught up into the whirl of her new life that the old life seems like a dream, she has no time to think during the day, and at night she is tired and falls asleep at once and does not stir till morning. No time to think—yes, that is the solution of the mystery, that is the reason Hester has stepped out of the old life and is so comfortably ensconced in the new.

I take up Tim's letter. He continues:

"There is not much chance of getting you out here at the moment, I'm afraid. You will see by the papers we are having some unpleasantnesses. Perhaps by the autumn things will have settled down and you and Annie could come to Egypt for the winter. If not we shall just have to grin and bear it until I can get home—that won't be soon! The trouble is everyone wants to get home and regulars will have to stick it out until the world settles down. I suppose it will in time! In my humble opinion demobilization is going too fast. (We have had enough bother winning the war and we should not throw away the fruits of victory by dispersing our armies before everything is settled.) But this opinion is too unpopular to pronounce aloud, indeed if I pronounced it aloud in mess it would cause a mild riot. It was funny your meeting Roger Elden in the train, I remember him well—an awfully nice fellow—I am glad he came through all right. I remember him asking about your photograph. He was interested in it because it was like his wife. Elden's wife died when their first child was born, so this clears up your little mystery, doesn't it?"

PULASKI-PERRY REG. LIBRARY
LITTLE ROCK. ARKANSAS

It clears up the mystery completely, of course. Major Elden remembered my face because I was like his wife, not because I was particularly beautiful or interesting. Fortunately this does not disappoint me at all. As a matter of fact my mind has been so occupied with other matters that I had almost forgotten Major Elden.

Tim continues: "I have got a parcel for you and will send it by hand with the first person who takes the road for home. I hope the contents of the parcel will be acceptable, it was a little difficult to choose. I rather like the pink silk pyjamas and wish with all my heart I could be there to see you wearing them . . ."

The writer becomes rather silly at this point but just at the end he pulls himself together again. "Oh, about that dream of mine. It was a very vivid dream—but here is Bollings to take the letters to the post. I will tell you all about it in my next . . ."

Saturday, 23rd March

It is early morning. I awake to hear the door opening and am aware it is Hope with my tea. As the sight of Hope's uncheerful countenance is a bad beginning to a day I shut my eyes firmly and play possum. Hope's method of calling me never varies, she marches in like a grenadier, slams down the tray and marches out again. There are no fine points about it. If the bursting open of my bedroom door does not rouse me from my slumbers the rattle of the teacup close to my ear has the desired effect. Once or twice I have slept through this to be awakened by the crash of the door which signals the departure of Hope. Today, however, she is unusually quiet. Her step is scarcely audible and the tray is deposited upon my bedside table without a sound, and—wonder of wonders—I can hear her moving about my room putting things straight, shutting the windw and switching on the electric fire. I open one eye and peep at her over the folded sheet . . . and it isn't Hope at all!

"Annie!" I cry, sitting up in bed with a bound.

Annie gives a startled yelp. "Lor'!" she exclaims. "And me thinking you were asleep! What a fright I got!"

"But, Annie, you weren't coming till next week!"

"I know," agrees Annie. "But what with one thing and another . . . to tell the truth there was such a crowd in the house and I got a bit tired of washing dishes."

"But surely—"

"Oh, it was my own fault, of course. I said I'd do the dishes to give Ellen a bit of a rest, but I didn't bargain for doing it even on for the whole family."

She comes and stands beside the bed and we look at each other with satisfaction. It is delightful to see Annie again, it makes me feel more like myself; for Annie is a part of my real life in which Tocher House is only an interlude. The sight of Annie makes Tim more real to me and brings Bryan and Betty nearer.

"Sit down, Annie," I say, moving my feet to one side and making room for her.

Annie sits down. "But I can't stay long," she warns me. "I've got all this floor to wake and half the second floor."

"You're not going to be overworked, are you?"

"I'll take good care of that," declares Annie.

"I'm sorry your holiday wasn't a success."

"It wasn't as bad as that, really," says Annie thoughtfully. "I enjoyed the first bit all right, but Ellen and me didn't seem to have much in common. She's my own sister, of course, but somehow I felt a bit out of it. Ellen said I'd changed—well, perhaps I have. It's funny, isn't it?"

"I'm sorry," I tell her, and so I am; especially as I have a feeling it is largely my fault. Annie has changed (in my opinion for the better) but is it for the better if it alienates her from her family?

"You needn't be sorry," says Annie. "It's just that I've got used to different ways, that's all. Ellen has got Bert and the children and she's quite happy in her own way. I've got Bill and you and the Colonel and Bryan and Betty, so I'm all right. I'll have children of my own someday and I'll see to it they're properly brought up—not like Ellen's children. Pictures three nights a week!" exclaims Annie scornfully.

"Meals all anyhow, going to bed any time they like, and little Ellen refusing to drink milk! No wonder they're pale and puny and always having colds!"

"I hope you didn't—"

"I told Ellen," says Annie, nodding. "It wasn't a bit of good and I knew it wouldn't be, but it was my duty to tell her, and I didn't mince it either. It was my duty," says Annie, with conscious rectitude.

I have a momentary feeling of sympathy for the unhappy Ellen, a sacrifice on the altar of Annie's duty—or at least Annie's conception of her duty. Whether or not her conception was right it is difficult to say.

"This isn't a bad place, is it?" continues Annie in conspiratorial tones. "I got here late last night and cook gave me a hot supper which I didn't expect, really. The food seems good and I've got a comfortable bed. The only snag so far is that Clara. She's a misery, isn't she?"

"Clara?"

"Of course she's had a good deal of trouble," admits Annie, with a judicial air. "She hasn't had a bed of roses, exactly, what with her father drinking himself to death and being jilted by the man she was going to marry at the very last minute, and getting her front teeth knocked out in a bus accident—but all that wasn't yesterday by any means and she might have got over it by this time."

"Who is your unfortunate friend?" I enquire, but Annie is wound up and takes no notice.

"Other people have troubles," she continues. "They don't just sit down and brood for the rest of their lives. It's my belief Clara would be all the better for a good shake-up. I'd like to shake her up and tell her to get on with it."

I can see the missionary spirit alight in Annie's eye. She will think it her duty to shake up the unfortunate Clara.

"Oh well," says Annie with a sigh. "There's always something, isn't there? I like somebody with a bit more life about them—but you can't have everything, it wouldn't be good for you, I don't suppose. I'll just have to bear with Clara as best I can."

"Annie, who is Clara?" I enquire.

"Clara!" exclaims Annie in amazement. "You know Clara!"

"No, I don't. I never *heard* of her."

"Clara, the head housemaid!"

"Hope!"

"That's right. Clara Hope."

"Oh, I thought it was Hope something!"

"Hope on hope ever," says Annie chuckling. "She doesn't, that's the whole trouble . . . but if I don't get on with my work there'll be wigs on the green so I'd better go."

She leaves me with a good deal to think of one way and another . . . and first I think about Annie herself and my relationship with her. We have been good friends for years, Annie and I, but today we seem to have moved a big step further. She has never spoken to me so confidentially before, never taken me right inside and showed me her feelings so plainly. Perhaps it is because we are now both employees of Miss Clutterbuck, but I prefer to think it is because we find ourselves together in strange surroundings.

Monday, 25th March

On coming downstairs rather early for dinner I am interested to see a good-sized salmon displayed upon the hall table. It has been killed by Mr. Stannard, of course, or perhaps by his son. These two gentlemen have been fishing industriously ever since their arrival at Tocher House, but this is the first fruits of their labor. Erica does not like the Stannards; the father is a short thickset man with a white moustache stained with nicotine from innumerable cigarettes; he is a London business man—business unspecified—and his aitches are not always secure. Captain Stannard is tall and lean and dark; he has a slightly vague look about him, as if he were thinking of something else (something that gives him no pleasure to judge from his expression). Mrs. Stannard is so small and quiet and frightened as to be almost invisible to the naked eye. In Erica's opinion (trenchantly expressed) the Stannards are a blot upon the landscape, for not only are they substandard (the horrible pun is Erica's), dull and unsociable, but they can't kill salmon. (It is, says Erica, a very bad advertisement for Tocher when people go out and flog the water for days without result. She wishes she had never taken the Stannards; she wishes they would go away; sometimes, when more than usually irritated, she wishes they would fall into the river and be drowned.)

But lo and behold the Stannards have killed a salmon— quite a nice one, too—and if there is any doubt in my mind as to the perpetrator of the deed it is immediately dispelled by the sight of Mr. Stannard himself, lurking in the shadows of the hall and craving his due meed of praise and approbation.

He shall have praise in full measure, not only because he thoroughly deserves praise, but also because I feel eager to reward him: the salmon is pleasant to look at and will make a most welcome addition to the menu of Tocher House.

"Yours?" I ask, smiling encouragingly.

"My son caught it," says Mr. Stannard, coming forward with a beaming face. "It's a nice fish, isn't it, Mrs. Christie? You know about salmon, I expect."

"It's a very nice fish, Mr. Stannard."

"Six pounds," says Mr. Stannard. "At least *nearly.* Not very big as salmon go but it gave Tom a good bit of sport. Three-quarters of an hour it was, before I got the gaff into it."

"Excellent!" I exclaim.

"It was the Priest's Pool—that's what they call it . . . Tom hooked it there about 'alf-past two, and away it went. I never was so excited in all my life as when I heard Tom's reel running out—never. You know, Mrs. Christie, it's what I've been 'oping for—you might almost say praying for. I said to Mother only yesterday, I said, if I could just gaff a fish for Tom that's all I want, I said. I daresay you think that's a bit silly."

"I've got a son, Mr. Stannard."

"Oh!" he says doubtfully. "You've got—oh yes, you mean you can understand; but it's more than that, really. You see Tom is all we've got—now."

"I see."

"Yes, his brother was killed, you see. They were twins,

you see. Well, it was a funny thing but there was something
between them . . . something more than . . . just being
brothers. We couldn't understand it, really, Mother and I.
It was—it was—"

"Affinity," I suggest.

"Well, perhaps," agrees Mr. Stannard doubtfully. "Perhaps it was infinity. Mother and I used to say they knew
what each other was thinking—it was like that. Well, you
see, when Dick was killed it went pretty badly with Tom.
It was as if something *went out* of Tom. He didn't say
much, but he stopped caring about things—didn't care about
anything anymore, didn't care what 'appened. I said to
Mother it was just as if we'd lost more than Dick, as if we'd
lost 'alf of Tom, too. Silly of course but that's 'ow I felt about
it, Mrs. Christie."

The little man pauses and looks at me to see how I am
taking it, and I am taking it so hard that I find some difficulty in saying I am sorry, very sorry indeed.

"Yes, I can see you are," he says nodding. "Well, that
was 'ow it was when Tom got demobbed, and the thing was
what was Tom to do. So I said to Mother we'll go to Scotland and fish—that's what we'll do. And that's what we
did."

"I hope it's being a success."

"Not at first it wasn't—and I don't mind telling you I
was beginning to think we'd made a mistake coming 'ere.
I began to think Mother was right and we ought to have
gone somewhere a bit more lively. We fished and fished; but
most of the time Tom didn't seem to be there at all—it was
almost frightening, really—but today when 'e got into that
fish Tom was different: all excitement, and rushing up and
down the bank, and thinking 'e'd lost it, and finding 'e

'adn't! I tell you it was 'a crowded hour'," says Mr. Stannard nodding. "'A crowded hour of glorious life' and I do believe 'e forgot about Dick just while it lasted. Yes, I do believe 'e wasn't thinking about Dick at all. I was staggering about in the pool with the gaff and suddenly I heard Tom laughing—laughing at me, 'e was," declares Mr. Stannard delightedly. "Laughing quite hearty. Mother couldn't believe it when I told 'er; but it was true."

"He'll come right in time, Mr. Stannard."

"That's what I say to mother. Give him time, I say. Don't fuss him. Don't notice anything."

"I'm sure you're right."

"Yes," says Mr. Stannard, nodding. "Yes, that's right. That's the way to do—and perhaps someday there'll be a girl —a nice, pretty little girl—that would be best of all. I *did* 'ope there might be one or two *here,* to tell the truth, Mrs. Christie."

He's absolutely right of course and I tell him so (whilst hurriedly reviewing the damsels at present residing at Tocher, and deciding regretfully that there is none sufficiently alluring to take Captain Stannard's mind off his troubles).

"Oh well, it can't be helped," says Mr. Stannard with a sigh. "She'll come along one of these days when we're least expecting 'er—that's what I say to Mother—and meantime if 'e can catch a few more fish—"

"Oh, I *do* hope he will!" I exclaim.

People are now beginning to drift down the stairs and assemble for dinner so our conversation is at an end. Mr. Stannard and the fish are suddenly the centre of an admiring circle. Mrs. Potting is enquiring with interest as to the habits of "Scotch salmon"; Mrs. Ovens is exclaiming rapturously over its size and color.

"My son caught it," Mr. Stannard is saying. "Gave him a good bit of sport before I got the gaff into it . . . yes, my son caught it this afternoon . . . yes, 'is first salmon, gave 'im a good bit of sport . . ."

"What a fuss to make!" says Erica as we sit down at the table together and unfold our napkins. "Silly, common little man! You'd think nobody had ever killed a salmon before!"

"No, Erica!" I cry, almost in tears. "No, you mustn't—honestly—he isn't common or—or silly—he's—he's—"

"Great Scott, what on earth has happened to *you!*" exclaims Erica, looking at me in blank amazement.

Having been told (or perhaps commanded is the mot juste) to take the afternoon off and to stay out till dinner time, I decide to climb Puss-hill and see what the hares are up to. There is a small car standing in the drive, just outside the front door, and a tall man in a very new brown tweed suit with his head under the bonnet. He is not one of our guests, I can tell that at once even though his back view is all that is visible, but he must be the guest of a guest and as such demands my sympathy and perhaps my cooperation.

"Can I help you?" I enquire advancing towards him.

He looks up and exclaims, "Mrs. Tim! What on earth are you doing here!"

I look at him, and it is a moment or two before I can "place" the man. I know his face, of course, but where have I seen him?

"Elden," he says, holding out his hand.

"Of course—Major Elden—you look different—I mean not being in uniform."

He smiles and says he feels different too, feels just a little lost, to be perfectly frank about it, "And I'm just plain Mr. Elden, now. I decided to drop the major when I doffed his crowns—not being a regular, you see."

"I see."

"And you approve?"

"I'm not going to answer that one."

Mr. Elden smiles and says, "Of course you approve. You know perfectly well it's the sensible thing—but never mind that, tell me what you're doing. Are you staying in the hotel?"

I tell him I am helping to run the hotel and ask him jokingly if he wants a room.

"Well—no," he says. "I'm—well—I'm staying in Ryddelton for a bit and I just came over to see a friend. The fact is—I say are you frightfully busy, Mrs. Tim?"

He looks so forlorn that I am obliged to take pity on him and invite him to come for a walk and after some discussion we set forth together, taking the path through the wood. We have not gone very far before I begin to regret my impulsive invitation, for my companion seems depressed and withdrawn; there is a sort of barrier between us and we can neither speak to each other naturally nor remain silent in comfort. Before, when we were immured together in the railway carriage and we did not know each other at all, we had plenty to say and it was easy to talk, easy to get to grips and to discuss things that mattered; now a queer awkwardness has arisen and we are both embarrassed. I have a feeling he wants to tell me about his private affairs but does not know how to begin, and although I am quite ready to listen to him it is difficult for me to open the subject.

At last he says, "You were wrong, weren't you? I mean we have met again."

"I've forgotten everything," I assure him.

"But I don't think I want you to have forgotten!"

"Then I remember everything, of course. What about Margaret?"

He smiles, but rather sadly. "It's no good," he says. "I've been given my marching orders—I feel rather shattered, really. I still can't understand. I still feel—it's quite unreasonable of me, I suppose—I still feel that Margaret is fond of me."

We have reached the gate and he goes forward to open it. The gates are all in a very bad condition, they lean drunkenly against their posts and are secured by pieces of rusty wire which require a good deal of manipulation. I can see his hands are shaking as he twists the wire.

"I *am* sorry!" I exclaim. "Are you quite sure she has made up her mind? Have you seen her? What did she say?"

These questions break the ice. He explains that he has seen her today and she was adamant. It is all over. He is not to see her again, not even to write.

"You saw her today?" I enquire.

"I came here on purpose to see her. I had written several times and she never answered, so I felt it was the only thing to do. I *had* to see her."

"You mean she's actually *here*?"

"That's why I came," he repeats. "She's staying here at Tocher House, so I came over this afternoon and—"

"Miss McQueen!" I exclaim in amazement.

"Yes," he says. "Margaret McQueen. You've spoken to her, perhaps?"

We have now fastened the gate securely so we walk on, taking a path to the left which skirts the edge of the wood (somehow or other I don't feel strong enough to tackle the steep slope of Puss-hill) and we walk along in silence because I don't know what to say, and because I am busy fitting the pieces together and forming the picture. The pieces fit so well that I am amazed I did not realize the two stories were really one—amazed and annoyed with myself. I could have thought over the problem quietly and decided what to

say instead of being taken by surprise and rendered speechless. I must be careful, that is obvious. I have no right to be-
tray a confidence, no right to meddle in this affair . . . but,
on the other hand, dare I stand aside and let these two nice
people drift apart for want of a friendly word?

"I suppose I shouldn't have come," continues Mr. Elden
after a long silence. "I suppose I should have waited, or at
least warned her I was coming. I thought I had only to see
her and everything would be all right—but it wasn't."

"What happened?"

"We met in the lounge. It was a mistake, of course, I
see that now. How could I speak to her properly with a
whole lot of frightful people sitting round pretending to
read newspapers, but really trying to listen to every word we
said? It was impossible from the very beginning, the atmosphere was all wrong. I couldn't say—all the things I wanted
to say. I asked her to come out with me but she wouldn't.
It was no use, she said. She kept on saying it was no use.
She kept on asking me to go away and not think about her
anymore."

"She's very tired, you know."

"I know," he says wretchedly. "She looks ill—"

"She may feel different when she's had a rest."

"She says she won't. She says she's made up her mind.
It's absolutely definite—quite hopeless."

There seems little to say to that, so I change the subject
and ask about his future plans, and he replies that he is staying in a hotel in Ryddelton and had intended to stay on and
do some fishing, but perhaps he should just pack up and go.
But where shall he go, that's the question—it isn't easy to
find rooms nowadays.

It seems dreadfully sad that he has been abroad all these

years and, now that he has come home, there is nobody to welcome him, no relative to whom his homecoming is a joy, no house to throw open its doors and invite him to come in.

"Don't look so sad, Mrs. Tim," says Mr. Elden, smiling rather forlornly. "I'll get over it, all right. I can take it."

"I am sad. It's so lonely for you."

"I've got Sheila," he replies. "She'll be coming for her holidays soon—that's another reason why I must find rooms somewhere."

"Stay on in Ryddelton," I tell him. "Yes, I think you should. You needn't meet Margaret. I'll keep an eye on her for you."

"But that would be splendid!" he exclaims. "That would be grand! If you could just keep an eye on her and see she's all right. The thing I dread more than anything is losing sight of her—losing her altogether. If she were to leave here and go away . . ."

I assure him that *that* shall not happen. If she leaves Tocher I shall keep in touch with her, but there is no talk of her going away at present.

Mr. Elden is inordinately grateful for this small favor —could anyone do less—and says I am a real friend and he will never forget my kindness as long as he lives—and more to that effect. It is all quite ridiculous, of course, because I have done nothing for the man. I tell him not to be silly. I tell him, also, to think about Margaret as little as possible, to fish the Rydd and enjoy himself, to make friends with other people in Ryddelton and have a good time.

Mr. Elden smiles quite cheerfully and says it's excellent advice and he will take it.

Our path has led us to the brink of a little burn which falls in a cascade of sparkling water over a shelf of rock.

There are pussy willows here with soft pale-grey catkins, and another kind of willow which has pale-green fluffy catkins covered with yellow pollen, all glinting with diamond drops from the spray of the waterfall. I ask my companion if he has a knife and immediately he produces one and climbs up the rock to cut branches for me. The highest branches are much the prettiest, of course, and Mr. Elden performs alarming feats of daring to procure them and becomes even more cheerful in the process. (Reflect, as I watch him in some anxiety, that men are very like little boys and are easily amused and comforted.)

We scramble down by the side of the burn and presently find ourselves amongst trees; there are oaks and chestnuts and beeches, all very gnarled and distorted by great age. The oaks especially are veterans of the forest with twisted trunks and stunted branches, some of them are hollow, others have lost most of their limbs, others again have fallen and lie rotting on the ground. Mr. Elden says the wood should be cleared, it is in a disgraceful condition, but he supposes it is a question of labor. I agree with him in principle of course, but the wood is very beautiful . . . It is sheltered here and these ancient trees are beginning to put forth tiny green buds, pale as jade and delicate as lace. Spring is always a miracle, but here it is more miraculous than usual; these old, old trees are still full of life, the sap has stirred within them, the sun has warmed and quickened them. Even the fallen trees are not all dead, some of them are budding.

We walk on, looking about us, and suddenly I catch sight of a grey wall with ferns growing in the crevices.

"Ruins!" I exclaim, pointing to it.

"Ruins, undoubtedly," agrees Mr. Elden. "Some sort of castle, perhaps. Shall we explore?"

This needs no answer. Breathes there a man with soul so dead that he can refrain from exploring a ruined castle? We push through brambles and nettles and discover a high archway of stone and, stepping over the tumbled masonry with which it is partially blocked, find ourselves in a large oblong courtyard. There is no roof and on two sides the enormously thick walls have disintegrated into piles of rubble masked with trailing ivy, but the third and fourth walls are still standing and tower above us, windowless except for narrow, slanting slits. At one time this great hall—or courtyard—has been paved with flags but these have been cracked with frost or raised from their bed by the roots of trees; grass grows in the crevices and wild willow herb (not yet in flower of course) and there are primroses in the sheltered corners. At one end of the ruin there is the remains of a tower, a thick square building with a narrow doorway through which can be seen a flight of stone steps.

"Interesting," says Mr. Elden looking about him. "Some border chief's stronghold, I suppose. Enormously thick walls, aren't they? Shall we climb the tower or clamber over the ruined wall and have a look at the view?"

We decide to look at the view, and as there is a convenient gap in the wall we make for that and leaning upon the trunk of a fallen tree we gaze out over the sunlit landscape. We can now see that the castle is situated upon a high crag which juts out from the woods and has a magnificent prospect over the river, far below, and over fields and woodlands and meadows which slope upwards to the moors. Just below us, and part of the castle itself, there is a sheltered terrace carpeted with soft turf, where—Mr. Elden suggests—the chief and his lady wife used to take the air when their day's activities were over. I agree that it must have been a delightful little promenade, it is a charming spot even now, but I can see no way of getting to it.

"This place must have been practically impregnable," says Mr. Elden thoughtfully. "Of course you could knock it to bits in half an hour with a gun or two placed on those hills, but these terrific walls would have stood a good deal of battering with cannon balls. As a matter of fact," says Mr. Elden, looking round with interest, "as a matter of fact this place would be a pretty tricky target with that false crest. Not much good for twenty-five pounders but just the sort of job for the old five-five with delay fuse. If you wanted to tackle it with direct fire . . . yes, see that ragged sort of wood over there, Mrs. Tim?"

"Where, exactly?"

"One o'clock from the white farm," says Mr. Elden. "Got it? A ragged sort of wood. Lovely for a single gun position. I'd bring it up overnight of course and then, first thing in the morning, let 'em have it over open sights. About two thousand, it looks to me, but that dead ground is a bit misleading. If you couldn't get a position there," continues Mr. Elden. "Let me see now . . . yes, it would be better to take it on as a pinpoint target; get your O.P. somewhere on that ridge and the guns about three thousand in the rear— then fifty or so rounds from a single gun at three-five hundred would do the trick nicely. There wouldn't be much left of the castle, I can assure you."

This reaction to the "ivied tower" is very much the same as Tim's would be—allowing for the fact that Mr. Elden is a gunner and Tim an infantry officer—but Mr. Elden is not a professional soldier, so he has not Tim's excuse. I point out to him that he is now a civilian and should react in a civilian manner, and admire the beauties of the mossy walls instead of battering them to pieces. He should fall into raptures over the view—so I tell him—the budding trees, the rushing stream and the moory hills, instead of using the landscape as a firing plan and the farms as his dial for locating gun emplacements.

Mr. Elden is slightly damped and says you can't learn a new way of thought all in a minute.

After a bit we leave our outlook post and wander round. We avoid the stair, which looks rather dangerous, but we find a low archway in the wall leading to a narrow passage, dark and dank, with moss growing on the walls.

"A dungeon!" exclaims Mr. Elden bending his head and disappearing from view.

I follow him carefully and with reluctance, for to tell the truth dungeons do not attract me and I have a feeling that this one may be full of skeletons—or rats; but it is not a dungeon at all, it is the chief's private passage to his terrace and in a few moments we are standing on the terrace in the blazing sunshine, all the more golden after the dank darkness of the tunnel through which we have come.

"Lovely!" I cry, flinging myself down on the grassy turf. "Absolutely heavenly! Warm and sunny and green . . . and so secluded! The chief was a lucky man, wasn't he?"

Mr. Elden sits down beside me and lights a cigarette.

"Can't you imagine the chief?" I continue. "Tall and burly with a golden beard—or was it red? He hunted all day, or led raiding expeditions and returned with hundreds of head of cattle, stolen from his English neighbours. He was fierce and bold, the terror of his enemies, but loyal to his friends. His wife adored him—she was tremendously proud of him, you know."

Mr. Elden smiles and says it sounds a man's life. He

wouldn't mind changing places with the chief—except for the red beard. Beards are too horrible for words.

We are silent after that, silent in a pleasant friendly way, enjoying the sunshine and admiring the view. Presently we discover that it is getting late so we return through the dark tunnel and take the road home.

Feel very chirpy this morning, and trip down to breakfast to find Erica eating porridge in a businesslike manner.
As is usual at breakfast our table is screened from public
view and I am now aware that the reason for this curious
dispensation is that Erica cannot endure the sight of her
guests so early in the day. She finds it difficult to endure the
sight of them at any time of day, but at breakfast the sight
of them is utterly unbearable.

I take my seat and unfold my table napkin and intimate
that I intend to have a go at the store cupboard this afternoon unless my employer has any objection. Cook and I will
do it together and make a list of everything.

"You and your lists!" says Erica dourly. "The store cupboard is well enough as it is, and anyway you can't do it
today because it's the work-party."

"Work-party!" I exclaim with rising inflection.

"We have it once a month," says Erica. "We've had it
all through the war and they still want the garments so we'll
go on having it."

"Here?" I enquire.

"In the drawing room," replies Erica. "A woman called
Miss Frost comes in a car and brings the stuff. Some of the
neighbors come, and nearly everybody staying here comes
too—all the women, I mean."

I make further enquiries and manage to elicit a little

more information on the subject. Nobody seems to be much
good at sewing, Erica declares, but I shall be able to help
Miss Frost and show people how to put the things together.
She adds that she never could set a stitch and doesn't intend
to start now, but she reads to them—it keeps them quiet.

The prospect of the work-party ruins my whole morning. I envisage myself setting seams, trying to fit pyjamas together and wrestling madly with shirt collars and cuffs.

After lunch Erica and I go up to the drawing room to
rearrange the furniture; we push the chairs about and carry
in a solid table for the sewing machine. Erica says suddenly
that she hopes I'm liking it here.

Reply—quite truthfully—that I'm liking it very much.

"You didn't like it at first," says Erica bluntly.

"You didn't like *me* at first," I retort—for I have discovered that the way to "take" Erica is to stand up to her boldly
and give as good as you get.

"I though you were wet," says Erica frankly. "Let's put
these two chairs together near the window."

"Wet!" I exclaim. "You trampled on me!"

"You lay down," she returns. "I always trample on
people if they lie down at my feet; what else can one do?"

"Help them up," I suggest.

Erica pretends not to hear. She says, "We'd better put a
table over here—a small one. The fact is I got a bit of a
shock when I saw you standing on the platform. Grace had
told me about you of course, but I didn't realise you would
be so young, or so good-looking. I don't mean Grace told
me you were old and ugly," continues Erica, as she sets her
shoulder to an enormous settee and moves it into place as if
she were an elephant, trained in lumber work. "She didn't
of course. It was just the impression I got."

"Quite."

"And I knew you had a son of sixteen—or is it seventeen? No woman has the right to look young and pretty with a son of that age."

"Rather sweeping," I reply, with a chuckle. (Grace told me that Erica was old and fat and ugly but I don't intend to reveal this, of course.)

"Not sweeping at all," replies Erica. "And talking of sweeping I wonder how long it is since Hope swept under this sofa."

"Six months," I suggest, glancing at the accumulation of dust and fluff.

"I'm in despair about Hope," declares Erica in such tragic accents that I can't help laughing.

"You may laugh," she says. "Spread the dust sheet, Hester. It's death on the Hoover, all those cursed pins."

"Why do you keep Hope?" I enquire, as I move a chair and smooth out the sheet.

"Keep Hope!" exclaims Erica. "My good woman, I've sacked Hope half a dozen times. She won't go—nothing will make her go. What can I do when she crawls about on the floor and licks my shoes?"

"I don't know, I'm sure."

"This place would be a thousand times easier to run without Hope," continues Erica. "She quarrels with everyone, she mopes and moans and complains about her food to Cook . . . I get quite desperate sometimes."

"But couldn't you—"

"The fact is Hope is fond of me," says Erica in lugubrious accents. "Oh yes, I daresay it seems funny to you—evidently it does."

"It isn't that," I gasp. "I mean it's quite natural Hope should be fond of you—but you don't seem pleased."

"Natural! It isn't natural. I can't stand it. She's got a— a *crush* for me," declares Erica, standing four square in the middle of the room with her hands upon her hips. "A schwärmerei or whatever you call it—quite horrible in a woman of Hope's age for a hag like me."

"So that's why she hates me!"

"Hates you, does she?"

"It's rather alarming, really," I add, taking up a cushion and arranging it on the sofa.

"That'll do," declares Erica. "Don't fidge fadge with those damn cushions. What do you mean when you say alarming?"

"Nothing much. It always alarms me when people hate me."

"You ought to cultivate toughness," says Erica firmly.

At this moment, while I am still swithering whether or not to reveal Hope's delinquencies in the matter of tepid hot-water bottles and such like trifles, we are interrupted by Mrs. Ovens opening the door and looking in.

"Oh, *there* you are, Miss Clutterbuck!" she exclaims.

"As large as life and twice as natural," agrees Erica in ponderous jest.

Mrs. Ovens giggles and says she just wanted to ask if she could have her room for another week.

Erica frowns and says this isn't the office.

Mrs. Ovens says, Oh she *knows* that, but nobody was *in* the office, and she just thought dear Miss Clutterbuck wouldn't mind her *asking,* and she wanted to see Mrs. Christie, too, and ask for another bath towel. "Two birds with one stone," says Mrs. Ovens brightly.

"Hrrmph!" exclaims Erica, emitting smoke.

"I do so *adore* Tocker," continues Mrs. Ovens in persuasive accents. "It's so Scotch, isn't it? So quaint. I just feel I can't go away till I have captured the Scotch atmosphere and crystalized it."

"Are you coming to the work-party?" enquires Erica abruptly.

"Oh—" says Mrs. Ovens doubtfully. "Oh, is it today? Oh yes—*definitely,*" says Mrs. Ovens who has suddenly made up her mind to propitiate Miss Clutterbuck with a living sacrifice and so retain her room. "Yes, of *course* I must come, though of course, as you know, I'm not *very* good at sewing. What are you going to read this month, Miss Clutterbuck?"

Miss Clutterbuck says she doesn't know.

"A scene from Jane Austen," suggests Mrs. Ovens. "Dear Jane, how I *adore* her! And it *will* be all right about my room, Miss Clutterbuck?" she adds in honeyed accents.

Miss Clutterbuck says she supposes so and with that Mrs. Ovens departs, leaving the little matter of another bath towel undecided.

"Well, you're very quiet all of a sudden!" exclaims Erica. "What are you thinking about, hrrmph!"

"About that lady."

"Nasty piece of work!"

"Erica," I say in a lower voice. "There's something odd going on between her and Mr. Wick. Perhaps I should have told you before, but—"

" 'Something odd!' " exclaims Erica fiercely. "What a way to talk! I hate mimsey-mouthed people—why can't you call a spade a spade!"

I am so roused by the accusation of euphemism that I tell Erica in Elizabethan language exactly what I suspect.

Erica immediately retorts that she didn't tell me to call it a blue-pencil shovel. She adds that if she had known before she wouldn't have allowed Mrs. Ovens to stay on.

I then enquire sweetly whether her guests' morals are Erica's affair. Erica replies by telling me the sort of place she is *not* running. The conversation waxes more and more Elizabethan in tone and is unfit to record further.

Miss Frost arrives by car with a large hamper which is carried upstairs by Todd and the chauffeur and is evidently very heavy. When opened it is found to contain rolls of felt-like flannelette and an assortment of garments in various stages of completion. Erica is reasonably polite to Miss Frost (perhaps because the lady is not staying in the house nor paying for her food) and introduces her to me, saying that Miss Frost has been doing this valuable work for years, going all round the county and holding work-parties for the Red Cross.

"First for the Red Cross and now for U.N.R.R.A.," says Miss Frost brightly (she calls it oonra, mouthing it as if it were a foreign word). "The great thing is to send the garments where they are needed most, Mrs. Christie. Nothing else matters at all. Miss Clutterbuck's parties are always *most* successful so I hope we are going to have a full house *today*."

Erica says she has told everybody to come; she doesn't think they'll dare not to. I feel sure she is right for her guests stand in such awe of her that they accede to her requests meekly. They are frightened of her—and no wonder; they don't know how to take her; they are never sure whether her rudeness is meant to be amusing or not. One would think that her curt manner and the malevolence she exhibits towards her guests would drive them away and the place would be empty, but it doesn't work like that. Lately I have begun to think that Miss Clutterbuck is actually a draw. People who have stayed at Tocher talk about her to their friends: "Quite a character," they say. "Orders you about like a sergeant major—she won't give you a room unless she likes the look of you—a most eccentric creature." Whether because Miss Clutterbuck is a draw, or whether because Tocher is well-run and in apple-pie order the fact remains we could fill the house three times over with the greatest of ease. Most houses are shabby nowadays, but not Tocher. Somehow or other Erica has managed to keep it perfect. She loves her house and grudges neither time nor trouble where Tocher is concerned, and the money which pours in from her unwelcome guests, is immediately poured out again in improvements and repairs. The money earned by the house is spent upon it lavishly. In this way Erica strives to propitiate the shades of her ancestors.

Miss Frost looks round and asks for a cutting-out table, as large and solid as possible, and this is just being carried in when the ladies begin to assemble. Some are strangers, middle-aged or elderly, in well-cut tweeds, carrying chintz bags full of sewing materials. These are neighbors from the surrounding country houses; they greet Erica by her christian name and chat about mutual friends. The hotel guests arrive either singly or in couples and choose their seats with care; some show preference for a window seat, explaining that there is a better light; others shun the windows as plague-stricken areas, murmuring the word "draught." Amongst the latter is Mrs. Maloney who seems to spend most of her waking hours avoiding currents of air which she imagines have a baneful effect upon her rheumatism, her neuralgia and her catarrh.

There is a perceptible coolness between the two groups

—Erica's neighbors and Erica's guests; they don't mix at all.
The neighbors obviously disapprove of the guests, disapprove
of their abodement at Tocher House (I hear one murmur to
another as they take their seats, "What a menagerie! How
can Erica . . ."); while the guests, feeling themselves at
home on their own ground, showed marked antagonism to
the interlopers. All this interests me considerably, but I have
no time to study the ladies as I should like, for Miss Frost
has already started to unpack the hamper.

"Mrs. Christie will help you," says Erica, handing me
over on a plate.

"How nice," says Miss Frost. "Perhaps you will give out
the work. Who would like to make a dear little frock?"

Nobody volunteers for the job but Miss Frost seems undismayed. She is an old hand at the game and is aware that
parties such as this must be cajoled with flattery and managed with tact. She hands me a pile of cut-out garments and
requests me to distribute them.

"We always have *such* a good party at Tocher," says
Miss Frost with a beguiling smile.

My task sounds easy, but it is less easy than it sounds,
for the ladies are very modest and unsure of their skill.

"Oh, I couldn't make a nightdress!" says one.

"Could I have something *very* easy?" pleads another.

"Miss Frost gave me a handkerchief to hem last time,"
declares a third.

Mrs. Maloney holds up the leg of a pair of child's knickers and exclaims, "What's this? Is it a sleeve? Where is the
rest of the nightdress?"

Fortunately there are some who seem more knowledge-
able and accept what they are given and get to work without any fuss; amongst these is Margaret McQueen (who

takes a boy's shirt and seats herself in a corner) and a fattish woman with a red face who says she will make a pyjama jacket if someone else will take the trousers. Also amongst these is the lady I met in Ryddelton standing in the fish queue, the lady in the grey tweed suit. She smiles at me in a friendly manner and asks how the dogsbody is getting on.

Miss Frost cuts out. She stands at the table in the middle of the room and wields an enormous pair of scissors in a reckless sort of way—quite alarmingly reckless to my way of thinking; crump, crump, go the scissors, flashing like silver in the rays of the sun—crump, crump, crump—crump—crump, crump . . .

I seem to have been assigned the thankless and most arduous task of overseeing the other members of the party, not by direct orders, but by unanimous impulsion. I would far rather take a piece of work and settle quietly in a corner like Margaret McQueen, I would rather wrestle with the pyjama trousers which have been refused by everyone in the room; but no, it is my task to go from one to another, to pin things together and try to make them fit. At first it is the guests only who bleat helplessly for "Mrs. Christie," who hold up weird-shaped bits of material and ask which piece goes where, but the neighbors soon learn and bleat for me too.

"Oh, Mrs. Christie, would you mind . . . this is a cuff, isn't it?"

"No, it's the yoke. It's a little frock, you see."

"Mrs. Christie—please! Look at these sleeves! Both for the same arm, or doesn't it matter?"

"Mrs. Christie, could you come here a moment? Oh, thank you so much . . . you see I've sewn that to that. It doesn't look right, somehow."

"No," I agree. "No, it *does* look rather queer. As a matter of fact this is really the yoke—not the sleeve. At least I think so, don't you? What a pity to have to unpick it—such neat stitches!"

I catch Erica's eye after this tactful little speech and there is a twinkle in it.

The party is now in full swing, everyone is busy, and Mrs. Maloney lifts up her voice and enquires if Miss Clutterbuck is going to read.

"That *would* be nice," declares Miss Frost, pausing with her scissors in the air.

"Oh, she *is*," declares Mrs. Ovens. "She said she would —didn't you, Miss Clutterbuck? She's going to read a scene from Jane Austen."

"Charming!" cries Mrs. Maloney.

"How delightful!" exclaims Miss Dove.

"I do *adore* Jane!" Mrs. Ovens declares.

Several other ladies admit to a like partiality for Miss Austen and urge Miss Clutterbuck to begin.

"All right," says Erica—quite graciously for her—"If everybody wants me to read I suppose I'll have to. Before I begin I'd better explain that Manders Court is the property of Mr. Rivers. Caroline Rivers is his niece and has kept house for him for some years—ever since his wife died—but now Mr. Rivers is going to marry again, so Caroline will have to leave Manders Court. Fortunately Caroline is an attractive young woman and has several suitors for her hand. The scene I am going to read takes place in the summerhouse where Caroline has an assignation with Mr. Redwell."

There is a murmur of pleasure in the pause that follows; the ladies nod and smile and say to one another that it is a most amusing scene, one of Miss Austen's best . . .

Mrs. Ovens is heard to remark that Caroline Rivers is her favorite amongst Miss Austen's heroines. Miss Dove says she prefers Fanny Bennett, but agrees that Caroline is delightful, too.

Oddly enough I have no recollections of Caroline Rivers, but as I am very busy tacking Mrs. Maloney's knickers together and showing her how to insert the gusset I have no time to think about it seriously.

Erica waits for the murmur of talk to subside; then, without more ado, she opens a large shabby volume and begins to read:

In a few moments Caroline reached the summerhouse and seating herself upon the wooden bench she endeavored to compose her thoughts and to prepare herself for the coming interview. It was not yet half an hour since Mr. Redwell had found her in the stillroom and asked her to meet him here, but during that short period Caroline had made up her mind as to her course of action. She was aware that Mr. Redwell intended to propose (his manner had been urgent and his request for an interview had been couched in language which could leave no doubt as to its significance) and Caroline had decided to accept him. It was true that Mr. Redwell was many years older than herself, that he was dull and stupid, that his mind was exclusively occupied with the improvements which he was making upon his estate and that his appearance left much to be desired, but Caroline was willing to overlook such minor defects in a man of Mr. Redwell's position. It was necessary that she should marry, and marry well, for she was accustomed to the comforts and conveniences of wealth without the means to gratify her taste, and as Mr. Redwell's wife and the mistress of Fountains Place her position would be assured.

Caroline could envisage herself walking in the rose garden, sitting upon the terrace admiring the peacocks, or visiting the stables which were the admiration and envy of every gentleman in the county. She saw herself in the house itself, ordering the staff—she had already decided upon several alterations in the decoration of the drawing rooms. It would be delightful to invite the County to a dinner at which she would play the part of hostess (a part for which she was admirably fitted by nature and upbringing). Seated at the long table, glittering with silver and glass, Caroline could see herself dispensing hospitality and conversation to her assembled guests. These thoughts and visions were so extremely pleasant that Caroline had little difficulty in relegating Mr. Redwell himself to the background. It was a pity he could not be eliminated entirely from the scene, but that was not possible.

At this stage in her daydreams Caroline suddenly awoke to the realization that some time had passed and she was still alone. Four o'clock was the hour named by Mr. Redwell for the assignation, it was now twenty minutes past four and Mr. Redwell had not come. One would have expected him to be here before the time arranged, to be ready and eagerly awaiting her arrival; it was unpardonable that he should be twenty minutes late.

There has been some misunderstanding, thought Caroline and she rose to go, for she was not accustomed to be kept waiting in such an inconsiderate manner; but she had scarcely taken one step when she saw Mr. Redwell, attired for riding, hastening towards her down the path.

"Miss Rivers!" he exclaimed. "Excuse me, I beg. It was impossible for me to be here at the appointed hour. I have received a most disquieting message from Fountains Place which necessitates my immediate departure. My horse is saddled. I must go instantly. There is not a moment to lose."

"Some accident has occurred!" cried Caroline in alarm.

"Not an accident, exactly," replied Mr. Redwell in hurried tones. "Word has been brought that my gardeners, through some foolish misapprehension of my orders, are moving valuable plants—moving them to make room for a rockery! It is essential that they should be stopped immediately. I cannot risk sending a message which might be ignored or misunderstood. I must go myself to prevent any further mistake and to retrieve the damage if humanly possible. My acacias!" cried Mr. Redwell, almost wringing his hands in the violence of his emotion. "My beautiful acacia heterophylla which I caused to be brought from North Africa with so much trouble and expense and which only now is beginning to recover from the journey and to make good progress! How could Anderson so grievously have misunderstood my instructions! It is inconceivable!"

Caroline listened to these explanations with growing amazement. To her it was inconceivable that Mr. Redwell—or indeed any man—should be so upset over an acacia. She was aware that he took an inordinate pride in the rare plants which he had collected from all over the world and which flourished more or less successfully in the sheltered spots in his garden, for she had suffered periods of intense boredom while he recited their names and habits; she had been forced to listen while he lamented the laziness and incompetence of his gardeners or the incidence of green fly upon his roses . . . all this she had managed to endure, achieving patience by the reflection that the gardens at Fountains Place were important not only to their present owner but also to his future wife; she had even managed to persuade herself that it was for the sake of his future wife that Mr. Redwell was planning so many improvements and alterations in his domain . . . but this was too much.

"You understand, I know," continued Mr. Redwell. "I

cannot explain further. I cannot linger here, wasting time . . . and indeed there is no necessity to do so for you are a sensible woman and we understand each other perfectly. The very fact that you have come to meet me at the appointed hour shows that you have no foolish pride—and this is all to the good. Your birth and upbringing have fitted you admirably for your position as my wife and the mistress of Fountains Place. There is no more to be said . . ."

He pressed Caroline's hand and was gone.

Caroline sank back upon the bench, agitated beyond measure at his extraordinary behavior. Everything he had said was wrong, everything he had said and done served to show Mr. Redwell in a most unbecoming light—"I cannot linger here, wasting time." Was it wasting time to propose with due decorum to the lady he desired to make his wife? "The very fact that you have come to meet me . . ." Could she have done less than accede to his request for an interview? "There is no more to be said." In Caroline's opinion there was a great deal more to be said. Mr. Redwell was taking too much for granted.

Mr. Redwell's assumption that Caroline's acceptance of his suit was a foregone conclusion was positively offensive to a woman of delicate taste and the more Caroline thought about it the more indignant she became. His folly disgusted her; the impropriety of his conduct was insulting; his conceit, his selfishness, his indelicacy were too flagrant to be pardoned or overlooked. It was fortunate, thought Caroline with mounting anger, it was fortunate indeed that her discovery of Mr. Redwell's real nature had not been delayed. What misery it would have been to find herself tied to a negligent husband, to one who had no perception of values and no consideration for her feelings.

Caroline had reached this conclusion and was congratulating herself upon her escape when she heard footsteps approaching and, on looking up, she saw that the invader of her privacy was Mr. Berringer. Like Mr. Redwell he was attired for riding, but there all resemblance began and ended, for Mr. Berringer was tall and dark with fine eyes and a dashing air. In any other circumstances Caroline would have welcomed the company of Mr. Berringer for they had much in common, but at the moment she would have preferred no company but her own.

"Redwell has gone," said Mr. Berringer, pausing at the door of the summerhouse and looking down at the fair occupant with an admiring gaze.

"Yes," agreed Caroline. "Yes, he has gone."

"He seemed in a hurry," continued Mr. Berringer. "I heard him call for his horse. Some important matter has called him home to Fountains Place."

"A very important matter," agreed Caroline, trying to compose herself and to behave as if nothing had occurred to distress her.

"It must be important indeed," declared Mr. Berringer. "I can think of nothing of less importance than a fire, than the contingency of Fountains Place being burnt to the ground and reduced to a heap of ashes which could have induced him to leave Miss Rivers sitting alone in the summerhouse." He said this with such a droll inflexion, with such a delightful blend of gallantry and humor that Caroline found herself smiling involuntarily.

"He is gone," continued Mr. Berringer with a gesture of his hand. "His horse is galloping furiously down the drive—it is a fire at least!"

Caroline laughed.

"But, no," declared Mr. Berringer, looking at her carefully. "No, it cannot be a fire, Miss Rivers would find it impossible to laugh if Fountains Place were in jeopardy."

"I have no interest in Fountains Place," returned Caroline, blushing.

Mr. Berringer observed the blush and was silent for a few moments. When next he spoke it was with a much more serious air. "Miss Rivers," he began in diffident tones. "Can I have understood aright? Forgive me for pressing a matter which is liable to cause you embarrassment, but I cannot leave it unexplained. Is it possible that you have refused Redwell? Is that the explanation of his hasty departure?"

"I have neither refused nor accepted his proposal," replied Caroline in a low voice.

"Good Heavens!" exclaimed Mr. Berringer. "Good Heavens, I can scarcely believe it! I was aware—forgive me but I could not help noticing that Redwell was paying you marked attention, and indeed this could cause no surprise in one who, had his circumstances been more affluent, would have been in the field himself."

Caroline was extremely confused. She could not endure the thought of wounding Mr. Berringer's feelings, for, although she had never for one moment envisaged Mr. Berringer as her future husband, she was by no means oblivious of his charms. It is true that these charms were not supported by wealth and position; they consisted of delightful manners, an exceedingly personable appearance and of a humor which matched her own.

"Mr. Berringer," said Caroline at last with earnest resolution. "I will not misunderstand you and, believe me, I am indeed sensible of the honor you do me, but—"

"Miss Rivers!" he exclaimed, interrupting her with an outstretched hand. "Miss Rivers, before you say more I beg you to hear me. I beg you to allow me to speak. I have no right to ask you to consider my suit—except the right of a man who regards you with admiration, with devotion and with a deep appreciation of your goodness of heart. It is this goodness of heart which gives me hope that you will at least listen to me with sympathy."

He paused for a few moments, and then, as Caroline did not forbid him, he continued earnestly, "I would have spoken before had it not been for Redwell. What had I to offer Miss Rivers in comparison with the position she would occupy as the mistress of Fountains Place? What was I? A country squire with a comfortable but unpretentious house, a few small farms and a modest competence. It would have been the height of folly to enter the running, to obtrude myself upon your notice—but now, now that Redwell has gone, and gone without your acceptance of his suit, I should be a coward indeed if I did not put my fate to the test. What have I to offer Miss Rivers? My hand, my heart, a deep and sincere affection and a lively appreciation of her beauty and grace."

Caroline was quite overcome by Mr. Berringer's eloquence and by the manly way he had spoken. His modesty and delicacy of feeling moved her inexpressibly.

"Position is not everything," murmured Caroline.

"Not everything," he agreed in earnest tones. "Position and wealth are much to be desired, but to my mind mutual affection and harmony of mind and intellect are even more important. Can it be possible that you feel as I do on the subject?" He hesitated and then continued, "Oh, Miss Rivers, will you allow me to hope?"

It was impossible for Caroline to reply. She turned her head aside.

"I have offended you!" cried Mr. Berringer in alarm.

"No, no," replied Caroline.

"Tell me," he begged. "Tell me that you will think of what

I have said. Tell me there is hope—that at least you are not altogether indifferent to me."

"I could not be—indifferent—" whispered Caroline, and raising her head she looked at Mr. Berringer with an expression of true sensibility.

"My dearest girl! My sweetest Caroline!" cried Mr. Berringer in accents which betrayed that his feelings were almost too deep for words.

Caroline's agitation was extreme but Mr. Berringer was so considerate towards her, so full of good sense and proper feeling, that in a few minutes she was able to overcome her embarrassment and compose herself sufficiently to give him the assurances he so earnestly desired. A few minutes more and Caroline was able to persuade herself—and him—that he had always been the object of her secret affections and that never in her wildest moments had she intended to become the wife of the egregious Mr. Redwell and the mistress of Fountains Place. Mr. Berringer was only too happy to believe her, too happy to doubt that this indeed was the case, too joyful to be critical. Nor were Caroline's feelings less joyful; hers was the exquisite pleasure of knowing herself beloved of a man whom she could trust and admire, whose intellect was lively and whose delicacy of feeling matched her own, a man who appreciated her not only for her outward graces but for her qualities of mind and heart.

Caroline could have no regrets. Her future home, though lacking fountains and peacocks, would not lack comfort, affection and intellectual companionship; and her future husband, though lacking the wealth and position of Mr. Redwell, was a model of manliness, humor and good sense.

When Erica has finished reading and closed the book

everybody thanks her effusively and a babble of conversation breaks forth, amongst which can be heard individual remarks. Mrs. Ovens is telling the world how much she enjoys the delicate satire of Jane Austen; Mrs. Maloney is agreeing with her; Jane is inimitable, declares Miss Dove. Mrs. Stannard says, "And Miss Clutterbuck reads so well, doesn't she? It's a pleasure to listen."

I look round the room from one to another, everyone is pleased and satisfied. I am pleased too, of course, for the reading has been most enjoyable and Erica's voice is an admirable instrument for its task, but . . .

"So you knew!" says Erica's voice in my ear (she has come up behind me while I was looking at the other members of the party).

"Er—yes," I reply doubtfully. "It was like Miss Austen, but not *quite* Miss Austen—if you know what I mean."

"Nobody better," says Erica drily.

"And Miss Austen would never have allowed her heroine to refuse a good match and be fobbed off with an ordinary country squire."

"I believe you're right," says Erica with a very thoughtful air.

"Why did you do it, Erica?"

"Huntigowk, of course. This is the first of April."

"Yes—but—"

"Austen was too good for the likes of them. Don't you agree?"

"Yes, as a matter of fact—"

"*Dear* Jane, *how* I adore her!" says Erica, copying the honeyed accents of Mrs. Ovens with ludicrous effect. "Makes me sick—hrrmph," says Erica blowing out smoke.

"Erica, what *was* it?" I enquire, for this has been puzzling me all along. "If it wasn't Austen what was it?"

"Clutterbuck, of course," replies Erica with a grim smile.

Tuesday, 2nd April

Annie has settled down splendidly at Tocher and despite her apprehensions she seems to get on with Clara Hope none too badly. It is pleasant to see Annie about the house, to meet her on the stairs or to find her dusting my bedroom or washing the paint. It is delightful to be awakened by Annie in the morning and to have a chat with her about matters which interest us both.

"That Mrs. Ovens!" says Annie as she puts down my morning tea and fetches the cushion from the armchair to prop me up. "She's no better than she should be—and her husband in Germany, too."

"Miss Clutterbuck is worried about her."

"Why worry!" says Annie. "She's bad, that's what. It wouldn't matter whether she was here or somewhere else, it would be just the same."

"Not the same for here," I reply, somewhat muddled, for to tell the truth I find Annie's ideas a trifle difficult to follow at this early hour of the morning.

"Miss Clutterbuck can tell her to go," says Annie. "There's nothing to stop her and she would enjoy the job if I know anything about what she's like."

Annie goes after that and I sip my tea and think about things—chiefly about Erica. Annie thinks she knows what Miss Clutterbuck is like, but does she? Do I, for that matter? I thought I knew what she was like in the first half

154

hour, but how wrong I was! Erica is like an unexplored country and my discoveries about her resemble the discoveries of an explorer who penetrates its fastnesses and is surprised at every step. Who would have thought at the first sight of that uncompromising figure that it contained a heart of gold? Who would have thought that beneath the tough shell and behind the screen of the offhand manner there is a sensitive soul? Yesterday's affair has cast another new light upon Erica Clutterbuck—who would have thought she could write? She says herself—I pressed her for information—that she can't write, not really. She can copy other people to a certain extent, but what use is that except to take in a lot of silly hypocritical sheep and have a joke? Erica calls it a jape. It was an excellent jape, she thinks.

(At first I had an unworthy suspicion that I was being taken in, and that the scene, though not from Austen, was from some other early eighteenth century novelist, but Erica showed me the sheets of manuscript concealed in the shabby book—a dozen sheets written in her own unmistakeable hand; written posthaste in pencil and to me utterly illegible of course. "It's very clever," I told her, gazing at her with something like awe. "Clever!" said Erica scornfully. "There's nothing *clever* about it. Don't be a fool.")

That was last night, of course. This morning I think it all over and fill in some more details in the map of Erica Clutterbuck.

After lunch, when I am passing through the lounge, I am hailed by name and looking round I see a woman sitting by herself on a sofa drinking coffee and smoking. It is not one of the "guests," it is one of Erica's neighbors.

The woman was here yesterday at the work-party and is associated in my mind with a child's flannelette nightdress of a peculiarly vivid pink.

She waves and beckons, "Mrs. Christie!" she says. "I was here yesterday; you remember, don't you? But of course you won't remember my name—if you ever heard it—I'm Ethel Cummin."

"Shall I tell Miss Clutterbuck you're here?"

"Not now," says Mrs. Cummin (she is wearing a wedding ring). "Sit down and talk to me for a minute. Erica won't be specially pleased to see me. She rather hates it if any of her friends come to Tocher but I just felt I had to have a decent meal which hadn't been cooked by me—I get like that sometimes."

I sit down somewhat reluctantly for I have plenty to do and although my duties include talking to Erica's guests they do not include talking—or listening—to her neighbors. Mrs. Cummin seems chatty and I have a feeling that the role of listener will be mine.

"That's nice," says Mrs. Cummins, making room for me on the sofa. "I like a nice quiet chat after lunch, don't you? Now first of all tell me about yesterday."

"About yesterday?"

She nods. "Who was Caroline Rivers? Which of Jane Austen's novels does she come out of?"

"I—I can't—remember . . ."

"No, neither could I, so I went home and hunted for Caroline—and I couldn't find her!"

This doesn't surprise me in the least, so it is very difficult indeed to register amazement, but I do my best. "Couldn't you!" I exclaim.

"I was interested in the creature," explains Mrs. Cummin. "There was something rather attractive about her. I liked the blatant way she washed her hands of Redwell and immediately was ready to switch over to the other man. I wanted to find out more about her; what sort of life she had had before she arrived at the summerhouse, and whether she married her country squire and how it turned out. I have a feeling she may have regretted the peacocks when things went wrong and possibly crammed them down the squire's throat. You can't help me at all?"

"No, I'm afraid not."

Mrs. Cummins sighs. "I have a whole set of Austen novels, she isn't in any of them. Where does she come from, Mrs. Christie?"

"You should ask Miss Clutterbuck," I reply.

"Mphm!, perhaps I might, though, as a matter of fact Erica and I aren't exactly buddies. She must be difficult to work with."

"I find her easy to work with. She always says exactly what she means, so you know where you are. There's no nonsense about her."

"She must be making a pile out of this," says Mrs. Cummin looking round.

I make no comment.

"All the same I don't know how she can do it," continues Mrs. Cummin, thoughtfully. "I don't know how she can bear to throw her house open to Tom, Dick and Harry—it would drive me mad . . . I know what I shall do about Caroline!" exclaims Mrs. Cummin, reverting to her previous subject with a sudden and somewhat alarming leap. "I shall ask Sheila Gray to find out about her from Erica. Yes, that's the thing—I hate mysteries, don't you?"

"You have been warned," I say later to Erica, reporting the conversation. "Sheila Gray will be on your tracks in half no time, and you will have to confess everything."

"Not I," replies Erica, smiling. "I shall say the episode was taken from an unpublished novel—and so it was. The novel has not been written yet, of course, and it is by Erica Mary Clutterbuck—not by Jane Austen—but there is no need at all to go into details of that kind."

"You will have some difficulty in satisfying their curiosity."

"Poof!" says Erica.

"I'm curious, too," I tell her. "I want to know more about Caroline."

"There is nothing more to know," says Erica firmly.

Wednesday, 3rd April

Receive a letter from Betty which announces that she will arrive in Edinburgh on Tuesday and she supposes I will meet her at the station. This necessitates a discussion with my employer and, after some difficulty, I discover her in the cellar amongst the wine bins. Erica says I had better go to Edinburgh on Monday, stay the night and meet Betty on Tuesday. It will be good for me to have a break and if I have begun to think myself indispensable I can get rid of the idea here and now.

"And I may as well warn you," says Erica in her usual downright fashion. "I may as well warn you that I don't like children."

"You don't—"

"No," says Erica firmly. "I can't bear the little darlings. They bore me stiff. You may think this very unnatural— I can see you do—but it isn't as unnatural as you might suppose, nor so uncommon. A great many people don't like children, but few have the courage to say so. It is the same with music. People would rather suffer tortures than admit to being unmusical."

"But Erica, if you don't like children—"

"I needn't see much of Betty," says Erica in reasonable tones. "She will be out all day, I suppose. Don't worry about it."

"I do worry."

"You needn't. I shan't bite Betty."

"She had better have her meals in the other room with Mrs. Everard's children."

"Oh well," says Erica. "If that wouldn't upset you."

I leave her counting her wine, and go upstairs full of apprehension. Betty is large and full of high spirits, she is friendly and impulsive. When Betty is in the house the house seems full of Betty. Of course Tocher is a big place so one hopes she will not make her presence felt to the same extent, but still . . .

There is so much going on in Tocher House, so much coming and going, and such a lot of work to do that I find it very difficult to keep up my diary and to decide what to put into it and what to leave out. The most important part of my duties—so Erica insists—is to talk to people and especially people who are staying in the house by themselves and are slow in making friends with their fellow guests. Some of them show no desire for my company and these I abandon most thankfully and leave them in peace, but others are pleased to be talked to and co-operate agreeably. I hear a good many strange stories from my new friends—some tragic beyond belief and others extremely funny—for the fact is that these people seem to regard me as a safe repository for secrets. I am quite outside their lives so they can talk to me without reserve.

They come to Tocher for a week or ten days—and then they disappear, never to be seen again, and a new lot of people arrive to fill their beds and to sit in their seats, a new lot of people with an entirely new lot of problems. But some of the guests remain and—like the poor—are always with us, and amongst these are Mrs. Maloney and Margaret McQueen.

Mrs. Maloney is a very lonely person, for the poor woman is such a bore that she is shunned by her fellow man (and woman) as if she were the plague. Sometimes I wonder whether she notices that people avoid her, and, if so, whether she knows why. Could she—if she tried very hard—amend her ways, cease to be a bore and become a popular member of society? Because she is lonely I am sorry for her and because I am sorry for her I allow her to talk to me a good deal and listen with what patience I can muster to her interminable reminiscences.

Margaret McQueen is quite different, of course. Having promised Mr. Elden to keep an eye on her it behoves me to establish good relations between us. At first it is difficult, but when she discovers that I have no intention of referring to her troubles she becomes quite friendly. We talk about books and compare ideas about various subjects and find that we have a good deal in common. It is to Margaret I fly with my anxieties about Betty and my apprehensions as to how she and Erica will hit it off. Margaret is very comforting. She says Miss Clutterbuck's bark is worse than her bite and, if I like, she herself will help to amuse Betty and keep her out of the way. She is fond of children—especially little girls; they don't bother her at all.

"I shouldn't like to take complete charge of a child," says Margaret, referring obliquely to our first conversation. "But I should enjoy going for walks with Betty. Children don't interfere with one's private thoughts."

The linen room is now my pride and joy with everything in its place neatly labeled and listed. It takes me a quarter of the time to count out the weekly change of linen for the guests of Tocher House—but it still takes time. I am in the middle of the pleasant task when Erica appears at the door and says there is a man in the office asking for me.

"Tell him to go away—seven, eight, nine," I reply abstractedly.

"I did," says Erica. "I said you were busy, but he wouldn't go."

I enquire what sort of man, to which Erica replies that he is tall, good-looking and impertinent. I take down two pairs of hemstitched sheets for number four and remark that I know nobody answering to the description.

Erica says, "You had better go down. He's very importunate."

"Does he want money?"

"He doesn't look it. He's wearing a very nice tweed suit and driving a Bentley—no, I don't think he's a beggar."

"Who can it be!"

"If you'd go downstairs you'd see. I've no patience with people who turn an envelope over and over and examine the postmark and try to guess who wrote it. If they'd open it they'd spare themselves the trouble."

"Not if it's from you."

"Less of your cheek," says Erica. "And anyway the man is not from me. He wouldn't disclose his name and he hasn't a postmark on him."

"Postmark Bombay," says a well-known voice from the landing—it is Tony Morley! Tony Morley, clad in a Lovat tweed suit, looking bronzed and weatherbeaten but otherwise unchanged!

"Tony!" I shriek, and dropping a whole pile of pillow cases I fling myself into his arms.

"Heavens!" exclaims Erica. "Why didn't you tell me you were the woman's husband?"

"Because I'm not—worse luck," replies Tony, hugging me tightly.

"Not?" enquires Erica doubtfully.

"No," says Tony. "This, my dear Miss Clutterbuck, is merely the welcome received by a hero returned from the wars."

"Returned from the dead!" I cry, clinging to him—how large and solid and comfortable he feels!

"Well—in a manner of speaking," he agrees.

"And you're alive!" I cry. "You're alive and whole!"

"Complete in every detail—arms and legs all present and correct."

"O Tony, I can hardly believe it . . . When Tim and I said good-bye to you in that frightful churchyard, with all the tombstones and the wind whistling round, I was sure I should never see you again."

"I shared your fears."

"You remember it, Tony?"

"Perfectly," says Tony gravely. "No detail of that afternoon has escaped my memory. You were wearing a fur coat and a small brown hat with a white wing in it—"

"It was awful!"

"Not at all. I thought it a very fetching hat."

"I mean everything was awful—there was a horrible sort of uncertainty about everything."

"We stood alone, but undismayed—"

"You said you would come back when you had drowned Hitler in the Red Sea."

"You said, take care of yourself."

"Idiotic, wasn't it?"

"Well—slightly," agrees Tony. "But the underlying idea was good, and anyhow here I am."

I hug him again. "O Tony! You saluted and marched away. It was almost more than I could bear."

"You had been pretty severely tried that afternoon," he reminds me.

Erica has been listening to this somewhat crazy conversation in a trance of astonishment. She now awakes from it and turns to go.

"Erica!" I cry. "This is Tony Morley. He's a Brigadier now—I've known him for centuries."

Erica says she gathered I knew Tony pretty well and, that being so, I had better take the afternoon off and talk to him. We enquire as to Tony's plans and learn that they are fluid; if Miss Clutterbuck has a room vacant he will stay for a day or two before going on to Edinburgh. Erica immediately says number eighteen and she will tell Todd to take up the luggage. She then goes away.

"You're exactly the same," declares Tony looking at me with interest. "Everyone else is six years older—how do you do it, Hester?"

"Not really," I reply. "I'm different inside. Nobody could live through—all that—and remain the same. I've lost my sparkle, Tony. I've gone flat, like stale champagne."

"No," says Tony seriously. "Perhaps you are a little different, but you aren't flat. I rather think you have matured into hock, but I'm not sure, yet."

"How did you know I was here? Or didn't you?"

"I knew," says Tony. He removes a pile of linen from the blanket box and sits down comfortably. It is a good place to talk, quiet and warm and private. It is my very own place and we can talk here without interruptions. "I knew," says Tony. "Because I touched down at Cairo on my way home. Brigadiers fly when they're in a hurry, it's one of the few advantages of being a Brigadier."

"You saw Tim!"

He nods. "Tim is in the pink. His quarters are comfortable, his food is nourishing and the riots aren't getting him down. Does that satisfy you?"

"What did he say?"

"Quite a lot," says Tony thoughtfully. "You wouldn't expect me to repeat our conversation word for word. As a matter of fact some of it is unfit for your ears, my dear."

"Is he missing me?"

"Not a bit," declares Tony gravely. "The Egyptian women are very attractive indeed—some of them. They have rather a curious smell, of course, but one gets used to that in time."

"Will you be sensible, Tony!"

"Why should I, Hester?"

We look at each other and smile.

"Oh well," he says. "If you want me to be sensible . . .

Tim sent you his love and a parcel which I will deliver in due course."

"Do you know what's in the parcel?"

"I do. It was necessary that I should know what the parcel contained in case of difficulties with the customs. Silk pyjamas and cami-knicks," says Tony unblushingly. "Six packets of hairpins, a length of silk and a couple of roll-ons—not bad for old Tim, in my opinion."

"Marvelous of Tim!" I agree, smiling.

"I am also the bearer of a love-gift from Bollings," continues Tony. "It is for Annie, of course. I gathered that Tim and Bollings went shopping together for mutual support, and I must confess I should like to have been there to see the fun."

"Me, too!" I exclaim, laughing.

We continue to talk, and while we do so I resume my task of counting out the linen, but I am somewhat hampered by the feeling that Tony is regarding my activities with a disapproving eye.

"I don't like it at all!" exclaims Tony suddenly.

"I like it quite a lot, Tony."

"Nonsense," he says. "There's no need for it. Tim said I was to make you chuck it."

"Why?"

"It's most unsuitable," says Tony, looking down his nose.

"You're old-fashioned, that's what's the matter with you. You're the sort of man who likes a woman to sit with her lily-white hands folded in her lap—or embroidering a tapestry—while her lord and master rides out to do battle in her honor."

Tony says he didn't know he was that sort of man.

"Well, you are!" I cry in annoyance. "You would have liked to find me at Winfield, dropping tears over my needle-work—you *know* you would!"

Tony says not tears.

"Tears," I repeat angrily. "Tears and idleness and lily-white hands. What sort of life is that for an active woman?"

Tony says it sounds a trifle dull, but—

"Of course it's dull—dull as dishwater! Isn't it a hundred times better to do something useful? How would you like to have nothing to do, day after day, except cook and dust the drawing room?"

Tony says not much.

"Well, then!"

"Well, then," says Tony. "But you could do something else, couldn't you?"

"Something ladylike, I suppose."

"The way she gave you the afternoon off!" says Tony indignantly.

"It was decent of her—it means she'll have to do my work as well as her own."

"Let her," says Tony. "Her back is broad enough. Anne of Cleves was a sylph in comparison."

"How do you know?"

"Never mind. Don't stray from the point, Hester. You will just pack your things and come with me on Monday."

The incidence of Tony's anger has turned mine to mirth. "Is this a dishonorable proposal?" I enquire chortling.

"It is not," says Tony. "If a dishonorable proposal—as you call it—would have interested you at all I should have made one years ago. My intention is to take you straight to Charters Towers. My mother will look after you."

This fairly takes my breath away for Lady Morley is a terror and I would sooner starve in a garret than bear her company—but of course I can't explain this to Lady Morley's son, and Lady Morley's son is obviously enchanted with his plan; he enlarges upon the delights awaiting me at his ancestral home and adds that he has Tim's wholehearted approval. They talked it over, says Tony, and agreed that nothing could be better. It will be so nice for Lady Morley to have me and so nice for me to lead a quiet peaceful existence in pleasant surroundings. I shall have nothing to do, of course, says Tony (who evidently thinks this is a draw), and I shall have butter from the home farm and a glass of milk every day.

When he has quite finished and I have regained my breath I smile sweetly and say an elopement would be much more fun.

"You little devil!" exclaims Tony. "It would serve you damn well right if I took you at your word."

The afternoon is fine and warm, for Britain is enjoying the delights of an anti-cyclone. Tony and I wander out into the garden after lunch and feed the pigeons with some crumbs collected from the dining room. I do this quite often and the pigeons have begun to know me quite well; they fly down from the trees with a whirr of their lovely wings which shine with rainbow colors in the sunshine. When we have used up all the crumbs we find a sequestered seat and settle down for a good talk about old times and about the adventures we have had since last we met, and we talk about Tim and his activities in Egypt. Tony enquires about the house at Cobstead which belongs to Tim's Aunt Posy, and which is to be ours when Tim can get his release from the Army. It has waited for us for six years and it may have to wait another six years before Tim is allowed to send in his papers. Tony says six years is pessimistic—it may be three—and on that we are silent.

"Tim told me to ask about the diary," says Tony at last in a more cheerful tone.

"It's coming along," I reply. "Sometimes I write a lot and sometimes I don't write a word for days. It depends on how I'm feeling."

"Are you feeling good today?" he enquires gravely. "I mean you really must write a full account of our meeting and describe my manly charms . . . Anthony Morley stood six feet two in his stocking soles . . . why stocking soles, I wonder!"

"Not shoes," I explain briefly.

"Why not bare feet? He might be wearing silk stockings or woollen. It's idiotic, isn't it? Well never mind, we must get on with my description. Anthony Morley stood six feet two in his bare feet—"

"On his bare feet—"

"Don't interrupt, Hester. His hair was blond, slightly silvered at the temples, it swept back from his high forehead to the nape of his neck. He was slim, with long legs," says Tony, with an admiring glance at those appendages, "and the—"

"No, you don't understand," I say firmly. "That isn't the way it's done. In fact, it isn't done at all, because people who know you know what you're like, and people who don't know you would far rather imagine you for themselves."

"How could they?"

"They take a Brigadier they happen to know and endow you with his physical characteristics."

"Good Heavens!" cries Tony. "Brigadiers sometimes have bow windows."

"I can't help that."

"But supposing they don't know a Brigadier?"

"In that case they take a Colonel and exaggerate him slightly."

"Most unsatisfactory," says Tony. "There must be some way of indicating the appearance of your characters without giving a description of their eyes and hair and teeth. I *do* grant you that's boring. Personally I always skip it in a book."

"There you are!"

"Let me see," says Tony thoughtfully. "If I were describing you I should do it like this: 'Looking at Hester, Tony decided she should always wear a blue frock, she should always sit on a green garden seat with a background of dark shiny rhododendrons. The golden sun found sunbeams in her hair and the bright blue sky was no bluer than her eyes'. You see the idea," says Tony with a wave of his hand. "It's all done by kindness, it's description without tears."

"It tells you practically nothing," I object.

"It tells you a good deal," contradicts Tony. "It gives you a distinct picture of Hester sitting on a garden seat; and not only that, it gives you a character sketch as well. For instance there is the woman who looks her best in the ballroom, and the woman who is irresistible sunbathing on the plage, and the woman who is at her most attractive when sitting by a cosy fire—the intime atmosphere of the boudoir is her milieu. The moment you hear that Hester is at her best in a sunny garden you know at once whether or not she's your cup of tea."

I am about to answer this extravagance in a ribald manner when two figures stroll by, amongst the trees. They are arm in arm, their heads are close together and they are talking so earnestly that they do not see us. They stroll past and disappear.

"Honeymooners, obviously," says Tony.

"No."

Tony looks at me with raised eyebrows. "Oh, it's like that, is it? And you aren't surprised."

"I knew—at least I thought—and Annie told me. Her husband is with the B.A.O.R. Isn't it horrid?"

"Hm'm," says Tony.

"What does one do?" I ask.

"You do nothing," says Tony firmly. "If Anne of Cleves likes to take steps that's her affair. Don't meddle with things that are not your concern."

"Yes—I mean no, I won't," I reply meekly.

After dinner I find Tony in the lounge talking to the American ladies. They beckon to me to join them and make room for me between them on the sofa. Mr. White-smith is one of the party and they are discussing Indian Politics—a subject which is too controversial to be comfortable. In fact before many moments have passed I have begun to wish I had not accepted the invitation to join them.

Mrs. Dene Potting says she cannot understand the Indian problem, Britain should treat the Indians in the same way as the United States treats her Indian population.

They are completely happy in their reservations, nobody interferes with their liberty and they can live their own lives.

Mr. Whitesmith says the population of India is about four hundred millions—so he believes—but the Brigadier knows better than he does, of course.

Mrs. Wilbur looks thoughtful and says they would require larger reservations.

Mrs. Dene says earnestly, "No, Darthy, that wouldn't solve the problem. India must be returned to the Indians and the British Army must leave the country."

Mr. Whitesmith says he hopes the Brigadier will contradict him if he is wrong but he is under the impression that the withdrawal of the British troops would lead to civil war.

Mrs. Dene says incredulously he can't mean the Indians would fight against each other.

Mr. Whitesmith says he means just that—but the Brigadier will be able to tell them about it because he has just come back from India.

They all look at Tony. I look at Tony, too, and send up a silent prayer that he will not be naughty.

Tony lights a cigarette with care and says, "Well, you've asked for it; I could talk all day without telling you half the complications and difficulties involved but I shall be merciful. You see nobody could understand the problem without having studied the history of India be-before the incidence of the British Raj. It's a history of constant war and unbelievable cruelty, a history of burning cities, looting, rape, murder and famine. India consists of a vast number of different races, and these races, owing to their racial habits and religious differences, cannot live together in peace. To take one cause of strife—the Moslem is taught by his religion that the pig is unclean, he loses caste if he touches a piece of its flesh. To the Hindu the cow is sacred. They use these little peculiarities to annoy one another in all sorts of ingenious ways—it's quite a game. Then of course there are the people outside India proper, the war-like people of the hills. The Gurkhas, for instance—they are a fine race, sturdy as ponies and brave as lions. I was talking to a Gurkha one day and I asked him what would happen if the British Army were to leave India. He smiled and said, 'Oh, Sahib, that would be a great day for us. We could go down to the big cities of the plains and take what we wanted.' They would, too," says Tony gravely. "They would come down in hordes and sack the cities—murder and loot would be the order of the day."

Mrs. Dene Potting says, "Well, I just can't believe it, Brigadier!" but she says it without much conviction. It is left to Mrs. Wilbur to thank the Brigadier for the interesting information, which she does with her usual social aplomb.

The party then divides. Mr. Whitesmith goes away, Mrs. Dene Potting talks to me and endeavors to persuade me to visit her sister-in-law, producing every inducement she can think of to lure me to America; while Tony and Mrs. Wilbur, ensconced together upon the sofa, carry on what is evidently a very intimate and amusing conversation in undertones.

These two ladies are leaving tomorrow and I am very sorry their stay has come to an end; they are interesting and ornamental, they are friendly with everyone and make for social pleasantness in Tocher House.

Today is warm and sunny with a few scattered clouds and a stiff breeze. Tony, to whom I have revealed the inward history of the Stannard family, has spent the golden hours fishing with Captain Stannard in the Rydd. This gives little Mr. Stannard the day off and he spends it in a deck chair in the garden shelter with a handkerchief spread over his face. He is not as young as he was and finds the unusual exercise of fishing tiring. It is extremely kind of Tony to bother with these people, who are not really his kind of people at all, but his benevolence is amply rewarded by their gratitude and by the day's basket which consists of two good-sized salmon in excellent condition. Captain Stannard is quite talkative in the lounge after dinner, scraps of his conversation with his parents drift to my ears. It is obvious that he has learnt a great deal about salmon-fishing from "the Brigadier" and hopes to put his new knowledge to good effect. As Tony is sitting beside me on the sofa, it is reasonable to suppose that he also is hearing Captain Stannard's account of the day and the supposition is confirmed by Tony leaning back and saying in a very low voice that he will get up and wring the young man's neck if he says Brigadier again.

"I bore it all day," says Tony in plaintive whispers. "He was so damn respectful—even when he was into a fish —that I longed to trip him up and throw him in the pool."

"You've done a good deed, Tony. Let that be your reward."

"I've got to go out with him again tomorrow," groans Tony.

I am about to comfort him by telling him that familiarity breeds contempt and that by tomorrow the young man's reverence for his exalted rank will have diminished, when Erica appears, looking somewhat distraught, and beckons to me to come.

I rise at once and make for the door.

"Major Ovens has arrived," says Erica in a low voice. "He's asking for his wife and she isn't in the house."

"She's out with that frightful young man, the one with the tan shoes," says Tony who has followed us into the hall. "I saw them go off in his car—in fact we met them in the avenue when we were coming back from the river."

"There!" exclaims Erica. "What did I tell you! I shouldn't have let that woman stay on."

A tall young man in uniform is standing at the other end of the hall with a battered-looking suitcase beside him. He now approaches and says he is sorry to give everybody so much trouble but he can't understand it at all, really. He wired to his wife to say he was arriving this evening—do we think she received the wire?

I am about to answer that she certainly received the wire for I gave it to her myself, but Tony is before me.

"That's it, of course," says Tony. "She can't have got the wire. I expect she's gone to the pictures in Ryddelton with a friend."

"Of course!" exclaims Captain Ovens, in obvious relief. "*That's* the explanation. I never thought of it, but I'm sure you're right. I got a bit of a shock when she wasn't here to meet me."

"Disappointing for you," says Tony in sympathetic tones.

Captain Ovens smiles and says, "Yes, it is a bit disappointing . . . sir." (Thus showing that even in plain clothes Tony looks the complete Brigadier.)

"Where are you now?" asks Tony. The question seems somewhat unnecessary, because it is obvious that the young man is standing before us in the hall at Tocher House, but Captain Ovens understands at once.

"At Kiel, sir," he replies. "Quite a good spot, really. You get sailing and that sort of thing. Have you been out there yourself, sir?"

Tony replies that he was in the Desert Campaign and afterwards in India. They begin to talk, but before they have got very far Erica interrupts.

"Captain Ovens had better have something to eat," says Erica firmly and hustles him into the dining room for a belated meal.

Tony and I are left standing in the hall.

"I think they've gone," says Tony in a low voice. "In fact I'm pretty sure."

"Gone!" I exclaim.

"Done a bunk. They had suitcases on the back of the car."

"But that's impossible! They couldn't bring down their suitcases without being seen."

"Isn't there a back stair?"

There is, of course. It leads to the kitchen passage and from thence to the backyard.

"That's what's happened," says Tony nodding. "They

could do it all right if they chose a time when there was nobody about."

I don't wait for more but turn and rush upstairs, two steps at a time, to Mrs. Ovens's bedroom.

The room looks much as usual with towels strewn upon the floor. One or two garments lying upon the chair and the bed gives it a tenanted appearance . . . but on closer inspection I discover that there are no toilet requisites upon the dressing table and the drawers and cupboards are empty.

At this moment Erica bursts into the room, bent upon the same investigation as myself. She looks round and exclaims, "Thank Heaven! I thought she might have gone for good!"

"She has," I reply, opening the door of the cupboard and displaying its vacuity.

Erica's remarks are unfit to record.

"I know," I reply. "I couldn't agree more."

Erica sits down on a chair and lets herself go.

"Yes," I agree, nodding. "Yes, she is. You've expressed my views exactly."

Erica pauses for breath.

"What are we to do with that nice young man?" I enquire anxiously.

"He's well rid of her," declares Erica.

"I daresay—but he may not think so—and somebody will have to tell him."

"H'm, that's true," says Erica thoughtfully. "D'you think Brigadier Morley would tell him?"

"Why should Brigadier Morley tell him?" enquires Tony, who has got tired of waiting in the hall and followed us upstairs.

"I wish you wouldn't do that!" exclaims Erica. "You're

always appearing suddenly where one doesn't expect you to
be—it's unnerving—like a jack-in-the-box or something."

"No," objects Tony. "Not like a jack-in-the-box, Miss
Clutterbuck. *He* appears *when* you don't expect him; in my
case time and place are equally uncertain."

"If Captain Ovens were a woman I would tell her,"
says Erica.

"I see the implication," says Tony, nodding. "This is
the first time in my life I have regretted the fact that I am
a man."

Erica is no fool. She understands at once. "Thank you
very much," says Erica. "You had better let him finish his
dinner first."

Saturday, 6th April

I was under the impression that Tony was fishing again today so am somewhat surprised to meet him on the stairs attired in a lounge suit. He seizes my arm and says he wants to speak to me and as I have a burning desire to hear what he has to say we repair to the linen room and shut the door.

"What is he doing?" I enquire.

"If you mean Ovens—"

"Of course!"

"Fishing," says Tony laconically.

"Fishing! But Tony, didn't you tell him?"

"Of course I told him. When have you known me flinch from an unpleasant duty?"

"But—but didn't he *mind?*"

"Really, Hester!" says Tony impatiently. "What an extraordinary question! Do you think any man wouldn't mind hearing the news that the wife of his bosom had gone off with another fellow and left him in the lurch?"

"What did he say?" I enquire, too full of curiosity to resent the unmerited rebuke.

"Quite a lot," replies Tony with a thoughtful air. "But he might have said a good deal more. I'm afraid the fact that I was a fairly senior officer cramped his style. Of course he was all for dashing after them then and there, but as we had no idea where to look for them it wouldn't have been very sensible, so I managed to persuade him to wait until morning. I let him get the worst of it off his chest and then sent him off to bed with a stiff whisky and soda and a couple of aspirins. He slept soundly."

"How do you know?"

"Well, as a matter of fact I looked in about two," says Tony with a slightly shamefaced grin. "He's a nice young fellow and I was a bit worried about him, you see."

"I see."

"It was quite natural that I should be worried about him," declares Tony, looking at me suspiciously. "I mean— after all—"

"Oh, *quite,*" I agree hastily.

"This morning—it was a bit after eight and I was in the middle of shaving—in came young Ovens, full of apologies of course, to say he had been thinking about it all night and had changed his mind."

"Changed his mind!"

"Yes, he has eight days' leave and has decided to stay at Tocher and fish for salmon instead of rushing about the country and trying to find his wife. I said I was delighted to hear it—and so I am. A week's fishing will do him a lot of good."

"But, Tony—"

"Besides," says Tony, talking me down. "Besides it suits me admirably. He and Stannard can flog the river to their hearts content and be as gloomy as they please. When you feel gloomy a gloomy companion is the best kind of companion to have."

"I don't agree."

"You're wrong," declares Tony. "They went off together this morning simply wallowing in gloom. It's the best thing for both of them, and—"

"He ought to do something about his wife. It seems so —so odd—"

"It seemed a little odd to me—just at first," admits Tony. "But when I thought about it . . . we're old-fashioned, Hester. The young of today are a bit ruthless, perhaps, but they see things clearly. They have the courage to cut their losses. Ovens said to me, 'If she likes the other fellow better, what's the good of me going after her and trying to get her back? There's no reason why I should, is there?' That's what he said—and I couldn't think of any reason why he should, can you?"

"Yes, I can. She's probably regretting it by this time."

"That's no reason at all," says Tony firmly. "She knew exactly what she was doing. He's better to let her go."

It is no use trying to argue with Tony he is far too clever and can make rings round me whenever he likes. Besides I am now half convinced that Tony is right which makes argument even more difficult.

"Don't worry about them," says Tony, smiling. "She's a little wretch, not half good enough for Ovens. You're worrying about them because you're thinking of your own marriage and what it means to you and Tim. Their marriage meant practically nothing."

Saturday is always a busy day so I have no time to talk further with Tony until the evening when we foregather in the lounge for coffee.

"This is a pleasant place," Tony remarks. "The country is lovely and the house very comfortable indeed. In fact

'Every prospect pleases . . .' You can co
tation."

"Not vile, Tony," I reply. "Some of them
of course, but—"

At this moment we are interrupted by Mr.
who approaches wearing a toothy smile and
Brigadier will join in a game of bridge.

"Very good of you," says Tony, "but the fac
a little tired tonight and intend to go to bed ear
to bed and late to rise," says Tony seriously. "Th
my doctor's orders—and before I retire I like a little
society as I find it induces health-giving slumber."

"But, bless me, it's only—only twenty past eight!"
claims Mr. Whitesmith, snapping open his watch and
sulting it.

Tony also consults his watch (which he wears on h
wrist) and says he makes it twenty-three and a half minutes past.

"It makes no difference," says Mr. Whitesmith.

"On the contrary," replies Tony. "If you were catching
a train it might make *all* the difference."

Mr. Whitesmith is too persistent to be ridden off like
this. "The night is young," he says. "We shall easily get
in a couple of rubbers before you go to bed."

"I play very slowly," Tony objects.

"Yes, but—"

"*Very* slowly," repeats Tony. "Bridge is a game requir-
ing intense thought."

Mr. Whitesmith is doubtful how to take this statement.
He hesitates and then looks at me and says it is just a
friendly game, nothing very scientific about it.

As I am aware that Tony is an absolute tiger at bridge

I am not surprised to see a slight shudder pass through his frame.

"Why not have a try, Brigadier?" says Mr. Whitesmith persuasively. "We play very low."

"Why not try?" I repeat, trying not to smile.

"It is no use," says Tony sadly. "I am not in the vein ... I'll take you on at backgammon if you like."

This offer does not attract Mr. Whitesmith.

"Or spillikens," says Tony. "Are you keen on spillikens?"

Mr. Whitesmith takes this quite well. "Bar jokes, Brigadier," he says. "The fact is we need a fourth."

"It is extraordinary," says Tony in a conversational tone. "It really is a most extraordinary thing how often people seem to need a fourth. Three people are constantly getting together, desirous to indulge in a hand of cards; but the fourth is missing, the fourth is reluctant, the fourth wishes to read or converse or drink or go to bed ... or, in the case of a female, to turn the heel of a stocking or finish off the hem of some garment unmentionable in mixed company. It seems to me that if someone could invent a card game in which three people—and three people only—could take part, that man would earn the undying gratitude of a vast number of his fellow creatures."

"Yes, but nobody has, Brigadier."

"Nobody has," agrees Tony. "How *strange* that nobody has! Surely it is not beyond the powers of a nation which evolved the mulberry, which perfected radar and helped to discover the atom bomb."

"You will have your little joke, Brigadier, but as a matter of fact bridge is good enough for me."

PULASKI-PERRY REG. LIBRARY
LITTLE ROCK. ARKANSAS

"And you, Mr. Whitebread, are good enough for bridge," replies Tony, smiling at him in a friendly manner.

Mr. Whitesmith does not know what to make of this (neither do I for that matter). He looks at the ceiling for inspiration and then looks at me and says he's sure the Brigadier is a bridge-man. And I, feeling that the joke has gone far enough and that Mr. Whitesmith deserves a little consideration, reply that the Brigadier is very fond of bridge, but as he is of a temperamental disposition it is no good trying to persuade him to play if he doesn't feel that way inclined.

"Ah—temperamental!" exclaims Mr. Whitesmith sympathetically—and goes away.

"Thank you, Hester," says Tony in a faint voice.

"Don't mention it, Tony."

"Temperamental is a useful word. I must remember it for future occasions. It had a most extraordinary effect upon Mr. Whitehouse, hadn't it? All the more extraordinary because it means nothing."

"It means swayed by moods."

"No, Hester, dear. It means nothing of the sort. Temperamental simply means appertaining to the temperament. The temperament may be choleric, lymphatic, nervous or sanguine. They all sound unpleasant, don't they? But perhaps when you said I was temperamental you really meant I was suffering from tempera—a form of distemper."

"Not *that* kind of distemper!" I exclaim.

"Yes," says Tony. "Yes, that's what you meant. I am suffering from tempera—no wonder I feel disinclined to play bridge. Please explain this to Mr. Whiteheart at your leisure."

"Whitesmith," I murmur.

"Whitebridge," says Tony firmly. "Whitebridge is the name."

Meantime Mr. Whitesmith has succeeded in capturing a fourth in the shape of Mrs. Maloney—she is his last resort —and having caused the table to be brought he produces the cards and the gamesters cut for partners and take their seats. Mr. Whitesmith has drawn Mrs. Maloney; Mr. Stannard and Miss Dove make up the four.

As they have settled quite near I suggest to Tony that we should move, but Tony replies he hasn't been to a pantomime for years and remains firmly seated.

Each of the players has his or her own peculiar manner of playing which makes it very interesting to watch. Miss Dove is an adept. She pauses for a moment and then plays without hesitation; Mr. Stannard is careful and concentrated as befits a businessman; Mrs. Maloney fumbles, hesitates, changes her mind and makes a running commentary upon the game; Mr. Whitesmith smacks down his card in a determined manner as if he were saying, "Take that, and make the best of it." But the fun really starts when the game is over and Mr. Whitesmith starts raking the ashes for his partner's benefit, and commenting bitterly upon her lack of skill.

"Look," says Mr. Whitesmith earnestly. "See here, Mrs. Maloney, if you'd played the king of diamonds Miss Dove would have been squeezed and forced to relinquish a heart giving up her guard in that suit. You see that, don't you? If you'd done that what would have happened next?"

"I don't know, I'm sure," says Mrs. Maloney faintly.

"You'd have continued with the king of spades and squeezed Stannard, because of course he couldn't have parted with a diamond without making your seven a master, so Stannard would have had to discard a heart and left himself unguarded in that suit. You had that double squeeze up your sleeve," says Mr. Whitesmith reproachfully.

"Had I?" says Mrs. Maloney in a bewildered manner.

"Then of course," says Mr. Whitesmith, warming to his theme. "Then of course you can get down to it. You've cleared the air and the whole thing is plain sailing. You lead the nine of hearts and finesse the queen, the ace drops the king and that gives us our contract."

"But she didn't," says Mr. Stannard, showing some anxiety—and indeed Mr. Whitesmith is now looking so pleased with himself that some anxiety seems justifiable— "Mrs. Maloney didn't play like that at all, so you haven't made your contract."

"I'm telling her what she ought to have done," explains Mr. Whitesmith.

"How could I know Mr. Stannard hadn't any more spades?" objects Mrs. Maloney. "I mean it's easy to say afterwards I ought to have done this or that, but for all I knew Mr. Stannard might have had the ace of spades and taken my king."

"You had the ace yourself," says Miss Dove with a titter. "You played it in the second round, Mrs. Maloney."

"Excuse me, *you* had the ace," says Mr. Stannard to Miss Dove.

"I!" cries Miss Dove indignantly. "Indeed I had not. Do you think I don't know what cards I held?"

"Perhaps there wasn't an ace," suggests Mrs. Maloney in conciliatory tones.

Her three companions look at her in amazement.

"I mean it may have fallen on the floor," she explains.

"You had it and played it," says Miss Dove firmly and she begins to scrabble amongst the tricks.

"Oh well, perhaps I had," says Mrs. Maloney—who is all for appeasement. "It wasn't trumps, was it? I mean spades wasn't trumps. I should have remembered if I had had the ace of trumps," declares Mrs. Maloney smugly.

Tony is shaking with laughter and I decide it is time for us to move.

Sunday, 7th April

Am sitting in the lounge after breakfast when Tony comes in and enquires what duties fall to a hotel assistant on Sunday mornings. I reply none, and add that I intend to go to the Episcopal Church at Ryddelton. Tony says good, he will have the Bentley at the door in half an hour. I am about to ask him whether he really wants to come but remembering in time that Tony likes churchgoing I refrain and the thing is settled.

The day is dull and cloudy, a soft mist covers the hilltops and it rains gently now and then, but after the long spell of golden sunshine there is something very refreshing about this gentle rain. Tony says that it makes him feel a new man—he has not seen rain like this for years—and the birds are enjoying it, too, for they are singing madly when we set forth in the car. The buds on the trees are ready to burst and the hedges are faintly green.

The church is moderately well-filled but the congregation consists mostly of middle-aged or elderly people. Are there so few young people in Ryddelton, or is it because the younger generation thinks churchgoing an unnecessary rite? I cannot help wondering what will happen when in due course these people die . . . will the younger generation, which will then be middle-aged, acquire the habit of attending Divine Worship? If not it seems probable that churchgoing will lapse completely and our churches will fall into ruins.

These thoughts sadden me. I try to remember my own feelings about churchgoing when I was very young and am forced to admit (if I am entirely honest with myself) that I went to church in those far-off days only because I was taken. The modern child is allowed more freedom and stays at home, so the habit of churchgoing is not acquired . . . should children be dragged to church willy-nilly, or should they be left at home in the hopes that, later, they will choose to go of their own accord? I decide regretfully that the problem is too difficult for me to solve.

During the sermon I glance at Tony and note that he is listening with rapt attention—and I remember he once told me he enjoyed sermons, and that no sermon, however long, was too long for him. This sermon could bore nobody. It is interesting and well-thought-out and earnestly delivered in a pleasant melodious voice. Mr. Weir gives us two texts: the first is from Isaiah, "For I, the Lord thy God will hold thy right hand saying unto thee, Fear not; I will help thee"; the second from the Epistle to the Hebrews, "Cast not away, therefore, your confidence which hath great recompense of reward." He asks us to note that these two texts taken in conjunction give us a promise of help and a piece of good advice, both of which are more than ever necessary in these troubled and unsettled times. Many people are full of unrest, and go through life burdened and miserable, beset by fears and doubts. These nervous disorders are the maladies of to-day, very serious maladies for which medicine can find no cure. If a cure could be found, if some clever chemist could invent a patent medicine which would banish fear, and make people happy and confident, everybody would flock to buy it and would persevere with it, steadily, grudging neither the trouble nor the expense. It would need no persuasion to induce people to take a course of the wonderful tablets, but no patent medicine will avail. There is a cure, of course. It is quite a simple cure and open to everybody. It is confidence in God.

Many people believe in God, says Mr. Weir, but often their belief is feeble—it is a milk-and-water belief which does not help them in the stress and strain of life. Others have lost all confidence and say so openly—but have they really tried religion? Have they tried it with the same resolution as they would try a patent medicine? Have they persevered with it steadily day after day?

Mr. Weir pauses and then says, "Have they tried giving their right hand to God?"

Man needs God, says Mr. Weir. There is a great recompense of reward for those who walk with God—perhaps the greatest is serenity. Man has always needed God. Savages who had no knowledge of God found they needed some sort of Divine Being to worship, so they invented idols and worshiped them. Take God away from man and you take a vital necessity from his life; he is like a lost child, crying in the dark, he is sick and does not know the cause of his sickness. But God is patient, God is waiting for him with a true and living promise: "For I, the Lord thy God, will hold thy right hand, saying unto thee, Fear not; I will help thee."

When we come out Tony says he thinks it would be a good idea to have a chat with the padre, and without waiting for my reaction—which is reluctance—he leads the way to the vestry and opens the door. Mr. Weir is discovered in the act of removing his surplice and when he emerges from its folds he seems somewhat taken aback to find two complete strangers looking at him; but Tony is equal to the occasion, he explains who we are and adds that he has just got back from India and is thoroughly enjoying the rain.

One thing leads to another and in a few moments the two men are deep in conversation about eastern religions. Mr. Weir has studied them in theory and Tony has firsthand knowledge of the subject, acquired during his travels in India and China, so they have plenty to tell one another and become quite excited. They discuss Lao-Tse, who founded Taoism, and agree that his teaching had much in common with the teaching of Christ.

"The Taoist lives in the present," says Mr. Weir nodding. "He takes no thought for the morrow, he practises humility and simplicity and is taught to return good for evil. How curious to think that these virtues were prized two centuries before Christ!"

Tony says St. Paul had a knowledge of Taoism and produces chapter and verse to bear out his contention. St. Paul bore his persecutions and afflictions with patience and used them to increase his spiritual stature—the Taoist welcomes afflictions and bears adversities in stillness and quietness, without striving against them or complaining, for in so doing he advances along "the Way". But, says Tony, the Christian is more fortunate than the Taoist for he need not walk the steep and stony path alone.

"Many do walk alone," says Mr. Weir sadly.

They continue the discussion. The subject is so interesting and absorbs them so completely that I begin to think we shall be here all day, but luckily there is a large clock in the vestry and, Tony's eyes lighting upon it, he is reminded of the passage of time.

"We must go," says Tony regretfully.

Mr. Weir objects—he has a thousand questions he wants

to ask. It is extremely difficult to tear ourselves away; he accompanies us to the car and stands with one foot on the step, still talking volubly . . . finally he asks if Tony will come to supper with him some night and continue the discussion at leisure.

Tony says he is going away tomorrow but will let Mr. Weir know if he comes back.

We shake hands cordially and say good-bye.

As we drive back to Tocher House I comment upon Tony's ability to get to grips with all sorts of different people and talk to them about things that interest them.

"Oh well," says Tony. "People like being talked to. They like it if you take an interest in them. Of course it isn't the slightest use if you only *pretend* to take an interest. However dull and stupid they may be they know at once if your interest is insincere—their subconscious mind is aware of insincerity and you get no further . . . we turn right here, don't we?"

"Yes, it's a bad corner."

Tony has been going about sixty. He slows down. "Mr. Weir knew at once that I was really interested and came halfway to meet me. When people go halfway to meet each other something happens—something important."

"Yes—but what is it?" I ask with interest.

"You give a bit of yourself and receive a bit of the other fellow, and you're both richer."

We roar round a bend in the road in a manner calculated to make the hair stand on end, but fortunately I have every confidence in Tony's skill as a driver so I remain perfectly calm.

"That's one reason why it's worthwhile to be alive," continues Tony. "It's a sort of immortality we can all achieve."

"Immortality?"

"Yes. We all want to achieve immortality. We all want to leave our mark upon the world. What use is it to have lived if we leave nothing behind us when we die. One way to achieve immortality is to have children, another is to write or paint—but not everybody can achieve offspring or works of art."

"I'm beginning to see."

"It's easy," declares Tony. "If we go about the world giving bits of ourselves to people we meet . . . it's worth-while having lived . . . we leave something behind us which goes on—and on."

He is silent after that. I reflect that if I have changed in the last six years Tony has changed too. Or perhaps not so much *changed* as developed and mellowed. He always had a solid foundation and even when he talked arrant nonsense there was wit and wisdom at the bottom of it.

"Am I going too fast?" enquires Tony suddenly.

"You can go as fast as you like," I tell him. "I'm never frightened with you at the wheel. Do you remember the day we drove over to Gart-na-Drium? We went like the wind. What has become of Alec MacDonald?"

"Gart-na-Drium!" exclaims Tony. "One doesn't forget days like that. It was a day in Paradise. We ate ambrosia and drank nectar and bathed in the Western Sea."

"I undressed in a little cave with pink flowers growing in the crevices of the rock. The sand was as white as snow! The sea was clear and green—it was like green glass with bubbles in it! Oh, Tony we shall never have days like that again."

Tony takes one hand off the wheel and lays it on my knee. "Don't talk like that, Hester," he says gravely.

"I feel like that sometimes. I can't help it. You know that bit in *The Trojan Women*—'Oh, happy long-ago, farewell, farewell!' "

"No," says Tony quickly. "I mean of course I know it, but you aren't a Trojan Woman. You haven't been seized by the enemies of your country and taken in captivity to a foreign land. You aren't eating your heart out in exile. You have been spared that fate—spared it by a very narrow margin, perhaps; spared it by a miracle or a series of what look very like miracles to any thoughtful person. There was a time when your fate, and the fate of thousands of others like you, hung by a very frail thread. People forget," says Tony earnestly. "People say, it was touch-and-go, but they don't really think what it means."

Tony has made me feel ashamed. "I'm not unthankful," I tell him. "I *do* realize what we have been spared—and our children. I just meant that those days of long ago were so carefree, so gay. They were golden days, Tony."

"There are good times coming," he replies as he slows down again to turn in at the gates of Tocher House. "Perhaps not the same sort of good times because we ourselves are changed and sobered by six dreadful years of war, but peaceful happy days. Tim will come home from Egypt and you'll settle down at Cobstead. Think about that."

"I do think about it, Tony—perhaps I think about it too much."

"How do you mean?" he asks as the car slides to a standstill at the door.

"The Taoist takes no thought for the morrow," I remind him.

"Oh!" exclaims Tony somewhat taken aback. "Oh—yes

—but it can't mean *that,* Hester. It can't mean we aren't to look forward to better times."

"What does it mean?"

"Too difficult," declares Tony, turning his head to smile at me. "Much too difficult. You had better consult Mr. Weir."

It is not until I am in my room, tidying myself for lunch, that I remember Tony did not answer my question about Alec MacDonald . . . so Alec has gone, too.

Monday, 8th April

Awake suddenly with the conviction that something out of the ordinary is happening today and after a few moments of dazed bewilderment I remember I am going to Edinburgh. Yes, I am going to Edinburgh with Tony, staying the night with Pinkie Loudon and meeting Betty tomorrow. All this is delightful, of course, and I am full of excitement . . . but beneath the excitement there is a slight feeling of apprehension, due to the coming of Betty to Tocher House. However it is no use meeting trouble halfway, so I banish my doubts and decide to enjoy myself.

Tony and I have breakfast early, in the empty dining room, and set off in the Bentley before the other inhabitants of the house have emerged from their rooms. The roads are clear at this hour, we skim through sleepy Ryddelton and over the hills. The valley of Tweed is green and peaceful, with the road winding along by the silver river and the hills scarred by peat hags and tenanted by black-faced sheep. It is a silver day. The sky is completely covered with shining white clouds, so thin and bright that one expects the sun to break through at any moment. Tony rejoices in the clouds, and says he prefers indirect lighting—it is certainly very restful to the eyes.

We chat in a desultory manner. Tony says he will spend a couple of nights in Edinburgh before going south. He has got a job in the War Office and pretends to dislike the idea.

"You like London," I tell him. "You have hundreds of friends and you will be able to go and see your mother every weekend."

"I shall be chained to a desk," he groans.

"Brigadiers are never chained—and think how useful you'll be to your friends!" I exclaim—very wickedly, I admit.

"That's all you care about," retorts Tony. "You think I shall be able to wave a wand and bring Tim home. Let me tell you I shall do nothing of the sort—even if I could, I wouldn't."

I abandon the subject hastily and enquire where Tony is staying in Edinburgh.

"At the club, I suppose," he replies. "Unless Pinkie could put me up."

"She couldn't possibly. Pinkie has only two beds."

"How happy could I be in either!" says Tony sotto voce.

I decide that I have not heard this remark, and am greatly aided in the matter by a large black-faced sheep which is sent by Providence to provide a diversion. The animal has been quietly grazing by the side of the road but suddenly, as we approach, it makes up its mind that the grass on the other side is more nourishing and tasty. It lumbers across in front of the car, necessitating the application of brakes.

"Dear creature," says Tony as we continue our way. "How I love dumb animals! And sheep are the dumbest of the brute creation—I could do without sheep."

"Without wool and mutton?" I enquire.

"I prefer silk and beef," says Tony firmly.

I leave it at that. The day is too lovely for bickering. I feast my eyes on the rounded hills, on the swiftly flowing river which leaps and gurgles in its bed of grey stones and pebbles, on the little plantations of firs and pines, clumps of them every here and there, planted as shields from the winter gales.

"I expect there were highwaymen on this moor," I remark.

"I shouldn't wonder," nods Tony. "It's a deserted spot—but what made you think of highwaymen all of a sudden?"

The curious thing is I was under the impression that my sudden remark was "out of the air," but now that I examine myself in order to reply I discover the source from which it sprung. Today I am worth robbing, for not only have I a goodly wad of notes—my salary for five weeks which I intend to spend in Edinburgh—but also, reposing in the recesses of my handbag, a diamond ring, the property of Margaret McQueen, which she has commissioned me to sell for what I can get.

"Well?" enquires Tony, who is waiting for an answer.

I tell him I am the bearer of precious jewels to be sold for a friend.

"For a friend?" he asks. "I mean you'd tell me if—"

"Yes, I would. I would, really, Tony," I reply quickly; and this is true for Tony is the sort of person from whom one could borrow comfortably.

"Let's see the precious jewels," he says, and pulling up at the side of the road he lights a cigarette.

At this very moment the clouds part and the sun pours through the gap, and the country is flooded with gold.

"How lovely!" I cry involuntarily.

"Perfectly beautiful!" agrees my companion in fervent tones. "There's a miraculous quality in light. I was in love with the silver day until I saw the gold."

For a few moments we admire the transformation in

silence and then we remember why we stopped. I produce the tiny parcel and disclose the ring.

"A pretty gewgaw," says Tony, taking it and moving it about so that the diamonds sparkle gaily with rainbow colors in the sunshine. "I'm rather partial to diamonds—nice glittery stones, aren't they? These are good, you know."

"Are they?"

"Yes—and I like the nice old-fashioned setting. It's an engagement ring of course. Who wore it, I wonder."

"I have no idea."

"Oh, I'm not *asking*," Tony assures me. "People who sell jewelry are always secretive—though why anyone should be ashamed of needing money I can't imagine—and anyhow the girl who wore it as an engagement ring has been in her grave for years. It's early Victorian, that's obvious. They went in for solid value in those days. You ought to get quite a decent sum for this ring—the friend is hard-up, I suppose."

"Yes, she's very hard-up."

"I wonder," says Tony thoughtfully. "I wonder what it's worth. Would you like me to come with you and help you to sell it, Hester?"

"Please do!" I exclaim in heartfelt tones—for to tell the truth I have been dreading the transaction.

"Right," says Tony. "We'll drive a good bargain. I happen to know of a fellow who deals in secondhand jewelry."

"It's very good of you—"

"I shall enjoy it," says Tony smiling.

This being settled we drive on and chat of other matters. I feel very tempted to tell Tony the whole story of Margaret McQueen and ask his advice as to whether or not I should meddle in her affairs or leave her to her own devices, but the secret is not mine to tell so my lips are sealed and my companion asks no questions.

Presently we reach the suburbs of Edinburgh and are struck by their unloveliness. There are rows of ugly houses, untidy dumps and squalid factories. Edinburgh itself is beautiful, the old town on the ridge running up to the castle, which stands like a crown upon the old grey crag, and the new town with its fairy vista of Princes Street and its dignified Adam squares. Edinburgh is like a flawless gem in a trumpery setting—the people who are responsible for the setting should be ashamed. Tony tries to soothe me by pointing out that this has happened to nearly every town in Britain, they have all been allowed to sprawl over the surrounding country in the same formless way. It was a bad phase, says Tony, marked by a complete lack of taste in architecture. The population grew and the small landowners on the outskirts of the towns sold their land to the highest bidder and did not care what sort of buildings went up as long as they got their money.

We park the Bentley (Tony says it is an unsuitable vehicle in which to drive up to the door of a dealer in secondhand) and set forth on foot to visit Mr. McBean. His place of business is not easily found, it is a small dark shop, somewhat uninviting, and filled with the oddest assortment of goods. There are pieces of furniture, shabby and broken; there is silver and plate, china and crystal trays of jewelry of all sorts heaped together in confusion. Mr. McBean is small and dark himself and despite his name there is nothing Scottish about him; he appears from the gloom at the back of the shop and asks what he can do for us.

"Would a diamond ring be of any interest to you?" Tony enquires.

His face changes. It is obvious that he thought we were buyers, his face for sellers is a different face, less genial and a good deal more sly. He replies cautiously that that depends . . . there are diamonds *and* diamonds.

Tony takes out the ring and lays it on the counter.

Mr. McBean seizes it with his very dirty fingers and examines it. "Thirty pounds," he says. "I'd give you more if I could but business is bad and nobody wants these old-fashioned settings nowadays. I shall probably have this on my hands for months . . ."

I am about to close with this offer at once but Tony gives me a little pinch so I shut my mouth tightly and remain silent.

"You're joking, Mr. McBean," says Tony smiling.

"Thirty-two," says Mr. McBean.

"No, no."

"Thirty-five."

"Listen," says Tony firmly. "You're wasting your time and mine. Unless you're willing to make a reasonable offer—"

"Forty."

"I said a reasonable offer."

"Forty is my limit."

Tony takes the ring and slips it into his pocket. "Come, Hester," he says. "Mr. McBean doesn't want the ring."

"Here, not so fast!" says Mr. McBean. "You tell me what you want for it, see? Then I'll see if I can come near it."

"I want a hundred pounds," says Tony frankly.

At these words Mr. McBean almost faints—but not quite. "What!" he says. "You want—you want a hundred! You want something, don't you? That's just nonsense. I can't afford to run my business on charity lines. I got to make a profit—see? How do I know if I can sell that ring? Might be months before I got a buyer—I got to take that risk. Let's have another look at it."

Tony hands it over and Mr. McBean sticks a magnifying glass in his eye and looks at it much more carefully than before.

"Well?" says Tony. "What's the verdict this time?"

"Look now," says Mr. McBean, confidentially. "I'll tell you what I'll do. I've said forty and you've said a hundred. We'll split the difference."

"Seventy," says Tony thoughtfully.

"That's my last word," declares Mr. McBean, putting down the ring. "That's square, that is. That's my last word and I wouldn't go a pound higher for nobody."

Tony considers the matter. "I think I can get eighty for it," he says.

"You won't," retorts the little man. "You won't get eighty—not in Scotland. I've made you a fair offer."

"I think you have—*now*," replies Tony smiling. "All the same I believe I can do better."

Mr. McBean is displeased. "Do as you like," he says crossly. "But if you take it away you needn't come back and expect to find the offer open. I'll give you seventy today but tomorrow it may be sixty."

"Thank you," says Tony, taking the ring and slipping it into his pocket.

"Remember what I said!" cries Mr. McBean in disgust.

"I shan't forget," says Tony calmly.

As we emerge from the shop I clutch Tony's arm. "For goodness sake give me the ring!" I cry. "Margaret McQueen will be tickled to death with seventy pounds."

Tony roars with laughing and says the American language is exceedingly descriptive. He accuses me of having

filched the expression from Mrs. Potting—which of course is
perfectly true—but the odd thing is I have used it quite un-
consciously in this moment of stress.

"Never mind the expression," I retort. "It expresses what
I feel *exactly*—which is what an expression is meant to do.
Please be sensible for a moment and give me the ring before
the horrid little man changes his mind."

"You would have taken thirty pounds for it, Hester."

"I know—you've been frightfully clever—but I'm sure
we ought to—"

"Trust your Uncle Tony," says Tony smiling. "As a matter of fact Uncle has taken rather a fancy to the ring, himself. He will give Miss McQueen eighty pounds for it."

"You!" I exclaim in amazement. "Oh, Tony, why? And
how do you know it belongs to Miss McQueen?"

" 'Margaret McQueen will be tickled to death,' " quotes
Tony laughing immoderately.

We have reached the car by this time but I hesitate before getting in. "Do you *really* want it?" I ask. "What do
you want it for?"

"What do you think?"

"It isn't a man's ring."

"Good Heavens, no!"

"Not—I mean you don't want it as an engagement ring,
Tony?"

"Who—me?" cries Tony in mock amazement.

"Why not?" I enquire putting on an innocent expression. "As a matter of fact I thought you and Mrs. Wilbur
Potting were getting on rather well together."

"Well!" exclaims Tony.

"She's a dear. She's pretty and witty—"

"So she is," he agrees. "Darthy Potter is a most attractive

creature—so is Marley—they're both darlings. It would be exceedingly difficult to choose between them. They have husbands already of course, but I don't suppose that would matter. Six months as Darthy Potter's husband would be delightful—and instructive. You advise that, Hester?"

"Six months?"

"Yes," nods Tony. "Six months would be just about right. After that we should part the best of friends. You must admit it's the civilized way to conduct marriage."

"Seriously, Tony?"

"Seriously!" says Tony, looking thoughtful. "No, Hester, not seriously. Come now, you should know me better by this time. I've dodged women for nearly fifty years and my technique is perfect. Is it likely I should be caught *now*."

It isn't likely, of course. Tony will never marry. He is buying the ring because he has taken a fancy to it, because he can easily afford to indulge his whim and last but not least because I told him the vendor needed the money badly.

"Don't look so sad, you little idiot," says Tony laughing. "You know perfectly well I should be a most uncomfortable husband. I shall keep the ring for your diamond wedding. Where are we lunching?"

Having lunched together, Tony and I separate and go our ways for I have some shopping to do and he has business to transact. I shop industriously—but without notable success—until it is time to make my appearance at Pinkie's flat. Pinkie is expecting me to tea. It seems years since I climbed the three flights of stairs for so much has happened in the interval, and perhaps this is why I have forgotten which is Pinkie's door. There are two doors on the top landing, one on the right and the other on the left—neither of them bears the name of Loudon.

I hesitate, and just at that moment the door on the left flies open and Pinkie rushes out.

"I've been listening for you with both ears!" she cries, embracing me warmly. "I had a sort of feeling you'd ring the wrong bell, and the man is never there which makes it even more awkward. People stand for hours outside that door and then go away thinking I'm out—it's perfectly sickening. Of course it isn't so bad if it's somebody I don't want to see, but it never is, really." She seizes my suitcase and leads the way in.

"D'you know what I've done?" continues Pinkie. "You'll think I'm mad, of course, but it was just a sudden impulse and I gave way to it before I thought it out properly. I've taken tickets for *Peter Pan!*"

"Tonight!"

"Yes, tonight," nods Pinkie. "We don't need to go if you hate the idea."

I am delighted at the idea and tell her so. It will be fun to see *Peter Pan* again.

"*That's* all right," says Pinkie, heaving a sigh of relief. "I've been wondering whether it was one of my silly impulses—but if you're pleased it isn't. We'll have a *thorough* meal now, shall we? Then we can have something light when we get home. Come and talk to me while I make an omelet."

Pinkie wants to know "all about everything" and while she knocks up an omelet I do my best to satisfy her curiosity. I tell her what I do at Tocher House and about the people there, especially about Erica.

"She sounds mad," says Pinkie as she folds the omelet and slides it onto a plate. "She sounds revolting, Hester."

"Then I haven't described her properly," I reply.

By this time the "thorough meal" is prepared and we sit down and do it full justice for Pinkie's appetite is as healthy as ever and the east coast air has made me extremely hungry. We wash the dishes, shut up the flat and walk to the theatre, still talking hard about an extraordinary variety of subjects interesting to us both. Pinkie and I are the unfashionable sort of people who like to be early at the theatre. We watch the people coming in and finding their seats, we discuss the curtain which is a queer medley of mediaeval figures, knights jousting while their squires look on, and boys with greyhounds in leash. There is something very exciting about the last few minutes before the curtain rises (especially if one has not been to a theatre for years) and I am glad I have not missed it.

Peter Pan has lost none of its old magic. Perhaps it is a little more boisterous than of yore, a little less fairylike and other-worldly. Celia Lipton who plays Peter is a gallant figure obviously enjoying her part, and Wendy is sweet and appealing. I am swept away into this half-fairy, half-realistic dream and the everyday world is forgotten.

Halfway through the performance Pinkie gives me a little nudge and murmurs something about tea, but I am so enthralled with Peter and Wendy that tea seems an unnecessary interruption.

"Don't let's bother," I whisper—and Pinkie immediately subsides.

The play is over, the curtain has fallen for the last time. As is so often the case in Barrie's plays we are left with an unresolved doubt in our minds. Peter is not really happy alone in his nest, he has chosen his way of life but it is a second-best choice. What will happen when Wendy grows up and leaves Peter behind? Will Wendy marry an ordinary human being and have ordinary human children?

We walk home, arm in arm; the night is warm and dark and above the jagged outline of the houses the moon is bright. We discuss the play and the actors, but chiefly Peter and Wendy and their problems. Pinkie seems a trifle distrait but my head is full of the play and I feel quite able to do most of the talking.

As we cross the West End Pinkie interrupts me to ask if I remembered to shut the sitting-room window before we came out, and I am able to assure her that I did.

"I was afraid so," says Pinkie with a little sigh. "I mean I was almost sure I saw you doing it."

"You told me to!" I exclaim. "You said there were cat-burglars in Edinburgh and we must shut everything securely!"

"Yes, darling, but I didn't know I was going to lose the key," says Pinkie reasonably.

"The key of the door!"

"Yes," says Pinkie. "I told you about it when we were in the theatre—don't you remember? I said I'd lost the key and you said, don't let's bother—and of course you were *too* right. It was no use spoiling all our pleasure by worrying about the beastly key until we *had* to. But now we *have* to," says Pinkie with another bigger sigh.

"Pinkie, I thought you said *tea!*"

"No, key," she replies, squeezing my arm. "*Key,* darling. Of course there's always the chance I may have left it in the door—I do that, occasionally—if not I'm afraid it's going to be rather a nuisance."

We hasten our steps. We climb the three flights of stairs. The key is not in the door.

"That's that," says Pinkie.

"What about the other flat?" I enquire, pointing to the door on the right of the landing.

"No good," replies Pinkie. "It's a man and he's always away from home. As a matter of fact I've never *seen* him. If one of the windows were open we might borrow a ladder, but I'm sure they're all shut—and it would have to be a fireman's ladder to reach this floor."

"A policeman," I murmur—for I have a tremendous faith in the initiative and resource of the police.

"If we could find one . . ." says Pinkie hopelessly.

We descend the stairs slowly. I have now begun to realize the extent of the calamity. What on earth are we to do?

There is no policeman to be seen (why should there be?) and anyhow, as Pinkie says, what could he do except conduct us to the Police Station for the night?

"Honestly, Hester," says Pinkie. "A policeman wouldn't be any help at all. We needn't waste time looking for one."

We stand for several minutes looking up at the windows. It is very cold by this time, and seems all the colder because the moon is so bright. It sails placidly in the western sky and casts jagged shadows of jutting eaves and towering chimney-pots across the street.

"I wish Peter were here," says Pinkie with a little shiver.

"Peter?"

"Peter Pan," she explains. "Wings would be useful, wouldn't they? I've often wanted wings."

This desire is fairly common, but I refuse to discuss the matter now. Instead I urge Pinkie to think of someone— some friend who lives near and could help us in our plight.

"The boy next door!" cries Pinkie. "Of *course*—why didn't I think of him sooner? It's a marvelous idea. How clever of you, Hester!"

The idea is not mine at all and I hasten to disclaim it.

The next door house is smaller than its neighbors and is not divided into flats. I am about to ask Pinkie if she knows her next door neighbors well enough to knock them up at this late hour, but before I can do so Pinkie has rung the bell. After a long wait (during which Pinkie explains that she does not know them at all) the bolts are withdrawn and the door opened by a middle-aged lady with grey hair and a somewhat forbidding expression. Her expression becomes even less cordial when she sees us and hears our tale of woe, and she shows no desire to help us nor to rouse her son who has gone to bed some time ago and is probably fast asleep. If I were alone I should now withdraw hurriedly and with profuse apologies but Pinkie is made of sterner stuff. Pinkie edges her way into the hall and explains the desperate nature of our plight, she informs the lady that I am extremely delicate and may get bronchitis or even pneumonia if some shelter cannot be found.

"What do you think we should do?" asks Pinkie anxiously.

The lady replies that she thinks we should go to a hotel.

At this moment a figure in pyjamas appears on the stairs and enquires what's up.

"Go back to bed at once, Adam," says his mother firmly.

"But what's up?" asks Adam. He begins to come down. His feet are bare, his blue-striped pyjama jacket is open in front and discloses a large expanse of well-developed chest; his brown hair is standing straight on end and his eyes are dazed with sleep. Suddenly he sees two strange females standing in the hall and, conscious of his déshabille, he gives a horrified yelp and sprints back to his bedroom.

"You see!" says his mother gravely. "Adam couldn't possibly do anything to help you. The only thing to do is to go to a hotel for the night."

"Yes," says Pinkie meekly. "Yes, that seems the only thing," but instead of making any movement in the direction of the door she still lingers. "It must be lovely for you to have him safely home," says Pinkie.

His mother agrees that it is. She adds that Adam was in Commandos which made it even more worrying.

"How marvelous!" exclaims Pinkie. "He must be terribly brave."

His mother laughs in a deprecating way and admits that Adam has been awarded the M.C.

"How marvelous!" says Pinkie again. "He's so young, too. You must be terribly proud of him."

His mother admits that she is.

All this is very nice, of course, but it is not getting us any further, and as it is already eleven o'clock I feel that something definite must be done; I tug Pinkie's arm in a gentle but purposeful manner and try to get her away. Pinkie takes no notice at all. She continues to enquire about Adam; and Adam's mother—as is the nature of mothers—is not unwilling to discuss her son. In fact she becomes quite animated on the subject and requires very little encouragement. We hear about Adam's prowess on the cricket field, before Hitler plunged the world into total war; we hear about Adam aged eight years old winning a cup for swimming. I feel pretty sure that at this rate we shall soon be hearing about Adam in his cradle but before we have reached this era a diversion is caused by the reappearance of Adam himself, this time quite decently attired in grey slacks and a blue pullover with a turtle neck.

Pinkie sees him first—can she have been keeping one eye on the stairs? "Oh, here he is!" exclaims Pinkie joyfully.

The young man's mother is not so pleased, she murmurs something about the lateness of the hour but nobody takes any notice.

"Come into the dining room, won't you?" says young Adam, throwing open the door and smiling at us both, but chiefly at Pinkie. "We could have drinks or something. You live next door, don't you?"

Pinkie says yes, she does, and adds that she has seen the young man out with his dog—a darling golden retriever.

"He *is* rather nice," agrees Adam. "Do come in. We've got some gin—"

"I really think it's a little late for drinks," says our hostess feebly.

"My dear lamb it's never too late for drinks," says Adam firmly. "Nor too early either, if it comes to that."

"But these ladies are going to a hotel."

"We'll all go to a hotel," cries Adam in delight. "We'll make a night of it—that's what we'll do. It's a grand idea— just give me five minutes to change into decent clothes—"

"It would be *lovely*," nods Pinkie. "We'll do it some other time, but not tonight."

"Not tonight?" he asks hesitating with one foot on the stairs.

"No," says Pinkie. "Mrs. Christie and I are a bit jaded tonight. All we want is to get into the flat. I've been *so* silly," says Pinkie, opening her blue eyes very wide and looking at him appealingly. "I've lost the key of the door—so you see?"

Adam sees at once. He is a most intelligent young man.

He smiles and says this is absolutely up his street. Pinkie couldn't have come to anyone better able to deal with the situation, says Adam cheerfully.

"We can't do anything tonight," objects his mother. "Tomorrow we can get a locksmith to come and take the lock off the door, but—"

Adam says there is absolutely no need for that, the point is shall he get out of his bedroom window and crawl along the coping stone, or would the roof be better.

"Adam, you'll kill yourself!" cries his mother in alarm.

"Oh!" exclaims Pinkie. "But that would be marvelous! The only thing is I'm afraid all the windows are shut."

This does not daunt Adam in the least. He explains that you can break a hole in the glass and put your hand through. "But perhaps the roof would be better," he adds thoughtfully.

"Our roof is higher, of course," Pinkie reminds him.

"A rope is the answer," says Adam without hesitation.

"You can't go up on the roof tonight," says his mother aghast.

"Of course I can!" cries Adam. "Our roof is child's play to some of the places I've been. I could go all over Edinburgh by roof—as a matter of fact I've often thought it would be rather amusing. Hold on till I find a rope."

He finds a rope and we all go upstairs (all except Adam's mother who has given up the unequal struggle in despair). We climb a narrow stairway and then an iron ladder and emerge through a trap door onto a flat zinc-covered roof.

"Gorgeous night!" exclaims Adam, sniffing the air like a young war horse. "Look at the moon! Look at the heavenly view over the Forth!"

It certainly is lovely, so bright and clear and windless. There is a faint smell of salt in the air from the far off sea.

In spite of his pleasure in the beauty of the night the young man wastes no time—he merely admires it en passant and goes about his task. To me his task looks formidable for the roof of Pinkie's flat is a whole story higher and there is no way that I can see of climbing the smooth stone wall.

"You can't do it," says Pinkie, who has come to the same conclusion. "I mean it's no use breaking your leg. We'll just have to—"

"Of course I can do it," declares Adam. He makes a noose in the rope, coils it carefully and flings it into the air; the rope curls upward uncoiling as it goes and settles snugly over a chimney. "There," says Adam, with satisfaction. "My hand hasn't lost its cunning. If that chimney pot is reasonably secure—and I think it is—

"You're absolutely marvelous," declares Pinkie earnestly.

Adam smiles at her, he swarms up the rope and disappears.

"Isn't he marvelous!" says Pinkie with a sigh of profound admiration. "It's no wonder we won the war. Adam gives me the sort of feeling that he could do *anything*."

I admit that I have exactly the same sort of feeling about the young man.

After a few minutes Adam's head appears over the row of chimney pots. "Hullo!" he says. "It's a piece of cake—the bathroom skylight—I'll meet you at the door."

Pinkie and I descend. We cannot find our hostess to say good-bye—but perhaps that is just as well. We let ourselves into the street and toil up the stairs. There is nobody on the landing and everything is quiet.

"You'd think he would be here before us," says Pinkie in some anxiety. "He hadn't nearly so far to go."

I put my ear against the door of Pinkie's flat but there is not a sound to be heard.

"What can have happened!" I exclaim.

"Perhaps he's lying on the bathroom floor with a broken leg," says Pinkie in horrified tones.

We look at each other in dismay—but at this moment the door of the other flat bursts open and Adam appears followed by another man, slightly older than himself; they both seem somewhat heated and upset.

"*There!*" cries Adam, pointing to us. "There they are. I told you—it was a mistake, that's all. I got in through the wrong skylight—"

"A damned funny mistake!" cries the other young man angrily. "You needn't think you'll get off with it so easily— I shall telephone to the police—you're nothing more than a burglar. If I hadn't happened to hear you—" He stops suddenly in mid-flight and gives an odd sort of choke . . . he gazes at Pinkie with goggling eyes.

Having known Pinkie for years, I have had plenty of opportunities to observe the impact of her personality upon susceptible members of the sterner sex so I am not really surprised to see the young man go down before her like a nine-pin. There is something positively dynamic about Pinkie. She is lovely to look at, of course, but there is more to it than that, for quite a number of girls are lovely to look at. What is it, I wonder. How can the thing be explained? I love Pinkie dearly but I cannot understand why the mere sight of her should have such a devastating effect.

"Oh!" says the young man, becoming very red in the face. "Oh, I'm . . . s'sorry."

"How dreadful for you!" exclaims Pinkie in sympathetic tones. "Of course you thought Adam was a burglar—and of course the whole thing is absolutely *all* my fault for being such a fool and losing the key. No wonder you're angry!"

The young man is heard to murmur that he isn't angry —not in the least—and of course he understands perfectly; he was in the middle of reading a detective novel which is probably the reason he leapt to the conclusion that Adam was a burglar . . .

Pinkie says of course he did—anybody would—and there are heaps of burglars about in Edinburgh; a friend of hers had her house burgled only last week.

Adam, who is getting slightly restive, says time is being wasted. He will go back through the young man's skylight and come down through Pinkie's. The two skylights are close together, says Adam, and he chose the first one because when he looked into the bathroom he saw a shelf stacked with creams and bath powders and things, and he was sure they belonged to Pinkie.

"They belong to my mother," says the other young man hastily. "She's here for the weekend. She goes in for bath powder in a large way."

"Well, I suppose you don't mind if I go up through your skylight," says Adam. "It would save a lot of bother."

"Not at all," says the other young man, cordially.

They both disappear and in a very few minutes reappear together at Pinkie's door, and having done this little job of work together they are now the best of friends.

"Isn't that lovely!" exclaims Pinkie, walking into her flat. "Isn't it lovely, Hester! We shan't have to spend the night in the streets. Do come in, everybody. I'm sure you want something to eat. I'm simply starving."

We all go in. Pinkie throws off her coat and dashes into the kitchen to see what she can find. The two young men vie with each other in being helpful. Adam carries in a tray with plates and knives and a loaf of bread, Pinkie follows with a tinned tongue and a dish of butter. Four glasses are produced and an assortment of bottles from a cupboard in the dining room. The other young man does yeoman service with a corkscrew.

"Cider for me," says Pinkie as she lays the table. "I expect Hester would like cider—there's beer and gin and vermouth—or whisky and soda. Guthrie can get any amount of it, so don't worry."

During these activities it has become known that the second young man's name is Frank and the others call him Frank without hesitation.

"Another knife, Frank," says Pinkie. "In the right hand drawer . . . oh, and a spoon for the jam while you're about it."

My job has been to blow up the fire, which was nearly out, and by the time I have got it blazing cheerfully the meal is prepared and we all sit down.

"This is a lovely party," says Pinkie rapturously. "It's the very nicest sort of party in the world, so unexpected and jolly. Half an hour ago we didn't know each other and here we are—all friends."

It is true, of course. As I sit back in my chair (for to tell the truth I am tired, not having the stamina of extreme youth to endure fatigue and excitement) I reflect that, although life today is less gracious and a good deal less comfortable than it used to be when I was Pinkie's age, the young of today have something that we lacked. They are so eager and willing to help one another, they are so unself-conscious, so frank and easy and sincere. They are generous and open-handed, sharing what they have and never counting the cost.

"It was nothing," Adam is saying. "I mean I liked doing it frightfully. I mean—well—to tell you the truth life is a bit dull nowadays. This time last year we were swanning along madly on tanks. It was tremendous sport—"

"I was at Sudlöhn with the Guards Armored," says Frank. "Yes, just a year ago, today. We found an egg-packing factory, bung full of fresh eggs and they doled them out to practically everyone in the Division. It was a great day, I can tell you."

"That's the sort of thing people remember," says Pinkie regretfully. "I mean people don't tell you about battles, they tell you where they got fresh eggs."

"Because they seemed more important," explains Frank. "There were skirmishes all the time. We were moving up pretty fast and the center line was so narrow that sometimes it scarcely existed at all—the fighting was an everyday job, but the eggs were a treat."

Pinkie gives him up in despair and turning to Adam enquires about his roof-climbing affrays.

"Oh well," says Adam, trying to play up. "Most of our roof-fighting was before we crossed the Rhine. There was one town we had to clear and we did it almost entirely by roof. We mopped it up good and proper taking it house by house. It was frightfully exciting because the Boches still had a lot of fight in them—or at least some of them had. You never knew whether they were going to throw up their hands or fight it out so you had to be pretty careful."

"I was wounded at Visselhoevede," says Frank, taking up the tale. "That was the eighteenth of April—a pretty big show, it was. We attacked the place from two directions. It was rather sickening to be wounded just at the end, like that. I should like to have seen it through."

We eat and drink and talk, but by this time I am so sleepy that I can hardly keep my eyes open, and although it is all extremely interesting I am not sorry when our visitors depart and we can go to bed. Just as I am dropping off to sleep Pinkie calls out to me that she has found the key, it was in the drawer of her dressing table.

Tuesday, 9th April

Pinkie and I have breakfast together. The little sitting room is flooded with sunshine and as spick-and-span and shining as a new pin—all traces of last night's carousal have vanished. On being questioned Pinkie admits that she always gets up early and does most of her housework before breakfast, in this way she provides a nice long easy day for herself. It is obvious that whatever she does suits her admirably for she is in blooming health and full of vitality.

Betty's train is due at twelve o'clock and as usual I find myself at the station far too early. Tim has tried for eighteen years to break me of the habit of being too soon for every appointment (a habit which he considers a positive vice and worse than the opposite extreme) but he has had no success and I still continue to waste my time in this reprehensible manner. As I wander up and down the platform I observe a number of people congregating—people of about my own age and very much my own type—and I realize that these must be "parents" like myself. Some of these people have met each other before and greet each other cordially, others walk past each other with elaborate disinterest. Nobody shows the slightest inclination to speak to me.

The train arrives at last. The doors are flung open and out pours a flood of girls, all arrayed alike in camel-hair coats and green berets, all carrying little suitcases and hockey sticks; they are all about the same size—or so it seems to me—they are all plump and rosy and full of the joy of life. In fact they are so alike that I am assailed by the conviction that I shall not recognize my own child and am quite panic-stricken in consequence—quite forgetting that if the worst comes to the worst it is more than probable my own child will recognize me. I am still looking wildly up and down when I am almost knocked flat on my back by a very large child throwing itself into my arms and shouting "Mummy!"

"Betty!" I gasp. "Goodness, how you've grown!"

"I haven't," says Betty, hugging me. "Or at least not enough to notice—I couldn't have in six weeks. Good-bye Sonia!" cries Betty disengaging herself and waving frantically to her friends. "Good-bye Jane—see you next term—good-bye Barbara—"

Somehow or other we extricate ourselves and Betty's luggage from the crowd.

After the first excitement of seeing each other has died down Betty becomes rather silent and it is not until we are safely in the train bound for Ryddelton that I begin to hear about school. The train is full, so we are jammed up together in a corner of the compartment, and at first Betty is stiff and unresponsive, her body is like a piece of wood; but presently she relaxes and leans her head against me and all is well.

"This is lovely," says Betty.

"Lovely. I've missed you frightfully."

"So have I, though I didn't really know I was missing you until now."

"I'm glad you didn't know."

"I'm glad, too," says Betty frankly. "Some of the girls are awfully miserable at first—but as a matter of fact there was such a lot to do at school that I didn't have time to miss anybody. It's very interesting—much more interesting than old Miss Clarke's—and of course I've got heaps of friends. We acted a play—it was *Midsummer Night's Dream*. I was Puck."

"Puck!" I exclaim in surprise—for there is nothing very fairylike about my daughter.

"Yes, it was tremendous fun scattering poppy dust on people's eyes. Have you ever seen the play?" enquires Betty.

"Not for a long time, I'm afraid."

"I'll tell you about it," says Betty eagerly.

The way is beguiled by Betty's exposition of *Midsummer Night's Dream* and presently we reach Ryddelton and are met by Todd and driven in a competent manner to Tocher House.

It is late when we arrive and Erica has retired to her room, but Annie is waiting for us and she and Betty greet one another affectionately.

"I can hardly wait till tomorrow to see everything," declares Betty. "It's a marvelous place, isn't it? Wouldn't it be a lovely house for hide-and-seek?"

I explain hastily that such a thing is impossible, she must be very quiet and good.

"Oh, I'll be good," says Betty nodding. "But I can't promise to be quiet, it's far too difficult. Some people are made that way so it's easy for them, but I don't seem to be able to *move* without making a noise."

Although I am very tired after all my adventures I lie awake for a long time worrying about the difficulties which loom ahead. Betty is larger than ever and more than ever full of abounding energy and life. I would not change her if I could, of course, for it is natural and right that a child of her age should be full of high spirits—but how am I to keep her in the background and ensure that she shall not annoy my employer? There are two problems here: first I must see to it that Betty has plenty of scope, for it is her holiday and I want her to enjoy herself; second I must see that she keeps out of Erica's way and does not upset the elderly guests with her chatter. I am too busy to look after Betty, and Annie has her own work—her days are full. There is Margaret McQueen, of course, but she cannot be saddled with Betty from morning to night.

I toss and turn. It is going to be very difficult. I decide that I shall have to leave Tocher House and take rooms elsewhere. Perhaps Betty and I could go back to Donford —Grace might find me some place to go. What a fool I was not to think of all this before and make arrangements for Betty's holidays!

Wednesday, *10th April*

Various matters over which I have no control conspire to make me late for breakfast and when I reach the dining room and slide in between the screens I discover Erica and Betty seated at the table eating bacon and eggs. This discovery surprises me considerably for I told Betty last night that she was to have her meals in the other room and Betty seemed to understand the situation and accept it as a natural dispensation. I am about to remove my child with suitable apologies but am prevented from speech by the cordial nature of my reception. Betty leaps up and hugs me ecstatically and Erica says she's thankful to see me and how was Edinburgh looking. Curry arrives with a plate of porridge and the next moment I have taken my seat at the table and said nothing.

It is obvious that I have interrupted a conversation and now that I am settled it continues amicably. The subject is hockey. Betty is a novice of course, but is tremendously keen on the game and when she discovers—by dint of questioning—that Erica when young was a member of the Scottish Ladies International team her eyes nearly fall out with surprise. They talk about bullies and shooting goals and other matters of importance and as I have never played hockey in my life I am obliged to hold my tongue.

Betty is finished first, she asks if she may go, and on receiving permission from her hostess goes with all speed to explore the domains. It is now time for me to tackle Erica.

"I'm sorry, Erica," I tell her. "I'm afraid Betty can't have understood the arrangement about meals."

"She understood perfectly," replies Erica, seizing the last roll and tearing it apart. "I saw Betty in the garden before breakfast and arranged for her to have her meals with us."

"But Erica!" I cry. "Why on earth did you—"

"Be calm."

"Listen, Erica. You said you didn't like children, so it will be much better—"

"I do *not* like children," says Erica firmly. "Pass the marmalade, please."

"Well, then—"

"Betty is a person—an individual. Say no more."

I disobey the injunction. "You may get bored with her chatter," I declare.

"You do your daughter injustice, Hester. Betty is quite sensible enough to see if her chatter is boring me and desist. Parents are always unjust to their children," continues Erica. "They are either foolishly fond or else they fly to the other extremes. A parent is biased by affection, prejudiced by familiarity which breeds contempt."

"I think you're talking nonsense, Erica."

"Possibly," say Erica calmly as she gathers up her letters and goes away.

My morning is so busy that I have no time to think about Betty, but she appears at lunch looking clean and tidy.

Erica enquires where she has been and what she has

seen, to which Betty replies that she has been a long way and it was lovely.

"I don't call that much of an answer," says Erica drily.

Thus challenged Betty becomes rather pink and says she didn't know Miss Clutterbuck wanted a full account of her morning's rambles. Sometimes people ask you things and don't really want to know.

Erica admits that this is true, but adds that she is not one of those people. If she asks a question she likes it answered thoroughly.

Betty looks a little thoughtful and then says it really *was* lovely; she went down the avenue and across the road and up through a field which was being ploughed by a man driving a red tractor, the earth which was newly turned looked good enough to eat—just like the chocolate truffles Mummy used to buy at Fortnum and Mason. There was a hawthorn hedge up the side of the field and it was covered with green buds which reminded Betty of the poem by Browning—"Oh, To Be in England Now That April's There." There were huge bushes of gorse—some of them in flower, all golden and lovely with the sun shining on the flowers. At the top of the field the earth was redder— not like chocolate—and there was a gate leading into a wood. The ploughman was sitting there having his dinner, he had cold tea in a tin can and some meat pies rolled up in a red cotton handkerchief. It was lucky he was there because there were doves in the wood—you could hear them cooing—and he was able to tell Betty that they were "cushat doos." (Betty thinks they are called that because of the lovely sleepy sound they make). She talked to him for a bit and then went on, skirting the wood. Here and there she saw chestnut trees with sticky brown buds, and the larches had green button buds on them. It was high up, of course. She looked down into the valley and saw little farms, whitewashed, with slate roofs—and one of them had a pond, shaped like an eye. It was as blue as the sea in the middle of a very green field and there were geese near it. Far in the distance she saw the town of Ryddelton, hidden in the haze of its own smoke. The sky was as blue as blue, says Betty, and the sun was warm and golden. She thinks Tocher is the most beautiful place in the world.

Erica listens to all this quite patiently (she could do no less having asked for it) but obviously she has had enough. When Betty pauses for breath she says, "You seem to have used your eyes to good effect. Use your teeth now."

Betty smiles and tucks into her dinner—nor does she utter another sound.

This episode pleases me and I address myself, silently, in the following words: My dear Hester, if you would cease worrying about things which have not happened you would spare yourself some grey hairs. You worried yourself silly about Erica and Betty—and you see how unnecessary it was. Erica and Betty understand one another very well (if you want to be quite honest they understand one another a deal better than you do). They are the same kind— in a way—or at least much more the same kind than you are. They will be very good for each other, that's obvious. Erica will benefit from having somebody in the house who has no fear of her and will take her at her word without the slightest hesitation, and Betty will take no harm from being gently squashed. You can sit back quite comfortably and leave them to work it out.

After lunch I pursue Margaret McQueen to her bedroom (she spends most of her time there for she shuns the society of the other guests) and I find her sitting near the window with a book on her lap; but she is not reading the book, she is gazing out of the window at the trees; her face is very pale and wears an expression of hopeless misery. I knew that Margaret was unhappy, of course, but today I have caught her off her guard and I am quite horrified at her appearance. Something will have to be done about Margaret, she can't be left alone.

"What do you want?" she asks looking round at me, her eyes vague, as if she had been far away and suddenly called back to earth by my entrance.

I hand over the eighty pounds in notes—and to tell the truth I am glad to get rid of them.

"Eighty!" exclaims Margaret incredulously.

"The diamonds were good."

"You couldn't have got all that for the ring!"

"Where do you think it came from?" I enquire jokingly.

This question is unanswerable, and Margaret does not attempt the impossible; she thanks me for my help and compliments me on my cleverness. It seems to me that the least she can do is to ask me to sit down for a few moments, but Margaret thinks otherwise; in fact she makes it plain that having been suitably thanked I should go away and leave her to be miserable in peace.

I hesitate for a moment and then sit down on the window seat.

"Did you enjoy yourself in Edinburgh?" enquires Margaret making the best of a bad job.

"Very much," I reply. "But I don't want to talk about that. I want to talk about your affairs, please."

"I told you not to," says Margaret fiercely.

"I know, but—"

"I can manage my own affairs perfectly well without interference from other people."

This opening is unpromising—indeed Margaret looks so disagreeable that I feel inclined to give up the struggle and leave her alone—but there is nobody else to help her.

"I think it's a good thing to talk to somebody about your affairs," I tell her in reasoning tones.

"I can't," she replies. "I don't want to. I wish I hadn't told you anything."

"I'm worried about you, Margaret."

"Don't worry, I shall get over it, I expect. People can't go on being miserable forever—or can they?" says Margaret listlessly.

"I wish you would see Mr. Elden."

"I *did* see him," she replies. "He came over one day and I spoke to him in the lounge."

"What good was that?"

"It was no good at all."

"Of course it wasn't. Why don't you give him a chance to talk to you privately?"

She hesitates and then says in a low voice. "He's in Ryddelton, you know. I can't bear it. I wish he would go away—if he doesn't go away I shall have to leave Tocher House."

"Where would you go?"

"Anywhere," she replies. "Some place where. I could get a cheap room—I've been making enquiries. I can't stay on here knowing he's at Ryddelton, so near—just a few miles away—it makes me feel quite frantic . . ."

"I wonder why."

"Because I love him, of course," cries Margaret, cover-

ing her face with her hands. "That's the awful thing; I
love him dearly. I knew it when he walked into the lounge
—I could have wept—I felt as if my bones had turned to
water. It's because I love him that I won't marry him."

"Why? I don't understand."

She hesitates. "Oh, what's the use of talking?" she says,
relapsing into listnessness again. "I've been over it all a thousand times. If you don't understand no amount of explaining will help. I've told you already he deserves somebody
better, somebody who isn't worn out and all on edge."

"But he wants you," I murmur. "He doesn't want somebody else."

"He wouldn't want me if he knew what I was like."

"Give him a chance," I plead. "Surely you can see him
and let him have his say. Tell him what you feel about it."

"I've answered that already. We're going round in
circles."

"You haven't answered it. You haven't told me why you
won't see him."

There is a little pause and then she says firmly, "Please
don't talk about it anymore."

The conversation is now at an end. The case seems
hopeless and I would fain take Margaret and knock her
red-gold head against the wall, so stubborn and stupid does
her attitude seem to me. Fortunately I have sufficient self-
control to refrain from such drastic measures, but I cannot
resist a parting word.

"I think you're mad," I tell her, as I rise and make for
the door. "You're making yourself miserable—that's your
own affair, of course—but you're making Roger Elden miserable, too—and all for a stupid quibble. Why can't you
make up your mind to marry the man and do your best to

make him happy?"

"You think I'm a coward!" exclaims Margaret, looking at me with a startled air.

"Of course you're a coward!" I cry and with that I go out, closing the door behind me and leaving her to her thoughts.

Friday, 12th April

Erica has had a cold for the last two days but nothing will induce her to stay in bed. Today however she has lost her voice and feels so wretched that she consents to go to bed after lunch. I suggest that the doctor should be summoned but Erica doesn't believe in doctors; she hasn't seen a doctor for years, croaks Erica, and if she goes to bed she will be perfectly well tomorrow. It is something to get her to go to bed and I leave the question of a doctor in abeyance; I administer an aspirin, fill a hot-water bottle for her and fly to my room where I proceed to heat a kaolin poultice which will relieve the congestion in her vocal tubes.

By the time this is ready, plastered on a piece of lint and carried along the passage between two plates, Erica is in bed. She is attired in the famous pink nightgown with the frill round her neck; her face is very red and her eyes are very bright and she is in the most appalling temper.

"What do you want now?" enquires Erica hoarsely.

"I've made a little poultice for you," I reply in dulcet tones.

"You're not going to put *that* on *me*."

"It will do you good—honestly, it will."

"It will not," she replies, holding her nightgown together across her chest and glaring at me. "It will not do me good because I am not going to have it on me."

"Please, Erica—"

"*No.*"

"Why not?"

"I hate poultices. They make a rash on my skin. I've got a very tender skin; I can't *stand* anything hot—"

"Erica, listen."

"I will not listen. Look at the horrible sticky mess— and hot as hell, I suppose. Take it away. Take it away at once."

"Come on, Erica. Don't be silly."

"Silly, yourself," croaks Erica. "You'll burn me—that's what you'll do. Go away and leave me in peace. I will *not* have the stuff on my chest."

I lay the poultice on the dressing table and approach my patient intending to reason with her, intending to persuade her into a better frame of mind, but at this moment the door opens and Hope appears.

"Oh, Miss Clutterbuck!" exclaims Hope breathlessly. "If only you'd told me I'd have come before—I didn't know you were ill."

"It's all right," I reply. "Miss Clutterbuck has a bad cold so she has gone to bed. I've given her a hot-water bottle."

"I'd have done it," declares Hope. "I can look after her. It's my job, Mrs. Christie."

The situation is extremely delicate and requires careful handling. I explain that I thought Hope was busy and that this is the reason I have taken it upon myself to play the part of nurse, but Hope is not easily appeased, she repeats that it is her job, not mine, to look after Miss Clutterbuck, and bewails the fact that she was not summoned to fill the hot-water bottle and prepare the bed.

"Don't be ridiculous, Hope," says Erica in a feeble croak.

"It's brownkitis you've got!" cries Hope in horrified accents. "Brownkitis or pewmonia—it's settled on your chest. I'll telephone the doctor to come."

"You will not," declares Erica. "I have a slight cold— that's all."

During this discussion the poultice has been lying upon the dressing table, cooling rapidly, and I decide to have a last try to place it upon my patient's chest. I take it up and approach the bed with a determined air.

"What's that?" asks Hope, looking at it.

"A kaolin poultice," I reply.

"She'd be better with a *proper* poultice, I don't believe in that newfangled stuff. Linseed and mustard is the thing, that's what the doctor would say."

"Kaolin is very good."

"Linseed and mustard," says Hope, firmly. "That's nasty and sticky. Miss Clutterbuck wouldn't like it."

As Hope is standing like a rock between me and the bed I am obliged to halt, we look at one another and there is a moment's silence. The situation, which on the surface might seem absurd, is not absurd to me; for I am aware that if Hope gets her way she will despise me forever and my relations with her will be impossible.

"Please move, Hope," I say as calmly as I can manage. "Miss Clutterbuck should have this poultice while it is hot."

Hope does not move an inch. "Linseed and mustard," she repeats. "I'll go and make it myself."

At this moment—while I am wondering what on earth to do and wishing with all my heart that I could see a way out of the impasse—a hoarse voice from the bed says plaintively, "How much longer have I got to wait?"

Erica has bared her chest.

The spell is broken; Hope moves; I advance and lay the poultice in the correct position. It is comfortably tucked in and covered with a large piece of cotton wool.

"How does that feel?" I enquire with solicitude.

"Very comfortable, thank you," says Erica aloud; adding in a low whisper "Curse you!"

I turn away hastily to hide my smile and busy myself tidying up Erica's clothes which she has flung down in a heap on the floor. Hope watches me for a moment and then departs, shutting the door behind her with unusual care.

"A nice exhibition!" remarks Erica.

"It was decent of you, I admit."

"I had no alternative. What could I do but allow you to put the blue-pencil thing on my chest?"

"It isn't too hot, is it?"

Eric does not answer that. Perhaps it was too much to expect. She says firmly, "Hope must really go this time."

"Not because of me. I don't mind—at least not much—and I'm only here temporarily as you know. Perhaps it would be better for me to go."

"You know perfectly well I wouldn't let you go."

"Leave it, then," I tell her. "Perhaps Hope will be better after this. Don't worry about it."

"I'm not worrying."

I have now finished tidying the room and am about to go.

"Hester!" says Erica, raising herself on one elbow and scowling at me fiercely. "Hester, you've got everything your own way, haven't you?"

"Yes, I suppose so," I admit.

"Well, don't take this as a precedent, that's all," says Erica crossly.

Betty and I have been invited to tea at the Rydd Arms Hotel with Mr. Elden and his daughter Sheila who has come there to spend the holidays. We borrow the car and set forth, attired in our best clothes as befits the occasion. Our host and hostess are waiting for us on the steps, they greet us cordially and soon we are sitting at a round table in the dining-room window indulging in a very ample tea. Although Sheila is just the same age as Betty she is much smaller and thinner, she looks delicate and has a sad little face which lights up into a very sweet smile when she is interested or amused. She and Betty are silent at first, measuring each other carefully, and the conversation is left to Mr. Elden and myself; but tea and scones have a mellowing effect and Betty's tongue begins to wag in its usual haphazard manner. Sheila's reserve vanishes swiftly and chat and giggles take the place of stiff politeness; they are getting along like a house on fire.

Mr. Elden watches the transformation with a pleased smile but fortunately he is too sensible to make any comment. We continue to discuss world affairs and agree that the prospect at the moment is far from rosy. The other conversation is much more lively, bits of it come to my ears between the gloomy remarks of Mr. Elden, and I realize that Betty and Sheila are comparing notes about school and Betty is telling Sheila all about *Midsummer Night's Dream*.

After tea the girls go out into the garden and disappear from view.

"It's grand," says Mr. Elden. "I wondered what would happen. Sheila is so shy that it's difficult for her to make friends. She's far too old for her age, but that's because she hasn't got other children to play with, I'm afraid."

"Betty is very young for her age."

"I know," agrees Mr. Elden. "She'll be very good for Sheila. I do hope you will let Betty come over as often as possible."

"And Sheila must come to Tocher—you, too, of course."

"Sheila would love to," he replies. "As for me I feel I had better stay away. You know why, don't you, Mrs. Tim?"

"I wish you could see her properly!" I exclaim. "If only you could see her and have a good talk I'm sure it would all come right."

"How can I force myself upon her?"

"You must," I tell him earnestly. "Do try to get hold of her. She's very unhappy, you know."

He says nothing in answer to this appeal and looks so stern and sad that I can go no further. I long to tell him the whole story and explain Margaret's attitude but somehow I can't.

As we drive home Betty and I talk about our afternoon's entertainment—Betty is full of her new friend. "She's nice," says Betty earnestly. "Oh dear, I do wish she could come to Dinwell Hall instead of that dull school she goes to! I'm sorry for Sheila, you know. I thought at first it must be rather fun to be Sheila, but now I don't."

"Why did you think it must be fun?" I enquire, struggling with the gears of the car.

"She can do exactly as she likes," replies Betty. "She can—really. She can choose her own clothes and do what she likes all the time just like a grown-up person. I thought that sounded fun."

"Isn't it fun?"

"No," says Betty seriously. "You see if you haven't anybody to keep you in order you have to keep yourself in order —so Sheila says. That's why she's a little sad and grown-up, you know. Did you notice she was like that, Mummy?"

"Yes, I did."

"That's why," says Betty with a sigh. "She has nobody to tell her to go to bed—her father just lets her go to bed when she wants to. You'd think that would be lovely, but it isn't. Sheila goes to bed at half-past eight every night because that's the proper time for someone who is twelve, and she can't choose the sort of clothes she wants, because they wouldn't be suitable and people would say, 'Poor Sheila hasn't got a mother to choose her clothes.' That would be awful," says Betty. "She couldn't bear them to pity her because it would look as if her father was neglecting her. She thinks her father is perfect. Perhaps he is—for a father," adds Betty doubtfully.

"I'm sure he does his best," I offer, shaken to the core at this revelation. "It's rather difficult for him. Perhaps we could help a little, could we?"

"If she would let us, but I don't think she would. She's sort of—proud," says Betty, trying hard to explain. "She wouldn't like people to interfere. There's only one thing that could really make things right."

"What's that?" I ask with interest.

"Well—I'm afraid it's a secret," replies Betty regretfully. "Sheila told me about it, but it's the most confidential secret on earth. I promised faithfully, cross my heart, I wouldn't mention it to a single solitary soul."

Erica has made a very rapid recovery; which I assure her is due to the beneficent effect of the poultice, but which she puts down to her own strength of will. The great thing is, says Erica, to make up your mind to get well quickly. Nothing else is any good at all. I persuade her to take one more day of leisure to complete the cure, and this she consents to do, chiefly because she is anxious to be in full fighting trim for a fête which is to be held at Ryddelton Park, tomorrow afternoon. The fête is in aid of the Thistle Foundation, to provide houses for seriously disabled soldiers. We have been hearing about this fête for some time, Erica has attended meetings to organize the arrangements and as she is a born organizer with dynamic drive most of the work has been done by her. She dislikes meetings intensely—or so she would have us believe—but I notice that she returns from them full of vim and vigor with the light of battle, and of victory, blazing in her eye. It is difficult to know whether to be sorry for the other members of the committee, who are obliged to bow their heads before her, or to envy them for having amongst them a woman who will shoulder all the burdens provided she is allowed to have her own way.

The last three days have been busy days for me, but the work does not worry me now, for I know exactly how to tackle it. The only thing that worries me is the way time flies, there are not enough hours in the day to accomplish all I want to do.

At lunch time I receive a letter from Tim and here at last is an account of his dream which I have been trying to get out of him for the last two months and which has teased my mind off and on since he mentioned it last February.

"You know how difficult it is to describe a dream," writes Tim. "And as a matter of fact you seem to have attached so much importance to it that you may find my description a bit of an anticlimax. The only important thing about it is I saw you so clearly. You were standing in a garden wearing a blue dress and there were pigeons flying round you. They were flying down from the trees and picking up crumbs which you were scattering on the grass. That's absolutely all. It doesn't sound much, but it made a great impression upon me at the time. It was so vivid that I wondered whether I had really *seen* you—silly, wasn't it? Talking of pigeons I was very interested to hear about Todd's. I hope Max won his race and brought glory to the Tocher loft. Todd sounds a nice fellow, I should like to have a talk with him someday. You, yourself, sound much more cheerful so perhaps after all it was a good idea to take that job, but you will have to give it up in the summer and go to Cobstead with Bryan and Betty for the holidays. I wish there were some prospect of my being free to join you but it is no use holding out any hopes of that. No chance of leave, either, I'm afraid."

There are several things to think about in Tim's letter: the dream, for instance. At first I feel a little disappointed, for it seems tame after all my lively imaginings, but after a few moments' consideration I decide there is something very odd about it, something rather alarming. I never fed pigeons until I came to Tocher House—months after Tim's dream. What is the explanation? Was it merely coincidence that Tim should dream of me scattering crumbs for pigeons, or was it prophetic—a shadow of things to come? If so my coming to Tocher House was foreordained, not merely the outcome of chance and my own impulsive action. Do I believe that everything in life is foreordained? No, I feel sure that we have a free choice, that we can take this path, or that. I could not bear to think that our lives are planned in advance; it would be incredibly dull to say the least of it . . . and if our actions were ordained beforehand all responsibility would be removed from our shoulders and there would be no credit in behaving well, no shame in behaving badly. No, I shall continue to believe that I came to Tocher House of my own free will . . . Tim's dream must remain an unexplained and unexplainable mystery.

Wednesday, 17th April

Erica comes down to breakfast in good spirits and says she is as fit as a fiddle. It is the day of the fête at Ryddelton Park. The hall is decorated with an enormous poster which gives full information about the Thistle Foundation, and a bus has been chartered to convey the guests of Tocher House to the scene of revelry. Erica—in her usual downright way—has made it perfectly clear that she expects all her guests to attend and to spend as much money as possible in aid of the disabled soldiers. It is decreed that Erica and I are to go early, in the car, which will then return to Tocher to fetch any members of the staff who can be spared from their duties. Betty is going with Margaret McQueen.

We meet at lunch as usual and discuss the arrangements. Everything seems to promise well; the day is fine, telephone messages from Ryddelton have announced the arrival of the band and of the Very Important Person who is to declare the fête open. The only piece of bad news amongst the good is that the fortune-teller who was engaged by Erica to come from Glasgow and exercise her art for the benefit of the wounded soldiers has developed acute appendicitis and is even now in a Glasgow hospital having her appendix removed.

"It's perfectly sickening," says Erica fiercely. "The woman promised to come."

"She can't help having appendicitis," says Betty reasonably.

"She's that sort of person," declares Erica. "She's the sort of person who *would* have appendicitis at the wrong moment . . . if only we had known sooner we could have got somebody else. Everything is ready and we've advertised a fortune-teller so people will be disappointed—besides it's always a tremendous draw and makes *pounds* at a fête like this."

"Mummy could do it," says Betty offering the suggestion hopefully.

"Indeed I couldn't!" I cry in alarm.

"Could you, Hester?" enquires Erica.

"Of course she could," declares Betty. "Mummy can tell marvelous fortunes with cards. It's absolutely thrilling —all about dark men and journeys and things."

"I couldn't, possibly."

"I believe you could," says Erica, looking at me with a gleam in her eye.

"No!" I cry. "No, you don't understand. I can tell fortunes to amuse the children, but—"

"That's settled, then," says Erica firmly.

I assure Erica it is anything but settled. How can I possibly tell fortunes to complete strangers? I am not nearly good enough for that. People will see through me and be furious; they will demand their money back. There will be a riot—

"Nonsense," says Erica, interrupting. "You can do it perfectly well. Just tell them what they want to know, that's all."

"How shall I know what they want to know?"

Erica does not hear this, of course. "Nobody will recognize you," she continues. "You're the very person for the job. I've got a black wig and we can do up your face—and the tent will be dark. Where did I put those curtains? I believe they're in the attic—"

I interrupt to enquire whether I was engaged to help to run a hotel or to tell fortunes disguised in a black wig. I point out that this is my afternoon off. I complain of a headache. I assert that my husband would object most strongly to the whole affair. I remind Erica that I have already put in four hours work and cannot complete my duties in less than three more hours . . . but Erica has an answer to most of my objections, and the ones to which she can find no answer she pretends not to hear.

Thus it is that at three o'clock on this beautiful sunny afternoon I find myself immured in a dimly lit tent, heavily disguised in a black wig and spectacles, and draped in a red cloak. The tent is extremely stuffy and it is all the more stuffy because of the blackout curtains which Erica has unearthed from the attics of Tocher House and brought along with her to produce the necessary atmosphere of gloom and mystery. Erica has done everything with her usual force and thoroughness. She has clothed and painted me and brought me to the scene of action in a closed car. I have been provided with a helper (a fat girl attired in a curious medley of garments which is Erica's idea of what a gypsy should wear). I have been provided with a name— Madame Katinka; I have been provided with a very ancient and dog-eared pack of cards.

"Speak with a foreign accent," says Erica as she arranges the folds of my cloak.

"What kind of accent?"

"Any kind—except German, of course. To Ryddelton people all foreigners are much the same."

"I don't like it, Erica. I feel the most awful imposter."

"You *are* an imposter," says Erica. "All fortune-tellers are imposters and everybody knows they are. It's just a joke."

"As long as everybody knows it's a joke . . ." I remark feebly.

Unfortunately my first victim is a young man—obviously a farmer—and as I had prepared myself for a woman this necessitates a rapid rearrangement of ideas. Instead of prattling gaily about dark men and cradles I must think of something to interest a man. His cards are no help, they are full of horrors and, as I have decided to avoid frightening people with coffins and bad news from across the sea, I cannot read them to him as they fall. I do my best for him but I can see he is not particularly pleased with his half crown's worth and is slightly sceptical of the fair lady whom I have invented for his benefit. My second and third victims are girls and very much easier to do. They help me a good deal by asking leading questions and giggle delightedly when I supply the answers they desire. Soon I begin to get into my stride and when Mrs. Maloney appears and takes her seat opposite to me I am ready for a little fun. The patience with which I have listened to Mrs. Maloney's stories is now rewarded and—secure in my impenetrable disguise—I delve into her past and reveal many curious incidents which have happened to her. As regards her character and her future I tell her exactly what she wants to know and she leaves the tent with a dazed expression upon her large fat face. Mrs. Maloney will be a good advertisement for Madame Katinka and my fame will be spread amongst the other guests of Tocher House.

Victim follows victim in swift succession and my helper is kept very busy ushering them in and letting them out. The people I know are much the most fun, of course. It is amusing to tell Miss Dove that she has a large circle of friends with whom she corresponds and to advise her that in her particular case the morning is the luckiest time for writing letters. Somewhat to my surprise Miss Dove is followed by Hope, dressed in her best clothes and looking a good deal less disagreeable than usual. Annie has told me quite a lot about Hope so it is easy to recreate her past and establish belief in my mysterious powers. The cards fall well for Hope, they are lucky cards. A dark man is coming towards her across the water with money in his pockets; there is a letter in the post which will bring her good news —all this I tell her faithfully and Hope is suitably impressed—but the last hand is different, the cards are all black, foretelling death and disaster, and as I have no wish to depress the woman and add to her gloom I must make up something more cheerful. I hesitate for a moment and then I say that lately a fair woman has come into Hope's life, the woman wishes her well and should be treated with consideration.

Poor Hope is somewhat taken aback at this pronouncement and goes away looking extremely thoughtful.

Time goes on and I begin to feel quite dazed . . . and then suddenly Mr. Elden appears and sits down in the victim's chair. He is wearing an indulgent smile; it is obvious that he does not believe in Madame Katinka's occult powers and is merely having his fortune told for a joke, or perhaps because Sheila urged him to try it. The indulgent smile annoys me—quite unreasonably, of course—and I decide to be very serious. The cards are shuffled and spread out upon the table; I study them carefully.

"What do you see?" enquires Mr. Elden.

I tell him that I see a tall slim lady with golden-red hair.

This surprises my victim a good deal and the indulgent smile vanishes. But I must not seem too clever so I play for safety with the usual patter about money and journeys and letters in the post.

Mr. Elden is bored. He interrupts to ask if there is any more about the lady.

I reply by telling him that the future is very vague.

"Vague?" he repeats questioningly.

I shake my head doubtfully and say that the cards cannot tell. It may be that the lady is going on a long journey in the near future . . . but it is not certain.

"Would another half crown help to clear things up at all?" enquires Mr. Elden.

At this I pretend to be annoyed and declare that I am telling him all I can. He may shuffle the cards again if he likes and wish a wish.

He shuffles the cards and I lay them out on the table.

"Do I get my wish?" asks Mr. Elden quite eagerly.

This gives me a grand opportunity and I seize it at once. I tell him that it remains in his own hands whether or not he will attain his wish. Prompt and vigorous action will bring him his heart's desire.

"Prompt and vigorous action!" repeats Mr. Elden in surprise.

I tell him there are obstacles to be overcome but happiness lies ahead if he can overcome them. He must not let things drift.

"Do you really see all that in the cards?" asks Mr. Elden incredulously.

"How else should I see?" I reply in sulky tones.

"Heaven knows!" exclaims Mr. Elden. He puts down a ten-shilling note and goes away.

This exciting interview is the climax of the afternoon, after it comes boredom and exhaustion. My head aches and I have no more ideas left; the tent becomes hotter and hotter and I can feel the grease paint melting and running down my face. At last I can stand it no longer and we shut up shop. My helper closes the doors and puts up a notice to say that Madame Katinka has finished for the afternoon. I clean my face, doff my disguise and emerge from the tent into the brilliant sunshine ravening for a cup of tea.

The first person I see on approaching the tea tent is Hope. I take action to avoid her of course (it is our habit to avoid one another whenever possible) but Hope pursues me and instead of glowering at me in her usual thunderous manner she smiles at me pleasantly and says it is a nice day for the fête, a change of heart so astounding that I can find no words in which to reply. Fortunately Hope does not seem to mind, she says she has had a very good tea and advises me to ask for chocolate cake which is kept "under the counter".

The discovery that Madame Katinka has made such a profound impression upon Hope is rather alarming, for it places an enormous responsibility upon my shoulders— a responsibility from which I shrink. Hope has taken my words to heart and has lost no time in acting upon them

—will others do the same? I sip tea and munch chocolate cake and reflect upon my afternoon's work with growing disquiet. Have my idle words altered lives, brought unsuitable people together and roused expectations of wealth which can never be satisfied?

So far Betty has behaved in an exemplary manner, but today she is late for lunch. She rushes in, panting, her hands unwashed, her hair unbrushed and her shoes covered with mud. I am quite horrified of course and reprimand her severely.

"Sorry," says Betty with a gasp. "I found a ruin and I was so busy exploring I forgot the time."

"Salvers Castle," suggests Erica, who seems quite oblivious of Betty's appearance. "Yes, it's a very interesting old place, it belonged to a Border Chief."

This is my castle, of course—the ruin which Mr. Elden and I discovered. I am delighted to hear that my Border Chief existed in fact. Erica says she has a book about the castle and will lend it to me, but Betty is more interested in the present than the past.

"It's a huge place," says Betty. "It's all covered with ivy. I expect there are jackdaws and owls—could we have a picnic there, Miss Clutterbuck? That would be gorgeous."

Erica replies that she does not care for picnics, but Betty can take her food and eat it in the ruins with the jackdaws if that's what she wants.

"It isn't," says Betty frankly. "I want you and Mummy to come, too. Perhaps Sheila would come and we could all play hide-and-seek."

Erica says she does not care for hide-and-seek. She's too old and fat.

"You're not old at all!" cries Betty indignantly. "And you're not fat, either. Fat people are wobbly like Mrs. Maloney. I bet your muscles are as hard as anything," and the temerarious child stretches out her hand and feels Miss Clutterbuck's biceps in a professional manner. "Hard as anything," she repeats, nodding her head.

Far from being resentful of this liberty Miss Clutterbuck smiles in a deprecating manner and admits that her biceps are not bad considering.

It is possible that Erica thinks she will hear no more of Betty's project of a picnic at Salvers Castle, or at any rate that she will hear no more of it for some little time, but knowing my child's persevering and importunate nature I am not in the least surprised when the subject is raised again at the dinner table.

"Could we have it tomorrow, Miss Clutterbuck?" enquires Betty with a persuasive smile.

"Have what?" says Erica.

"The picnic, of course. The weather is so lovely we ought to take advantage of it; we really ought. I could telephone to Sheila and ask her to come over—I'll organize everything if you just say yes."

"Oh well—" says Erica weakly.

"And you'll come!" cries Betty with flattering eagerness.

"I suppose so," says Erica, suitably flattered.

As this is the day for my biweekly shopping expedition it is arranged that I shall pick up Sheila in Ryddelton and bring her back to lunch at Tocher House. Betty, true to her word, has made all the necessary arrangements and Sheila is waiting for me at the post office at half-past twelve. Somehow or other she looks younger today, perhaps it is because she is happy and excited at the prospect of the picnic. She climbs into the car and sits down beside me and off we go.

Sheila is quite different from Betty, she doesn't chatter, she is much more reserved; in fact I find it a little difficult to make suitable conversation.

"Is your father fishing today?" I enquire.

Sheila hesitates and then says, "No, not today, Mrs. Christie."

"What is he doing, then?"

She hesitates even longer, this time, and then replies that he is going out.

I ask if she and Betty have decided what we are to do at the picnic—is it to be hide-and-seek.

"No, not hide-and-seek," says Sheila in a final sort of tone.

After that I decide that suitable conversation cannot be maintained and we accomplish the remainder of the drive in silence.

We all lunch together at Erica's table, and—as is to be expected—we discuss the arrangements which are now complete. Erica, who was very halfhearted before (and prophesied thunder and torrents of rain) has now changed her attitude completely and is as keen as the girls.

"It's a splendid day for a picnic," Erica says. "Couldn't be better—and there won't be any midges so early in the year."

"What about food?" I enquire.

"You mind your own business," says Erica jovially. "Betty and I and Cook have arranged all that. Leave it to us."

I leave it to them with the greatest of pleasure for I have plenty of other things to do—especially as I am to be out for tea and must cram all my work into the early part of the afternoon.

"I'll meet you at the castle about half-past four," I remark, as I rise from my seat at the table.

"No, Mummy!" cries Betty in urgent tones. "You must leave here at four o'clock. It's very important indeed."

"Important?"

"Everything is *timed*. We want you to arrive separately. Please don't be late. Sheila and I are going early because we've got to arrange things before you come."

"Is it a game?" I enquire.

"Sort of," says Betty mysteriously.

I am hard at work in the office when Erica looks in and says she's just off to the picnic and I am to follow at four.

"If I'm ready—"

"Whether you're ready or not," says Erica firmly.

"What is the mystery?" I ask with interest.

"I don't know, but Betty has taken a lot of trouble over it, so don't be late."

Erica vanishes and a few moments later I see her pounding across the lawn towards the woods . . . I can't help smiling to myself at the sight; Betty can now wind Erica round her finger with the greatest ease.

At four o'clock precisely I leave the house and wend my way towards the rendezvous. It really is a beautiful afternoon, the trees are budding and the birds are singing and the sun is shining like burnished gold. Sheila is waiting for me at the entrance to the castle—her eyes are shining like stars and she is a good deal more talkative than usual.

"Oh, Mrs. Christie!" cries Sheila, bounding towards me and taking my hand. "You'll do what we tell you, won't you? It's a sort of game, you see. Betty said you wouldn't mind—I hope it's all right."

I assure her that I am willing to play any part assigned to me, and so I am, for it is good to see Sheila looking happy and childlike, nothing could be better for her than to play childish games. I suggest to Sheila that we might have tea on the little terrace overlooking the Rydd but this is not to be.

"No," says Sheila. "That's where—well anyhow we can't. You're to go through the door and up the steps of the tower. Betty said so."

She leads me to the crumbling steps and releases my hand.

"Are you sure they're safe?" I enquire doubtfully.

"Oh yes," she replies. "Miss Clutterbuck went up and she's twice as heavy as you are."

Thus reassured I mount the stair and discover Erica sitting on a little platform halfway up the tower. The platform has a parapet, waist-high, and from here the view is magnificent, even better than from the terrace.

"How much do you weigh?" enquires Erica. "More than six stone, I'll be bound."

"Much more," I reply. "It was merely a façon de parler. As a matter of fact Sheila is so excited that she scarcely knows what she's saying. It's lovely here, isn't it? I suppose this was a lookout tower in the days of the Border Chief. The stones are quite warm with the sun; but I still think it would be nicer to have tea down there on the terrace, the turf is so soft and—"

"If you would stop prattling for a moment," says Erica sourly—the insult to her weight is still rankling—"Stop prattling and look *down there* at the terrace."

I lean over the parapet and look down . . . and exclaim in horror at the sight of a man lying stretched out upon the ground.

"He's not dead," Erica assures me. "He's entranced, that's all. Poppy dust has been scattered upon his eyelids. I witnessed the performance."

"It's Mr. Elden!"

"So I supposed," says Erica calmly. "Only a fond parent would allow such liberties to be taken with his person. As a matter of fact your daughter was anxious to besprinkle my eyelids with her nauseous herbs—not really poppy dust, she informed me, because neither she nor her friend could find any poppies (hardly surprising in the month of April) but pollen from catkins which they had collected with great difficulty and destruction to their clothes. Betty's knickers suffered severely . . ."

"It's the only decent pair she possesses!" I exclaim in horror.

"In that case she possesses no decent pair," says Erica with brutal candor.

There is a short silence while I digest this information and try to decide whether it will be possible to clothe my child's nether limbs in garments made from an old frock, no coupons being available.

Erica rises, lights a cigarette and leans over the parapet beside me. "Odd creature, Betty," says Erica in a ruminative voice. "Such a mixture of sense and inanity."

"We all are—if it comes to that."

"True, but it shows clearer in Betty. This picnic, for instance. She was most capable in her arrangements, and then all this mystery. There's a sixth guest expected, do you know who it is?"

"No, who is it?"

"I wasn't informed . . . merely drew my conclusions from the fact that there are six cups in the basket . . . I need my tea," she adds, plaintively.

"We should have had tea first and then played the game."

"My good Hester, I suggested that myself, but I was told the poppy dust must take effect before tea."

"What sort of effect, I wonder."

"It's *Midsummer Night's Dream,* you ignorant woman," replies Erica with a grim smile. "Mr. Elden is Lysander, of course. Surely you remember the tale."

"He woke from his trance and saw Hermia and loved her madly, didn't he?"

"Something like that."

"Who is Hermia? You, I suppose."

Erica sighs. She says, "I wasn't told but I have my suspicions."

"And you're willing to cooperate?"

"Oh, I'll go and waken the man if that's what they want," says Erica in resigned tones. "Anything short of kissing him —they wouldn't expect that, would they, Hester?"

I am about to assure her that she must certainly kiss Mr. Elden or the whole thing will fall flat when a diversion is caused by the sound of voices from the main part of the ruins. Erica and I with one accord move over to the other side of the tower and, looking down in that direction, we see Betty appear through the archway leading Margaret Mc-Queen by the hand and encouraging her to brave the nettles.

"It isn't much further—*really*," Betty is saying. "And it's such a lovely view. You'll be surprised, I know you will."

"The sixth guest," says Erica softly. "What a curious choice! She won't add to the gaiety of the picnic, will she?"

I cannot reply for the sight of Margaret has taken my breath away. What on earth will happen when she and Roger Elden meet and are expected to drink tea together in our company? Why didn't Betty tell me she was going to ask Margaret to come? Does Sheila know the state of affairs, or doesn't she?

"This *is* a weird place!" exclaims Margaret, pausing and looking round. "What enormously thick walls! Where's your mother? Is she waiting for us? Are we going to have tea here?"

"Presently," says Betty, dragging her on. "We're going to play the game first. You said you would."

"Oh, of course," agrees Margaret, following meekly.

"You go down there," says Betty pointing to the entrance of the passage.

Margaret hesitates. "I don't like dungeons," she objects.

"It isn't a dungeon," Betty assures her. "It's a passage

leading to a lovely terrace. I know it's a bit dark and the walls are slimy but you won't mind, will you? It will spoil everything if you don't play up."

Thus adjured Margaret bends her head and enters.

"Just go down and wait on the terrace," says Betty to her receding back.

Erica grasps my arm. "What's happening?" she enquires in a whisper. "She doesn't know he's there? Oughtn't we to do something, Hester?"

This is exactly the question I have been asking myself—oughtn't we to do something? But what can we do? It is obvious, now, that the whole affair is a deep-laid scheme evolved by Betty and Sheila and it is such an odd mixture of serpentine guile and childish nonsense that it fairly bewilders me. Will the plot succeed, that's the question. Will the surprise of seeing one another unexpectedly bring them together or drive them further apart? But I can do nothing to avert the meeting, it is too late, now. Events must take their course. All this flashes through my mind like lightning, and like lightning I decide that I don't want to be a witness to the scene. Nobody must see what happens when Margaret emerges from the tunnel and beholds Roger Elden lying on the grass.

I put my finger to my lips and motion to the steps. Erica obeys and we creep down silently, with our hands on the crumbling wall.

"Now perhaps you'll explain," says Erica as we reach the bottom.

"I can't," I reply. "It's all too difficult."

"Nonsense—you must. Why was I made to scale those precarious steps and dragged down again before seeing what happened when Lysander awoke? It would have been interesting. Miss McQueen seems an extraordinary choice for the part of Hermia. Does she know the man? You can surely answer that."

"Yes, she knows him."

"Oh," says Erica doubtfully. "Oh well, I suppose that's why they chose her. You knew she was coming to the picnic?"

"I didn't know she was coming. They told me nothing. I'd have stopped it if I'd been told—at least I think I would."

"Well, for goodness' sake let's have tea," says Erica and she moves towards the tunnel with a purposeful air.

"Not there!" I exclaim, clutching her arm.

"Tea," says Erica firmly.

"But not *there,* Erica."

Fortunately at this moment Sheila and Betty appear at the other end of the ruin and wave to us to come. They are carrying a large hamper between them and at the sight of this hamper Erica gives an exclamation of relief.

"Tea!" repeats Erica, throwing off my hand and hastening towards them with all speed.

We spread the cloth in a sheltered corner of the ruined hall and lay out the cakes. It is a marvelous tea of course, for Betty and Erica and Cook are all good doers and have seen to it that nobody shall starve. No conversation takes place while the food is being laid out except the requests concomitant with our task, requests to pass the scones, to put the chocolate cake out of the sun or to find the teaspoons.

"Are we waiting for the others?" enquires Erica when all is prepared.

The conspirators look at each other. "No," says Betty. "Sheila thinks—I mean we'll just start without them."

We start.

I notice that Sheila has chosen to sit upon a stone beside me from whence she can see the entrance to the tunnel without turning her head. She is pale, now. Her excitement has faded and her eyes are strained. Betty and Erica are gorging themselves cheerfully and arguing about the nests in the overhanging trees. They are rooks' nests, Betty thinks, but Erica is of the opinion they are only crows'.

"D'you think it was wrong of us to do it, Mrs. Christie?" asks Sheila in a low voice. "I thought it was a good idea, but now I'm a little frightened." _

I am about to reply when Erica chips in. Erica is never deaf to anything she wants to hear. "Why are you frightened?" she enquires.

Sheila twists her hands. "They used to—like each other," she says.

"Hrrmph!" snorts Erica.

The curious thing is that everything is now perfectly clear; the situation which seemed to me far too difficult and complicated to explain is explained in six words.

"It said in a book you should throw people together," says Betty, taking up the story. "At first we thought we would make them go up the tower and then break the steps so that they couldn't come down—at least I thought that would be a good plan, Sheila wasn't very keen on it. So then we decided the terrace would be better and the only difficulty was how to make them go there."

"You overcame that," says Erica in dry tones.

"We had to," says Betty earnestly. "We didn't tell any lies at all—not one."

"We acted lies," says Sheila. "I thought it was all right at the time . . . but now I see we shouldn't have done it."

"We didn't act lies!" cries Betty indignantly.

"We pretended it was a game," Sheila reminds her.

"It *was* a game."

"Not to me," says Sheila in tragic tones.

They all look at me—even Erica—and I realize that I am expected to pronounce judgment. It is a task for which I am singularly unfitted by nature, for I look at things from everyone's point of view and this muddles me. The people who can think and speak clearly are those whose ideas are cut and dried . . . but I shall have to try.

"It was wrong," I tell them gravely. "But you intended well, which is the main thing, and it looks to me as if your plan has succeeded."

"They've forgotten about tea," nods Sheila, looking relieved.

"But remember this," I continue. "When we do wrong we have to pay for it, and you will have to pay for it by going on with your pretense that it was only a childish game."

This is beyond Betty, of course, but Sheila understands and looks at me seriously. "It will be horrid to have a secret from Father," says Sheila with a sigh.

We finish tea—even Betty can eat no more—and still there is no sign of Lysander and Hermia. We chat in a desultory way. Erica smokes like a chimney. Betty and Sheila play "I spy" in a halfhearted manner which deceives nobody, not even themselves.

Presently Erica rises and shakes herself. "I'm going home," she says. "If you take my advice, Hester, you'll come home, too. It's far too cold to dawdle about here, and I've finished my cigarettes."

"Oh, please, Miss Clutterbuck!" cries Sheila. "Please don't leave us alone!"

"Go and see what's happened, then," says Erica.

"I couldn't!" Sheila exclaims.

"Why couldn't you?"

"Because . . ." says Sheila. "Oh, because they might not want me. I mean . . ."

"You go, Miss Clutterbuck," suggests Betty.

"No, Mrs. Christie should go," declares Sheila.

Erica and I refuse with one voice.

The matter is discussed earnestly and with some heat. None of us is willing to go down the tunnel and everybody thinks somebody else should go. Erica holds fast to her determination to return home and take me with her unless something is done at once to clear up the situation.

"Let's all go," says Betty at last. "We all think each other should go, so if we all go we're doing what everybody thinks best. You see what I mean, don't you?"

Erica says she sees exactly what Betty means, but disagrees profoundly. Betty and Sheila got themselves into the mess so they can get out of it themselves.

"We didn't think it would be like this," Betty explains. "We thought they'd make it up and then come out and have tea—"

"I didn't," says Sheila quickly. "I mean I didn't think at all about what would happen afterwards. I just wanted them to make it up and be happy."

"I don't care what you thought," declares Erica impatiently. "All I want is to go home before I catch a chill. You can come or not as you like, it's all one to me."

"They may be dead," says Sheila piteously.

This is ridiculous of course, but oddly enough it raises a feeling of apprehension in my bosom. It is as if a cold wind had started to blow. I realize that we cannot go home without finding out what has happened—glancing at Erica I see that she has realized this, too.

"All right," says Erica, after a short pause. "If we must go, we must. Lead on, Macduff!"

We all go down the tunnel together. Together we emerge onto the terrace.

Nobody is there.

For a moment or two we stand there in silence, looking round. The sun has hidden itself behind a low cloud; the wind is chill; the cawing of the rooks seems unnaturally loud and ominous. I, for one, am absolutely petrified with horror and can neither move nor speak, but Erica is made of sterner stuff.

Erica marches across to the edge of the terrace and looks down. "That's the way they've gone," says Erica, pointing. "It's a bit steep of course, but not impossible. In fact there's the remains of a sort of path . . . very sensible of them to go home. We'd better do the same."

The arrangement was that Todd was to take Sheila back to Ryddelton, and Todd, performing his duties with his usual punctuality, is waiting for her in the drive. Sheila says goodbye politely and is driven away. It is not until I see the car disappearing down the avenue that I realize I should have gone with her to afford her moral support.

"We shouldn't have let her go alone!" I exclaim.

"Why not?" enquires Erica.

"Something may have happened."

"For pity's sake have a little sense! Their bodies were not lying at the bottom of the cliff so it's reasonable to assume they got home safely," says Erica impatiently.

It is plain that Erica is cross and tired and fed up with

the whole affair so I refrain from further comment—and Betty has the sense to keep her thoughts to herself—but when we go in to dinner my first glance is directed to the table where Margaret always sits and I note that she is not there. Betty has noted this, too. She looks at me questioningly, but the question is unanswerable. Dinner is an unusually silent meal.

As soon as I can escape I run upstairs to Margaret's room and find it empty. She is not there. What has happened, I wonder. Where has she gone? Perhaps it is foolish to feel so responsible for Margaret, who is old enough (so one would imagine) to look after herself and her own affairs without interference from me, but the whole thing lies upon me like a heavy weight. Betty was the author of the plan, and Betty is my responsibility . . .

Very slowly I descend the stairs and sit down in the corner of the lounge. I provide myself with a book and pretend to read it, for I am too tired and anxious to talk to anybody. My thoughts go round and round. If everything is all right and they have "made it up" (as Sheila put it), the obvious thing would be for Margaret to dine with the Eldens. I decide that this has happened and heave a sigh of relief . . . but if everything is all wrong and Margaret and Roger have broken completely with each other the obvious thing would be . . . what? Margaret might return to Tocher House and go to bed, or she might wander miserably in the woods. She may be wandering in the woods, now, at this very moment. Perhaps I ought to go and look for her . . .

This is ridiculous, of course. Where should I start looking for her?

The evening drags on. One by one the guests sigh and stretch themselves and trail upstairs to bed. The clock strikes twelve; I am the only person in the lounge, and still Margaret has not come.

At ten minutes past twelve I hear the sound of a car approaching, it roars up the avenue and stops with a crunch of brakes, a moment later the front door opens and there is the sound of footsteps in the hall.

"There's a light in the lounge," says a deep voice, the voice of Roger Elden. "Everybody can't have gone to bed—" He appears in the doorway and looks about him as he speaks.

"Everybody has gone to bed except me," I tell him, rising from my chair.

"Mrs. Tim!" he cries advancing towards me eagerly. "Margaret, here's Mrs. Tim, the very person we wanted to see!"

Margaret lingers in the doorway. She looks so different that I should hardly know her for the same woman. Her eyes are shining, her cheeks are pink with excitement, her whole appearance is transformed.

"Come on," urges Roger. "Come and talk to Mrs. Tim. Come and tell her all about it."

"O Roger—I can't. Not tonight . . ."

"You needn't tell me anything!" I cry. "I can see everything is all right."

"Everything is splendid," declares Roger Elden smiling. "And it's all because of you and that crazy child of yours."

"What about your crazy child?"

"She was in it too, of course, but Betty invented the game—and what a game!"

"Childish nonsense."

"Perhaps—I'm not so sure. I hope you weren't worried about us."

"Worried is scarcely the word."

"I'm sorry," says Roger. "I didn't think—until afterwards. The fact is we just couldn't face *anybody* after what happened on the terrace, so we crawled down the cliff. It wasn't as difficult as it looked."

"We forgot—about everybody," says Margaret with a dazed sort of air.

"The whole thing was so—dynamic," explains Roger. "So sudden and unexpected, so absolutely—dazzling. I heard somebody coming down the tunnel and I opened my eyes expecting to see Miss Clutterbuck, and—"

"And you saw Margaret!" I exclaim.

"Dimly," says Roger, laughing. "I couldn't see anything very clearly because my eyes were bunged up with yellow powder."

"You saw quite enough," declares Margaret, smiling at him.

Roger nods. "I took prompt and vigorous action."

Somehow or other these words seem familiar to me. I repeat them in questioning tones.

"Yes," says Roger. "The fact is—it's rather silly, really—I went to a fortune-teller at the fête. She was a most extraordinary woman."

"Tell Hester about her," says Margaret, who obviously has been told.

"I don't believe in fortune-tellers," declares Roger. "They're usually idiotic, but this woman was different. She was hideous, of course, and frightfully dirty and disreputable—a regular old gypsy queen, a sort of Meg Merrilees—but there was something positively uncanny about the old hag, believe it or not."

"She told Roger to take prompt and vigorous action,"

explains Margaret, laughing a little. "And Roger took her advice."

"And got my heart's desire," adds Roger, smiling at her fatuously.

There is no more need for me—that's very plain—so I say good night as quickly as possible and make for the door, but Margaret turns and seizes my hand.

"It was you," says Margaret, smiling at me with tears in her eyes. "It was all you, really—fortune-tellers are nonsense. I was angry when you said I was a coward, but afterwards I saw—I saw it was true. O Hester, how can I ever thank you enough! I'm going to make Roger happy—it's going to be all right!"

Bryan has been staying with the Edgeburtons for a fortnight and is arriving at Tocher House today. He is to spend
a few days here and then go on to Aberdeen to stay with another school friend for the remainder of the holidays. All this
has been arranged by Bryan, who takes after me in liking to
have his plans cut and dried, and we have agreed by letter
that although it is very distressing to have so little time together it will be better if Bryan is not at Tocher House too
long. The summer holidays will be different, of course.
We shall spend them at Cobstead en famille—that also is
arranged.

As I am too busy to go to the station to meet Bryan, I
arrange with Todd to go. To be quite honest I am tremendously excited and yearning to behold my son, but as Erica
is extremely scornful and has teased me for days about Bryan
I am obliged to dissemble and assume a calm front.

We meet on the steps of the hotel under the eyes of the
assembled guests who are waiting for the lunch gong to
sound. Erica, also, is present and this being so I greet Bryan
with a cool kiss and enquire whether he has had a good journey. Bryan is equally calm. He has grown enormously, and
with his long slim legs and his long sleek head seems taller
and old for his age. In fact he is so "grown-up" that I feel
quite shy of him; he seems a different being from the cheerful schoolboy with the untidy hair, the Bryan who is familiar

to me. It is obvious that the assembled company does not disturb him; he takes them in with a smile—not really looking at them at all—and follows me into the house without a backward glance. As I lead the way upstairs we are both completely silent, perhaps because there is nothing more to say. For my part I am already deeply regretting that cool welcome and wishing with all my heart that I had thrown my arms round his neck and hugged him—and be damned to Erica!

It is too late now, of course. The deed is done.

We reach the third landing and I open the door of the little room with sloping roof, which is to be Bryan's room, and show him in.

"It's rather small," I begin, "but I daresay—"

Suddenly I am seized in a bear's embrace and almost strangled. The strong young arms are hard as steel. They go round me like a vice. "Darling!" cries Bryan. "Oh, *what* a dear wee Mummy! I'd forgotten you were so small."

"Bryan!" I gasp. "You're—breaking—my ribs!"

He gives me another squeeze, more gentle this time, and then releases me, and I collapse onto the bed, laughing in a slightly hysterical manner. Bryan laughs too.

"You're enormous!" I cry, looking up at him as he stands in the middle of the room.

"I know," agrees Bryan. "I've outgrown all my clothes. But I didn't realize how absolutely enormous I was until I saw you." He stretches his arms above his head and touches the ceiling. "Look!" he says grinning.

"You're a giant."

"As big as Dad?"

"I shouldn't wonder."

He smiles down at me. "Wasn't it funny?" he says. "All

those queer old beans standing about watching us—they don't know, do they?"

"No, they certainly don't."

"You said, 'Hullo, Bryan, did you have a good journey?'"

"You said, 'Yes, thank you. The train was well up to time.'"

"Ha, ha!" laughs Bryan in an uproarious manner. "It was rich, wasn't it? We took them in beautifully."

He sits down beside me on the bed and puts his arm round my waist. "Let's look at you," he says. "Are they decent to you here? Are you getting lots of food and not being worked to death? Dad says I'm to write and tell him honestly. I shall keep my eyes open and see what's what, and if I don't think it's all right there'll be trouble. Where's the kid?"

I inform Bryan that his sister is spending the day at Ryddelton with some friends.

"It's just as well," says Bryan. "I've got lots to tell you. It will be nice to have you all to myself."

The lunch gong sounds—a welcome sound to Bryan—and we go downstairs together, once more cool and withdrawn. There is a tacit understanding that this is the way in which we shall behave in the company of our fellow creatures, an understanding arrived at without words.

Erica has started her soup when we reach our seats. She glances at Bryan in a puzzled manner; it is plain he is different from what she expected and that she resents his coolness and poise. We talk about this and that—Bryan behaves beautifully and is neither too voluble nor too silent—but in spite of this I begin to feel as if I were skating on thin ice, ice that cracks in an ominous manner as I go. My nervousness is no help, of course; Erica senses it and becomes more gruff. It is her habit to trample upon people who grovel at her feet.

"I suppose you expect me to let you off for the afternoon," says Erica suddenly, scowling at me as she speaks.

This remark, though ungraciously worded, does not worry me unduly—for I am aware that Erica intends me to take the afternoon off and spend it talking to my son—but Bryan, not knowing that the thing is arranged and that Erica's scowl is used by her as cover for a kindly action, is plainly horrified at her rudeness and resents it on my behalf.

"There's no need for my mother to have the afternoon off," declares Bryan, getting very red in the face. "There's no need for her to be here at all, if it comes to that. My mother has plenty of friends to go to—people who appreciate her."

"You don't think I appreciate her?" enquires Erica grimly.

"It doesn't look like it," replies Bryan, boldly. "I was going to say you speak to her as if she were a scullery maid, only no scullery maid would stand being spoken to like that."

Erica laughs. "That's where you're wrong," she says. "I say what I think to everybody—it doesn't matter whether it's your mother or the scullery maid. Ask your mother, she'll tell you that's true."

Bryan is about to reply but I shake my head violently and he relapses into silence.

Fortunately we have finished our meal, so we need not delay our departure. Erica rises and goes without another word and I lead my son into the lounge.

"Crumbs!" exclaims Bryan, sinking down beside me on the sofa. "What a frightful woman! I suppose I should have held my tongue, but how could I when she spoke to you like that? Are you frightfully fed up with me?"

"No, of course not. It was the best thing you could have done."

"The best thing . . ." says Bryan, looking at me with eyes like saucers.

"She says what she thinks and she respects people who do the same. It's logical, but rather unusual."

"She was furious!"

"She was slightly annoyed, but she'll get over it and respect you for standing up to her."

Bryan digests this. "I think she's awful," he says at last. "Why on earth do you stick it? Why don't you go away?"

"I'm perfectly happy here. I like the work."

"Oh well," says Bryan in a bewildered manner. "If you *like* it . . . What have you got to do this afternoon? I mean can we do it together?"

"I've got the afternoon off."

"She said—" begins Bryan, looking at me in surprise. "She said—"

"It was all arranged beforehand. That's just her way."

"A mighty funny way!" says Bryan vehemently.

It is no use trying to explain Erica to Bryan, so we leave the subject and make plans for the afternoon. I suggest a visit to the ruins of Salvers Castle, and Bryan agrees and asks if we could take tea with us and have a picnic there.

"What did you do at Langmer's End?" I enquire, as we set off together through the woods.

"We rode a lot," replies Bryan. "It was tremendous fun. We helped to cut down trees—Sir Percy is selling a lot of timber. I liked Sir Percy. Hedgehog is frightened of him, of course, but I got on with him all right. I played chess with him every evening. He's too good for me—very wily—but he gave me a few pieces and it improved my game a lot."

"Why is Hedgehog frightened of him?" I ask.

"He looks rather terrifying—like an eagle—and of course he jumps on Hedgehog a good deal. He thinks Hedgehog is silly. Fright makes people silly," says Bryan in a thoughtful voice. "Hedgehog is an absolute terror, really. He's always getting into trouble. If he gets annoyed he goes for people twice his size without the slightest hesitation—if anybody calls him Percy he just sees red. I told Sir Percy that." Bryan smiles and adds, "I'd forgotten for the moment that the old man's name is Percy, too, but he didn't mind a bit. He laughed and said he used to do the same thing himself. After that he was nicer to Hedgehog."

"That was good."

By this time we have reached the ruins and Bryan is suitably impressed by its age and magnitude. He spends about an hour exploring and joins me on the little terrace for tea. We sit in the sunshine watching a heron circling over the river, its great grey wings outspread, circling higher and higher and then turning and sailing downwind in a slow stately dive. It is lovely to be here with Bryan—whom I adore—it is almost too perfect. The sun is warm, the turf is soft, there is a smell of gorse in the air—a golden scent. In the distance is the sound of the river chattering in its stony bed.

"He's very generous," says Bryan suddenly. "I mean Sir Percy, of course. When I went to say good-bye he gave me— what do you think! He gave me *five quid*. He said it was for playing chess with a disagreeable old man and I was to spend it and not put it in the bank . . . so I spent it. I had a whole afternoon shopping in London, it was fun."

"What did you buy?" I enquire.

Bryan puts his hand in his pocket and brings out a small parcel done up in tissue paper and opening it discloses a little necklace of blue beads. "I thought it was rather pretty," says Bryan, looking at it doubtfully.

"It's very pretty," I declare.

He drops it onto my lap. "For you," he says gruffly.

"Oh, Bryan!"

"It didn't cost much," he assures me. "I mean I had lots over for other things . . ."

Bryan has been here for two days and is leaving tomorrow, and this being so I must make the most of him. He has had his bath and got into bed and when I go in to say good night he motions me to sit down.

"Let's have a good old talk," says Bryan persuasively.

This was always his plea at bedtime, so it makes me smile.

"I know," says Bryan nodding. "It's like old times, isn't it? I used to think up all sorts of excuses to keep you talking."

I sit down on the bed. "Shall I tell you the story of the three bears?" I enquire.

"One bear is enough," replies Bryan seriously. "She's a terror. It's just as well I'm going away tomorrow—"

"I thought you were getting on better with her, Bryan."

"Yes," he replies. "Oh yes. We haven't actually come to blows, but I don't like her at all. She gets my goat."

"She's very kindhearted."

"She's rude," declares Bryan. "She may have a kind heart —I'm willing to believe it if you say so—but why should people have to put up with her rude manner?"

"You put up with Sir Percy," I remind him.

"That's quite different," says Bryan quickly. "He wasn't rude, exactly. He was just a bit crochety, and Sir Percy is old and ill. I'm terribly sorry for him. Miss Clutterbuck is as fit as a fiddle so she shouldn't need special consideration. You see, don't you?"

"Yes—but—"

"Everybody treats her as if she were an invalid or something!" exclaims Bryan. "Everybody kowtows to her as if she were a queen! And all the time it's only because she's got a devilish temper and they want a little peace—it's disgusting!"

I think about this seriously before replying. To a certain extent Bryan's dictum is true, yet it gives a completely false picture of Erica, a picture in which the really important features are missing. Bryan has seen the ungracious manner; he has not seen the woman who hides herself behind it, the woman of pure gold. If I were in trouble I would go straight to Erica, knowing I could depend upon her loyalty and strength and that she would stand by me through thick and thin without counting the cost. She has other good points, but this alone makes her a worthwhile friend. Why can't Bryan see the real Erica? It is all the more curious because Betty, who is less intelligent and much less sensitive, saw the real Erica at once.

"She's difficult to know," I tell Bryan thoughtfully. "I didn't like her at first. It's only when you get to know her that you realize—"

"Oh yes," agrees Bryan, interrupting. "I can see you like her and I can see she's quite decent to you according to her lights, but that isn't the point. The point is why should people have to bear her rudeness?"

"You don't understand her, Bryan."

"Listen," says Bryan earnestly. "Listen, Mummy. This is important and I want to know. You always say nothing excuses rudeness—it's one of your *things*—so why do you excuse it in *her*?"

I can find no answer and I tell him so.

Thursday, 25th April

Bryan's short stay at Tocher House comes to an end today and we set off together in the car for Ryddelton Station. He is going by the three o'clock train and seems a little surprised when I suggest starting shortly after two, but I explain that the car is old and unreliable and we must not risk losing the train.

It is colder today, windy and showery, with grey skies—and these tone in very well with my depressed mood. Bryan is such a dear that I hate parting from him, and he feels the same as I know by his forced cheerfulness and his repeated assurances that we shall all be together for two whole months in the summer holidays.

The car behaves well. It careers along merrily and even consents to be coaxed into top gear on level stretches of road. We shall be at the station far too soon, of course, and shall have to walk up and down the platform, getting thoroughly chilled before the train is due. I feel annoyed with myself for my over anxiousness. Why can't I behave like other people and take a chance?

Bryan is annoyed, too. His mood has suddenly changed —probably because of the imminence of his departure—and he has become tetchy and irritable. He points out there was no need to start so early, we shall be in plenty of time to catch the train before the one he wants to go by.

I agree that it looks like that, but you never can tell.

Bryan says what's the matter with the car? It's old, of course, and looks as if it had come out of the ark and the gears seem rather queer—unless it's the way I'm driving it.

I reply that the gears are more than queer.

There seems to be plenty of life in the engine, Bryan says.

I tell him to touch wood, but Bryan says no, it isn't a case for touching wood. You touch wood when you've been boasting about something. He isn't boasting.

"And anyhow," says Bryan crossly, "we oughtn't to pander to silly superstitions, they're absolutely pagan. They're a survival of belief in malignant gods, that's what they are."

At this moment the engine ceases to function. It simply dies. We drift very gently down to the bottom of a steep incline and come to rest at the side of the road.

"What's up?" enquires Bryan.

"It's stopped, that's all," I reply.

"Try the self-starter," suggests Bryan hopefully.

I try it with determination but without result.

"Let's see now," says Bryan, who has quite recovered his temper. "You've plenty of petrol, I suppose. Yes, the tank is full. It might be an air-lock, of course. I'll try cranking it."

He cranks until his face is crimson and I beg him to desist.

"It's no good," I tell him. "We had better walk. It's only about a mile and we might get a lift."

"I'll have a look at the carburetor, first," says Bryan cheerfully.

He looks at the carburetor, he takes out the plugs, he examines the magneto. I help him as best I can, handing him the tools and encouraging him with words of praise. To tell the truth I am filled with admiration and astonishment for he knows exactly what he is doing and he is doing it quite calmly and without the slightest fuss. If this had happened to Tim he would have been irritated beyond measure, he would have worked to the accompaniment of muttered curses and consigned the car to the nether regions—to which I am convinced it belongs. It is not so much that Bryan is better-tempered than Tim, but merely different and therefore annoyed by different things. I reflect upon this curious dispensation of Providence as I hand Bryan the box-spanner and send up a silent prayer that his wife—when he gets one —will appreciate him and assess his qualities at their true worth.

"Everything is perfectly all right as far as I can see," says Bryan at last in puzzled tones. "The engine *ought* to start. I'll crank it again."

He cranks it again, but nothing happens.

By this time it is a quarter to three and the situation is desperate. We decide to walk. Bryan seizes his suitcase and sets off down the road, I follow with his coat, his golf clubs and his handbag. No car passes, going our way, but several cars speed by rapidly in the other direction. We pound along in silence, for neither of us has breath for speech. Bryan's suitcase is heavy, his brow is wet with perspiration.

"We can't do it!" I cry at last. "It's three now—we can't do it."

"Yes, we can," grunts Bryan. "We're nearly there—but the train is signaled . . ."

He breaks into a run. We reach the station breathless. The train is actually starting to move when Bryan leaps in and the door is slammed behind him.

There has been no time to say good-bye, of course. I am left standing upon the platform gasping like a fish.

"Ye shouldn't run it so fine," says the stationmaster reproachfully. "It's folks like you makes trains late. If I'd not happened to see ye coming and held the train ye'd have missed it for sure. It's an express, too."

This is the last straw. The injustice of it is almost more than I can bear. "I didn't," I cry. "I mean it wasn't my fault. I'm always too soon."

"Ye weren't too soon today," says the stationmaster.

I am too dejected to explain, besides the stationmaster does not wait for an explanation, he has more important things to do than to bandy words with a foolish woman who has delayed an express. I sit down on a bench for a few minutes to recover myself and then set forth on foot to recover the car.

The car is standing exactly as we left it, which is not surprising, of course. When I see it—and not before—I realize that I should have telephoned from the station and asked Todd to come to the rescue. I am completely stranded, but it doesn't seem to matter. I am too depressed to care what happens to me.

It begins to rain gently, so I open the door and get in and, more from habit than anything else, I press the self-starter . . .

The engine immediately springs to life and purrs away merrily.

"You brute!" I exclaim. "I suppose you'll run home quite smoothly. You really are the most disagreeable car I have ever met," and so saying I let in the clutch, turn at a convenient gate and head homeward to Tocher House.

By this time the rain is descending in sheets and I am feeling quite as wet and dejected as the weather. I am in the mood when one forgets one's blessings and counts one's troubles, when nothing seems good and the world seems grey and drab. I have a son, but he has gone away. I have a husband, but I have not seen him for months. It may be years before I see Tim, it certainly will be years before we can settle down to a reasonably peaceful life. What is the use of being married when you can't be together? It is misery, no less. All very well for Tony to say think of the future—I *do* think of it most of the time but you can't live on hope forever. There are times—and this is one of them—when the savor goes out of life, when you lose heart, when you feel you can't go on, when you would give everything you possess for one glimpse of the person you love . . .

Thinking these thoughts and choking a little over a most uncomfortable lump which has suddenly arisen in my throat, I turn in at the Tocher gates, chug up the avenue and stop with a jerk at the door.

Erica is waiting for me; she rushes down the steps with a piece of paper in her hand. "It's just come!" she exclaims. "A cable from Cairo. I took it down over the phone—but it doesn't seem to make sense."

"From Tim!" I cry. "Is it from Tim? Is he all right?"

"No," says Erica. "It's from somebody called Max—"

"But I don't know anybody called Max!"

She hands me the paper. "I took it down most carefully," she says. "It's absolute nonsense, I'm afraid—unless it's some sort of code."

"We haven't a code—it isn't allowed," I reply as I seize it from her.

The message reads as follows:

MAX MEET SATURDAY FORTY NINE DAYS MIST

To me the message is perfectly clear and my spirits soar

with a bound. They soar so rapidly from the depths of despair to the heights of bliss that I almost faint with joy.

"Oh, how marvelous!" I exclaim. "I shall have to go—you won't mind will you—I'll come back afterwards, of course."

"But who is Max?" asks Erica, gazing at me in bewilderment. "And why forty-nine days mist?"

"It isn't Max," I tell her. "Max is Todd's pigeon."

"Todd's pigeon?"

"It means Tim is flying home. It couldn't mean anything else."

"Couldn't it?"

"No, of course not. He wants me to meet him on Saturday at the Forty Club—he's got nine days leave!"

"Mist?" murmurs Erica feebly.

"That *is* rather difficult," I admit, laughing joyfully. "That *is* a sort of code. It means a thousand and one salutations from Tim. You couldn't know that, could you? The rest of the message is perfectly clear."

"As clear as Christie," agrees Erica with heavy sarcasm.